Derek Power

Filthy Henry :
The Fairy Detective

A Filthy Henry novel

For K,
This would never have been written
without your encouragement and support.
I'm forever thankful.

Chapters

Chapter One

Michael held the door to the main bedroom closed, using all his strength to keep the handle in the upright position. It was the only way he could keep whatever was in the bedroom from getting out. He would have preferred if the door had been made out of ten-inch thick steel with a few deadbolts, but bedroom doors generally came in the wooden variety these days. Things like metal doors with multi-locks were classed both as a specialist item and a strange request to have installed in a house.

A creak on the stairs made him look over his shoulder to see Jane, his wife, coming up with two mugs of tea in her hands. She carefully sat down on the top stair and placed one of the mugs down on the carpet beside her.

"Still no sign of him?" Michael asked her, eyeing the second cup of tea with longing.

"No," Jane said. "But he'll be here."

On the other side of the door came the sound of something expensive falling over and smashing. This was followed by the pounding of little feet running across the floor.

"Little bastard!" Michael snarled.

"What's that going to achieve?" Jane asked. "You know there is nobody in there to hear you."

"Well it'll make me feel better," he said, irritated. "I still reckon it's just a herd of rats that we have and we just need to call in an exterminator to sort it all out."

"Pack," Jane said, taking a sip from her tea.

"Pack?"

"You said 'herd' and it's not. You don't have a 'herd of rats', you have a 'pack of rats'."

Michael stared at her, slowly counting to ten under his breath. She always picked the worst possible moment to treat him like one of the snotty-faced kids in her class at school. Even after he had agreed to let some witch-doctor into their house. A supposed exorcist who no doubt got his jollies on by prancing around in nothing but his birthday suit.

"Sorry, pack then," Michael finally said. "I still think that is what we have. Not some ghost."

"Then why are you holding the door closed?"

"To keep...whatever it really is in there. At least until your voodoo man shows up. Then it's his problem," Michael said.

Jane shrugged and took another sip from her drink.

Michael would have bet good money that this whole problem was Jane's fault. She was forever buying random knick-knacks from traders on the street because they told her some horse-crap story about the magical powers the object had. Things that promised good fortune. Powders that prolonged life and improved health. Stones that offered protection from the various types of wild tigers known to roam the Dublin suburbs. It was only a matter of time before she picked up something that actually was a little bit out of the norm. Something that did defy logic and reason and science.

Something that was properly cursed!

"This tosser is nearly an hour late," Michael said, looking at his watch. "An hour! I'd hate to have to rely on him if this was an emergency. Like a possessed girl shooting out vegetable soup all over the place."

"He's not a priest," Jane said, and make sure you don't go calling him one while he's here. I got his number through a friend of friend of my Gran's and she says he is the best at what he does."

Conning old bints out of their pensions, that's what he does, Michael thought. *Not hard to be good at that sort of gig.*

The doorbell rang.

"He's here," Jane whispered.

"He can't bloody hear through walls and you are sitting at the top of the damn stairs," Michael said. "Just go let him in. I'm getting tired holding this handle."

Jane went down stairs to answer the door.

Michael leaned back as far as he could, kept a firm grip on the bedroom door handle, and craned his neck to try and get a view of the hall below. He could just about see between the banisters. Jane had opened the door and greeted their late night arrival. She brought the visitor inside and closed the front door behind him.

Michael had spent the last few hours painting a mental picture of what their guest would look like. This tardy visitor was going to be some mad man, all crazy hair and thick bottle bottom glasses that enlarged his eyes to the size of melons. There would, not doubt, be a smell of old cabbages from him. All in all Michael expected to see somebody that would probably have considered a straitjacket as a required fashion accessory.

Which was an image that changed rapidly when the visitor stepped into full view at the bottom of the stairs. Standing in the hall, dripping slightly from the rain outside, was a man in his early thirties. At Jane's request their late night guest had taken off his rain soaked trench coat and hung it at the end of the stairs.

"You're an hour late. Do you know that?" Michael shouted down the stairs.

"Good thing I only charge for the hours I'm actually here then, isn't it?" came the reply. "Whose that then?"

"That's my husband, Michael," Jane said. "He has trapped the ... presence, I guess ... in our bedroom upstairs and is holding the door closed. I'll show you."

They both came up the stairs. Jane stepped just inside the bathroom doorway, allowing their guest to stand on the landing behind Michael.

"I'm Michael," Michael said. "You'll forgive me for not shaking your hand, kinda busy here."

"Not at all," the visitor said. "I'm Filthy Henry, the fairy detective."

"Filthy Henry? What sort of name is that?" Michael asked.

"The one that I just gave you," replied Filthy Henry.

"But you have to have a surname. Your first name surely isn't Filthy."

"I never give out my family name," Filthy Henry said, looking about the landing with interest. "Don't think I even remember what it is."

"Well I am not doing business with you until you do tell me your full name."

"Michael," Jane hissed.

Filthy Henry's stare snapped back to Michael, looking him directly in the eyes.

"Then it would seem like we have come to something of an impasse."

Michael adjusted his position so that he could get a better look at their visitor.

Filthy Henry's hair was a mixture of greys and ginger. He was tall, easily over six feet, but seemed to stoop a little to make himself appear smaller. The brown suit that he wore looked like it had seen better days, those days having been a few decades ago. His shirt had taken on that lovely grey hue that white shirts tended to over time. He was leaning against the wall,

13

nonchalantly, with his hands in his pockets almost as if waiting for something to happen.

"So what are you then? Something goes bump in the night and people call you to bump back?" Michael asked, feeling proud of the not so subtle insult.

Filthy Henry simply smiled.

"Not at all. Those things that go bump in the night; I'm one of them."

For God's sake, Michael thought.

"So, Jane," Filthy Henry said, turning to face her. "Tell me exactly what's been going on here."

"Well..." she began.

"Things are getting moved about at night. Stuff broken. Empty rooms making a lot of noise," Michael said, cutting Jane off.

Filthy Henry glared at Michael.

"I didn't know you were called Jane as well. Please, continue female Jane," he said, standing up straight and facing her.

"Now you just..." Michael began.

Filthy Henry turned quickly on the spot and pointed at Michael with his right index finger. The lights on the landing dimmed for a split second. Michael could have sworn that a blue glow outlined Filthy Henry's hand. It grew in intensity briefly, then leaped from the tip of his finger into the air.

"*Bí ciúin,*" Filthy Henry said, his voice echoing as if they all stood in a great empty hall.

Something invisible smacked Michael in the mouth, causing his head to jolt back a little. The lights returned to normal and the glow around the fairy detective disappeared.

"Now, if you wouldn't mind telling me the rest of the details," Filthy Henry said to Jane, turning back to face her once more. "It helps if I have all the facts."

Every button of Michael's had been pushed at this stage. Somebody had come into his home and told him to be quiet. In Irish! Bad Irish! If a teacher in primary school had never managed to make Michael obey such an instruction then this suit wearing muppet had no chance.

Listen you unmitigated tosser! Get out of my house right now and pray I never see you again!

That was what Michael said, or least tried to say. But in place of his voice there was silence. Nothing. Try as he might he could not say a single word.

I'm can't speak! He thought, panicked.

Jane had stopped blabbering on about their invisible tenant and looked over at Michael. He was furiously moving his lips, trying to talk.

"Em..." Jane said, shyly pointing at Michael.

"Oh don't worry about him," Filthy Henry said with a dismissive wave of his hand. "He will be alright in an hour. I just needed him to shut up while you told me the rest of the story. Rather irritating attitude problem he has there. Should see about getting him into some class that teaches manners. I know a good dog trainer if you want his number." To Michael he said. "Why don't you go and pop the kettle on, make Jane a nice cup of tea. There's a good lad. I can handle it from here."

Michael forgot all about keeping the door closed and let go of the handle. He clenched his fists and took a step towards the fairy detective.

Filthy Henry simply raised his hand up, gesturing for Michael to stop.

"Just think about this course of action sunshine," Filthy Henry said, a sinister tone in his voice. The shadows around his eyes had deepened as he stared at Michael. "You can either go make the tea and then sit down on the couch voluntarily or I can make you sit down while you soil yourself constantly for the next ten minutes. Your call."

Michael had never backed down from a fight. Never walked away from an argument. It was hard to admit defeat when you were never in the wrong to begin with. Right then, given that this strange man had somehow managed to take his voice, Michael decided that the best way to face this opponent was to advance in reverse.

He barged past Filthy Henry, giving him a not-so-accidental shoulder bump, and went down the stairs.

A victory was still a victory, no matter how small.

At the foot of the stairs Michael stopped and looked up at Jane. He gestured for her to follow him.

"It's alright," Filthy Henry said, stepping aside so she could get past. "I can handle things from here. Just go into the living room and do not leave it again until I come back down. No matter what you hear happening up here, stay downstairs with the door closed. Maybe you could tell Michael all about your day, Jane. I'm sure he'd love to hear that."

As she came down the stairs Jane was grinning from ear to ear.

"Well, first I rang my mam..."

Michael rolled his eyes and stormed into the living room.

#

Filthy Henry flicked the light-switch beside the bathroom door, plunging the landing into darkness. Whatever was in that bedroom needed light to see. It did not matter who your parents

16

were, an eyeball was an eyeball. The only difference was that some eyeballs could work better in less light than others.

Luckily Filthy Henry had a trick up his sleeve that helped him see in the dark, something that came from his innate magical nature. After all, to be a fairy detective you needed to see through the veil that separated the two worlds, otherwise you were just some madman running around the place. He closed his eyes for a second and turned on his fairy vision, his second sight that brought down the curtain and allowed him to see the man behind it. Actually, to be politically correct, it allowed him to see the fairy creatures that inhabited the world. The magical realm that existed right beside the normal world, hidden from sight.

He opened his eyes and looked around.

Immediately the world brightened, becoming varying shades of blue. It was like wearing night-vision goggles, only without the actual need to look like an idiot wearing night-vision goggles.

Filthy Henry did a quick magical reserve check.

So far he had only cast the silencing spell today, which barely cost any energy to begin with. This meant that he still had practically a full magical tank in him. More than enough power to cast one big spell, or a lot of little ones. Given the disturbances that Jane had told him over the phone there was nothing all that dangerous up here. It was going to be an open and shut case. But it always paid to be prepared.

He crept over to the bedroom door and pressed his ear against it, listening for any movement coming from the other side. There was nothing to be heard.

Reaching down Filthy Henry took hold of the door handle and slowly turned it, opening the bedroom door as quietly as possible. He peered into the room through the slight gap but could see nothing moving at all. The shades of blue, better than any military grade night vision scope, showed everything in perfect sapphire-tinted detail.

Filthy Henry slowly moved his head around the door to get a look at the rest of the room.

The room was your typical bedroom. A double bed in the centre of the floor, lockers on either side of it with lamps on them. Along the back wall stood a large wardrobe. The windows had their blinds pulled closed but a little bit of light from the street shone through.

Then Filthy Henry spotted movement on the far side of the bed.

There was a creature rummaging around in the top drawer, sniffing at things as it pulled them out before discarding them to floor and searching in the drawer once more. It was no taller than a foot and a half at the most, with a scrawny frame that would have made a weight-concerned skeleton consider going on a diet. Two elongated ears spread out like small wings on the creature's head, a pointed cap perched between them at what was probably meant to be a jaunty angle.

Filthy Henry was somewhat relieved at the sight of the creature. There was always the chance that one of these seemingly standard cases would result in a nasty surprise. It added a degree of uncertainty to the job that he hated. But here it was, nothing more than a simple Red-man. A child could handle one of these without resorting to magic.

Red-men were one of the lowest forms of fairy in the Fairy World. Mainly because they had very little to offer, very little to even justify being classed as a fairy. They were notorious for just being pranksters, although their definition of what constituted a prank was wildly different from the one shared by the rest of the world. Be it the human one or the fairy world.

A few centuries ago the King of the Fairies had tried to reclassify the Red-men race as deformed humans, wanting to trim the evolutionary tree of Fairy-kind and make them man's problem. It was not a bad plan, as plans went, only the execution part of it failed. The Fairy King had slightly lost his mind and made the declaration in the middle of his hall stark naked. It is kind of hard to follow the instructions of royalty while you are avoiding an accidental eyeful of wobbling genitalia. As a result the king was quickly removed from power and the Red-men continued being fairies.

Since the Red-men played pranks on whomever they wanted, regardless of race, it was not uncommon to find one living in a human house causing mischief. They had no real magical powers at all. It was as if the entire race had slept in on the day all the useful fairy parts were being handed out. They could avoid being seen by humans if they wanted to, a feat that was impressive as pointing out you could breath, but that was about it.

Filthy Henry brought up his right foot, quietly, and pulled his shoe off as silently as possible. He took aim and, like a ninja short on cash for throwing stars, lobbed the shoe towards the creature's head.

The shoe sailed through the air with the grace of a duck falling from the sky. It flew over the bed and connected with the side of the Red-man's head, knocking the creature sprawling to the ground. Filthy Henry wasted no time. As soon as the shoe had left his hand he fully entered the room, closed and locked the door behind him, then flicked on the light switch. His vision returned to normal, the blue outlines of objects gone.

Pocketing the room key, Filthy Henry walked around the bed and looked down at the Red-man as it rubbed its head.

The creature's skin was a dark shade of red, a maroon colour, thus where the race got its name. Originality was another thing that was lacking amongst the Red-men race. It had on a pair of blue shorts, tied around the waist with a length of rope. Its hat was a bright yellow colour, in no way matching anything about the creature.

Scattered on the ground around the creature were various

types of women's underwear. Bras, knickers. panties and what looked like a shoelace made from silk.

"That was bloody uncalled for," the Red-man said, glaring up at the fairy detective. "Wait, how can you see me?"

"Don't worry about that for the minute. Pass me my shoe," he said.

Filthy Henry held out his hand and clicked his fingers twice.

The Red-man did as instructed, tossing the shoe up in the air towards Filthy Henry.

"So," he said, catching the shoe and putting it back on his foot. "What the hell is a Red-man doing here? More to the point why are you trawling through women's underwear?"

It should not have been possible to notice, given his complexion, but Filthy Henry would have sworn that the Red-man went red from embarrassment. The creature stopped rubbing the side of its head. It suddenly found everything else in the room more interesting to look at, staring at anything to avoid looking at the fairy detective. As it looked around the Red-man tried just as hard to avoid looking at the assortment of underwear on the floor around it.

Sometimes it's just too easy, Filthy Henry thought.

"You're a cross-dresser," he said arching an eyebrow, indicating the array of garments on the floor with a nod of his head.

"No I'm bloody not!" the Red-man said. "It's just...the fabric...softener...stuff. Plus the material is so..."

The creature trailed off and simply sat there, staring at the floor. It reached out and picked up a bra, rubbing one of the cups against its cheek.

Red-men were one of the strangest races of fairy that Filthy Henry had ever dealt with. Aside from their penchant to play pranks they were easily addicted to scents and textures. No two enjoyed the same smells, but the addiction was always the same. A strange, overpowering, compulsion to get as much of the smell as possible. Right now this pathetic excuse for a fairy was caught with its hand in the fabric softened cookie jar. Getting rid of it was going to be as easy as pie.

"I'll make a deal with you," Filthy Henry said. "Rather than report you for breaking The Rules."

Instantly the Red-man's ears picked up, points wiggling slightly in anticipation.

"Really...?" it asked, sounding cautious.

"Really," the fairy detective said. "I've been hired to get rid of you, permanently. But what's a little underwear sniffing between friends, right?" He winked. "So here's what I propose. You can stay in the house for as long as you want and every night the humans will leave out three freshly washed pieces of underwear for you to enjoy. But you are to stop with this nightly raiding and I don't want to get called back here any time soon because things are still going bump in the night. Understood? You get your nightly fix and they get to think that for some reason they have magical underwear that keeps pixies at bay."

Filthy Henry watched as the creature considered the proposal.

The Red-man stood up, straightened what little attire it had, and held out a little red hand.

"You've got yourself a deal...mister...?"

"Filthy Henry," Filthy Henry said, taking the hand and shaking it firmly three times.

Two little blue sparks appeared, one over each hand. They floated into the air, joined together, then vanished in the blink of an eye.

The Red-man's eyes opened wide, its mouth doing likewise.

"The half-breed," it said in a whisper.

"One and the same," Filthy Henry said. "So just remember who you made a deal with, one that we've magically sealed. You don't want to see me again. I'm uglier than you are and who wants to see that twice in a lifetime? Now put all that crap back where it belongs and I will go tell your new hosts how to ensure their disturbed 'ghost' doesn't bother them any more."

#

"...which of course Mary did not like one bit. But she has been in such a mood these days nobody paid her any attention at all when the tea went all over her new dress."

Jane had been regaling Michael with the events of the past twenty four hours non-stop since the rat bastard fairy detective had sent them downstairs. Twenty minutes of constant verbal diarrhoea, which was fine normally because Michael could respond. Direct the conversation. Participate. But whatever Filthy Henry had done to him made talking entirely impossible and Jane was taking full advantage of her mute audience. It had to be some sort of hypnosis or something, like that guy off the television. There was no such thing as magic, it was all part of the con artist's act so that people thought he was really getting rid of ghosts and goblins from their house.

From out in the hall he heard the sound of footsteps coming down the stairs, then the door into the front room open and Filthy Henry entered.

"It's done," the fairy detective said.

Michael reached over to the coffee table and picked up a pen and pad. Quickly scribbling out his question he ripped off the page, crumpled it up slightly, and tossed it at Filthy Henry.

The fairy detective caught the note, opened it up, and read aloud.

"It's done then is it?" he said. "Why yes, Michael it is. Just like I said when I entered the room only two seconds ago. You should have no more problems with the ... spirit ... that occupied your upper floor. There is one thing you have to do though, to keep the spirit away."

"Oh," Jane said, "you mean you didn't kill it or exorcise it or whatever it is you do?"

"Well I didn't really have to kill it to make it leave, just find its weakness. If you leave a dinner plate out every night before going to bed with three pieces of freshly washed underwear on it the spirit will stay away. In particular your underwear Jane. We wouldn't want to risk any of Michael's skid-marks angering the spirit and bringing it back."

Michael frowned at this strange instruction and wrote another note, holding it up for Filthy Henry to read.

"No, Michael, I am not defecating on you," Filthy Henry said. "That's just disgusting and I know you used a different term on your little pad, stop looking so confused, but I wasn't going to sully the lovely Jane's ears by repeating it."

Jane blushed a little, which irritated Michael. Had she a thing for this muppet in the suit?

"So we do that every night and all the strange things around here will stop?" Jane asked twirling some strands of hair around her little finger as she looked at Filthy Henry.

The fairy detective nodded his head.

"In a week or two change the brand of softener you use. Then at the end of the month don't leave out a plate a few nights in a row. It will eventually get bored and move on."

A strange tingling sensation started in Michael's mouth, running along his tongue and spreading to his cheeks. He guessed it was an indication that Filthy Henry's little trick was wearing off. Which was great, because once he could speak again Michael had a long list of things he wanted to say to the freak in his sitting room. All of which would sully Jane's bloody ears!

"Now, the small matter of payment," Filthy Henry said, looking to Michael, " and I will be on my way."

Jane rose from her seat, walked over to Michael and grabbed his arm. She tugged him up and pulled out his wallet.

How come I have to pay for this if she wanted it? Michael thought, wishing he could scream it at her.

He snatched his wallet back from Jane, opened it, and pulled out fifty Euro.

Filthy Henry took the money and simply stared at Michael directly in the eyes.

"If I was you, sunshine, I'd fork over the rest of the bill. That is, unless you want this no voice thing to last for a few more years."

The fairy detective sounded like that statement was more a promise than threat. Something about how he was standing suggested that very few people ever tried their luck with him. Grudgingly Michael pulled out another hundred Euro and handed it over.

Filthy Henry smiled, took the rest of the money and put it all into his pocket.

"Pleasure doing business with you. Don't worry, I can show myself out."

He nodded at them both, and then left the room. Jane sat down on the couch and turned on the television with the remote, flicking through the channels. But Michael stood there, wallet in hand, feeling the tingle spread throughout his mouth and down his throat.

Tonight's events were grating on him. This random stranger had come into his home, did some hocus pocus, and walked away with three times what Michael thought the service was worth.

That could just not stand. He threw his wallet on the couch and followed Filthy Henry out into the hall.

There were several pieces of his mind he wanted to share with the suit-wearing muppet, magic tricks be damned.

#

Filthy Henry collected his trench coat from the end of the bannisters, pulled it on, then opened the front door and stepped outside. It was still raining, although not nearly as bad as it had been when he arrived. He pulled up his collar and buttoned up the coat.

He heard movement behind him and turned around to see Michael approaching, the glow of the silencing spell around his mouth fading rapidly as it wore off.

There's always one, he thought.

"List hen hare due," Michael said, fighting the residual effects of the spell to unload whatever was on his mind. "Due due thin kink due jar?"

Right now Filthy Henry did not want to deal with some irate moron who wanted to negotiate the fee. More so because these conversations usually ended up the same way, with fists flying about the place and the noses of fairy detectives getting thumped. Unlucky for Michael, Filthy Henry still had an abundance of magical energy left inside him since he had not needed to use any with the Red-man. Enough energy for one really long-lasting, funny, spell.

The one that sprang to mind would resolve the situation quite nicely.

He aimed his hand at Michael.

"*Siúlóid aon éadaí,*" Filthy Henry said, gesturing with a flick of his hand.

A little blue orb appeared in the air and rushed straight

towards Michael, hitting him directly in the chest. The man watched in amazement as his hands, seemingly with a mind of their own, started to take off his clothes. In under a minute he was fully naked, standing in the hallway, staring at Filthy Henry.

"M sore ee," Michael said, looking panicked and struggling to get control of his hands once more.

"I'd say you'll be more embarrassed than sorry in an hour or two," Filthy Henry said, turning around and walking down the driveway.

At the gate he looked back over his shoulder and saw Michael taking an awkward step forward, like a giant drunk baby learning to walk. He took another step, then another, slowly and stiffly making his way down the garden towards the gate. Rain hit his naked body and made it glisten in the streetlight. The look on his face was one of intense concentration as he tried to regain control over his seemingly wayward body.

That should learn him, the fairy detective thought.

Filthy Henry left the gate open, not wanting to hinder Michael on his walk, then headed home.

Chapter Two

"I don't want to drink it."

"Drink the damn thing or we'll never get this job done."

"Did you see how he made it? Did you see? He used needles to drain the blood and then mixed it with whatever was in those vials. Now you want me to drink that? Forget it!"

The argument had been going on for the past half an hour, pretty much the entire drive to the job. Jim O'Toole was getting more and more annoyed with every passing minute. He had started to contemplate force feeding the contents of a vial down his partner's throat, just to stop the stupid arguing.

In Jim's line of work, work that primarily focused on removing the ownership of objects from people in order to give said ownership to different people for a tidy profit, it was not unheard of to be asked to do some questionable things. Knock out an eighty-year-old security guard so you could swipe a priceless painting. Hold a toy gun up to a secretary's face, pretend it was real, and scream at her until she gave you the key to the safe. Heck an obviously insane crime lord had once paid them fifty thousand Euro to literally steal candy from a baby.

It was, apparently, one of the crime lord's life long fantasies to witness.

So Jim viewed the contents of the two vials in his hands as another questionable thing that had to be done in order to get paid. And the payment for this job was worth the inconvenience of drinking something disgusting.

Both he and his long time partner, in a criminal sense, Frankie Doran, had gotten the job through the usually channels. Which meant they had been out one night, having a few pints, when somebody of a shady disposition walked up and handed them an envelope of dubious origin without saying a word. No answers suggested, no questions thought up. A simple transaction.

The amount they would be paid had more zeroes in it than either of the crooks had seen in their lives. The job itself had been a two-parter. Part one had been accomplished with the greatest of ease. Jim generally frowned on animal cruelty, but again it was amazing how stupidly large sums of money could turn any frown upside-down. He and Frankie had been instructed to steal a specific cat from a ditzy artist type and bring it back to their employer. A task they managed to complete without any hassle at all. The end result being one dead feline and two vials of cat blood mixed with some secret herbs and spices. Vials that were currently in Jim's possession.

Vials of vileness which they were now required to drink in order to begin part two of the job.

"I'm not drinking it, end of," Frankie said, crossing his arms.

He was actually pouting. A grown man, built like a tank and sporting a shaved head, pouting like a child that had been asked to eat something healthy with his chocolate chip cookie.

Jim turned off the car's engine and took the key out of the ignition.

It was late, almost half three in the morning, and the street was deserted. They had just entered their destination into the GPS, newly acquired that day, and followed the directions. Why their employer had not just told them to drive to Conyngham Road and park facing the old stone wall of The Phoenix Park was a bit of a mystery. Almost like he wanted to add a cloak and dagger element to the job. Part-time crooks were all the same, seen five too many movies and thought it was all very glamorous. Figured it just was not a true 'heist' unless there was a flare of the mysterious thrown into the mix.

They had parked the car in an empty car park, tucked away nicely in a very dark and shadow filled corner, beside a single storey office building, facing the ancient stone wall that enclosed Phoenix Park. A wall that had been built sometime in the 1600's and was still standing. Not so much as a testament to time, but more in defiance of it.

As annoying as Frankie's point blank refusal was Jim could understand his reluctance. Never before had they been asked to drink something, disgusting or otherwise, in order to get a job done. But drink it they would because apparently part two did not start until the contents of the vials had been consumed. Why this was the case had become a question Jim had decided not to ask.

The trick to getting Frankie to take the strange concoction, Jim knew, would be to drink it first. Not that Jim found this a stomach satisfying strategy. He was, after all, considering taking a shot of animal blood, like some moody teenage vampire at a hip club from a soppy romantic book. There was no way that it would taste good in any...

A mental light bulb went off in Jim's head, illuminating a sneaky idea. He reached over, popped open the glove box, and rummaged around inside, his elbow brushing up against Frankie's inner leg.

"Can I help you down there?" Frankie asked, leaning back in the passenger seat. "Or do I have to leave some money somewhere before you continue?"

"Shut up, gombeen," Jim said. "I'm looking for that can of Red Bull you threw in here earlier."

Jim's fingers found the can. He grabbed it and took it out, leaning back over to his side of the car.

"Hey, you can't have that. I'll need it later," Frankie said, eyeing the can of heart-rate increasing drink like a hungry wolf.

"I'll buy you a new one," Jim said, opening the driver door and stepping out into the cold night. "Just need to get some air before we do this thing."

It was chilly outside the car, although the air smelled a lot better. Frankie had eaten something that was repeating from both ends of him. Which had caused the air in the car to become noxious.

Jim looked around the empty street, all law abiding citizens were tucked up safe and sound in their beds. He closed the driver-side door, opened the Red Bull, and placed the can on the roof of the car. If he had any morals, Jim knew he would have reconsidered his next actions. But that was the beauty of being a crook, your morals were long since gone. Sold on your first job in order to afford that lovely crowbar you cherished so much.

Taking one of the vials Jim uncorked it, tipping the contents inside the stimulating drink. He repeated this procedure with the second vial, emptying it completely before throwing both glass containers over his shoulder. They landed in a bush behind him with rustle of leaf and a clink of glass.

As the two fluids mixed inside the drink started to fizz, loudly. The metal container clinked a little, like it was being lightly crushed. Jim picked it up and sniffed cautiously at the opening. Whatever was inside now smelt worse than what Frankie had produced during the car ride here.

"Over the lips," Jim said to himself, downing half the potion containing power drink in one go. This was not the first time he had drank one of these energy drinks, so Jim knew how it should have tasted. He was fairly sure that the rusty metallic taste was the potion and not some god awful new flavour.

It went down warm and smooth, like hot varnish being poured down his throat. Jim felt like his stomach was already rejecting the drink, closing of parts of the intestine to redirect the fluids. He threw up a little in his mouth, clamping his hand over it to make sure nothing got out. With great effort everything was swallowed back down.

Jim grimaced at the thought of what he had just done and then gagged a little once again. He shook the can, heard the rest of the drink slosh around inside, and walked around to Frankie's side of the car.

The trick now would be to not seem like he wanted to throw up all over the place, while ignoring the sailor's knot that was tightening in his stomach. Jim took a couple of deep breaths to help steady himself, then opened the passenger door and handed the can to his partner in crime.

"You want the rest of this, I forgot how mank it tasted," Jim lied like a pro.

Frankie took the can and downed it in one. He crunched it up with his left hand and flung it out of the car, past Jim, without saying a word. This act was followed by a loud belch that smelt faintly of leaking batteries.

If it was going to be that bloody easy I wouldn't have bothered showing him the damn vials in the first place, Jim thought.

He watched Frankie for a few seconds. There was no change in the man at all. No indication that his innards were rebelling like a small country against their oppressive overlord. The rat bastard was fine.

"You feeling okay?" Jim asked.

Frankie shrugged, he nodded his head.
"Yea, think that curry I had at lunch had something bad in it though. Stomach is in a bit of a jock."
Clearly the best method to imbibe potions of dubious nature was to have some spicy food in your gut beforehand. Jim took a mental note of this. Then again he had high hopes of never having

31

to drink animal blood again just to get a job done. This was the big score, the one that every crook hoped to get at some stage. Early retirement with a big fat pay cheque, just like a useless politician. His dad would have been so proud, had he not disowned Jim after the first time his son had been sent to prison for a bungled burglary.

"Right, let's get started," Jim said, getting his mind back on the job and walking towards the rear of the car.

Unlocking the boot he opened it, reaching in to take out a large black duffel bag. Frankie came down to the rear of the car, took the bag from Jim and gave the contents a quick examination.

"No guns?" he asked, sounding genuinely disappointed.

"No guns, just those dart ones. Boss man said nothing is to be killed on this job."

"Aside from the cat."

"Well yea, obviously. But we didn't kill it, so that doesn't count. Anything we see moving in there gets a dart shot at it. He says we should have enough to knock out half the city if we wanted, so don't go sparing any. Apparently the juice in each of them could take down an elephant, so be careful not to prick yourself with the business end of one."

Frankie took out a dart gun from the bag, along with a ski-mask. He pulled the mask over his head, adjusting the eye slots so he was able to see out, and then tucked the gun into the back of his jeans.

Jim did the same with the second mask and gun, strapping the bag onto his back so that they had the extra ammo with them. He handed an extra clip of darts to Frankie.

"So," Frankie said, looking around at the buildings. "What we robbing then? One of these fancy pants apartments?"

There was nothing really on this street except for apartment complexes. Some had wonderful electronic gates that gave a sense of security, or the illusion of it at least. Others lacked even a fence to separate the garden area of the complex from the road. But their employer had been very precise with his instructions, Frankie had obviously tuned out as they were being given. They were to drink the vials only at this location and wait for a sign once the vials had been finished.

"No," Jim said, looking about the place. "I'm guessing we just wait and see what happens. Probably going to get 'the signal' from somewhere. A flash of a light or something."

"Well so long as we ain't waiting too long," Frankie said. "I'm getting hungry. Plus it's freezing."

Jim's stomach rumbled at the mention of food, but it still felt strange from the potion. He was giving serious consideration to stopping off at a hospital on the way home for a voluntary stomach pumping. The sooner the cat-tonic was out of his body the better. Lord only knew what it would do to his other body parts if he had to naturally pass it naturally out of his system.

Across the street a light caught Jim's attention. It was shining on the wall of the park and had not been there when they arrived. He walked to the front of the car and checked the headlights. Both still turned off, no beam of light coming from them and being reflected on the old stone wall opposite.

"Hey, Frankie," Jim said, gesturing with a flick of his head towards the light. "Have a look at that."

Frankie came over and stood beside Jim, staring at the wall across the street.

"They putting lights in walls now?" he asked.

Before Jim could respond the light grew in intensity, blinding the pair of them so much that they had to shield their eyes with their hands. As suddenly as it started it was over, the light vanishing in a blink. Jim lowered his hands and looked at the wall.

A hole had appeared in the stone work, one that could easily fit a football, where the light had been shining. Jim looked up and down the street, saw no cars coming, then crossed over. Frankie followed close behind. They stood on either side of the hole. Jim looked up at the windows of the apartment blocks for any sign they were being watched. It appeared no insomniacs were observing them, a feat that would have transformed the late night watcher from innocent bystander to pain-in-the-ass witness.

"All clear," Frankie said, who had also checked. "Was that hole there earlier?"

Jim shrugged. He examined the stone wall of the park carefully. It was as it always had been; old and stone and solid as the rocks it was built with. He slowly reached inside the hole with his hand, expecting his fingers to bump into stone as the hallucination was blown away by reality. Instead his fingers brushed against something cold and metallic, set inside the hole. It felt a little like a handle or lever. Gripping it Jim tugged hard, then pushed it down when the tugging failed to achieve anything.

A very loud click came from within the wall, followed by the sound of stone grinding against stone.

The stones directly above the hole in the wall started to move, wiggling about of their own accord. Each one bulged slightly, pushing away from the wall, before being sucked into the old barrier in a cloud of dust and dirt. Jim rapidly pulled his hand back out from the hole, taking two steps away from it. Frankie had already jumped off the kerb onto the road, gun in hand and aimed at the stones.

Jim was by no means a mason or brick layer, but he knew enough about walls and bricks to know that they generally did not move about on their own.

More stones started to wobble and wiggle in place, each one popping out a little before it too was sucked into the wall. With each one that disappeared three more started moving.

"Are you seeing this too?" Frankie asked Jim, eyes fixed on the stones.

Jim did not answer, mesmerized by what was going on. The strange potion their employer had given them was obviously some sort of mind alerting drug and way better than anything either of them had ever taken. To see strange things while you were high was normal, practically passé. For your friend to see the exact same things while also high was impressive.

Selling a concoction like that on the street could make a man very rich indeed.

After thirty seconds the hole in the wall had grown in size, thanks in no small part to the stones that kept disappearing. When the last section had vanished from sight there was an archway left behind, set into the wall as if it had always been there.

"That," Frankie said, "was pretty damn cool. You see that?"
"The wall just transformed like a bloody cartoon. You think I didn't see that?" Jim said.
What was even more trippy than the wall reforming itself so that it had a lovely new archway was what lay beyond the entrance. Logical if a hole appeared in a wall, let alone an entrance way, you would have expected to see what was on the other side. With this logical line of thought Jim figured the only thing they should have seen at that moment was the grass and hills of The Phoenix Park.

The last thing he expected to see was a long stone corridor lit with flaming torches. A corridor that seemed to go straight through the park. A park that had very few buildings in it, let alone ones built right beside the old stone wall.

"Is there some underground castle in the Phoenix Park that nobody has ever heard about?" Frankie said, walking up to the archway and peering inside.

"I have no idea," Jim said, pulling out his dart gun and cocking it.

"Here, did you spike my Red Bull?" Frankie asked, his mental penny finally dropping after the self arranging bricks.

"Of course I did, now build and bridge and get over it already," Jim said.

They both started to walk down the corridor, slowly and each as equally unsure of what was going on as the other. In their line of work, 'hostile acquisitions during nocturnal hours' as Jim liked to sometimes refer to it, you got used to seeing some strange things. People generally collected random junk that wound up being valuable or left their toys best used in the bedroom department drying on the kitchen draining board. So after your fifth or sixth robbery you sort of built up a tolerance for the strange.

But this was an entirely different level of strange. Safes behind ancient paintings, that was acceptable. Entrances in old public park walls that only opened after you drank down a cat blood drug laced potion, that was just not normal.

"I think I see someone up ahead," Frankie whispered, patting Jim on the shoulder then pointing further down the corridor. "We get a little closer," Jim said," then take whoever it is out. Boss-man said the dart will only knock them out. No killing, got it. He was very clear on that point."

"I heard you the first time," Frankie said. "You'd swear I never listen or something."

Both of them stopped moving and Frankie took aim. Jim looked down, trying to see whoever it was that was about to get a helpful prick into slumber-land. It was hard to tell in the flickering torch light, but there was definitely something up ahead. If it was a person then they were either sitting down or extremely short and fat.

Frankie took his shot, a little hiss of air was the only noise his gun made.

The dart found its target. Although in place of the thud sound of a falling body that Jim expected to hear there came a shattering, like a clay pot breaking.

They looked at each other.

"Don't think that was a person," Frankie said.

"Really?" Jim replied, sarcasm dripping from the word.

They continued along the corridor, Frankie slotting another dart into his gun, and came down to their pottery victim. Lying on the ground, smashed to pieces, was a white vase. Bits of it littered the floor. Beside the remains of the vase was a little display stand, now bereft of anything to display.

"That doesn't count as killing something," Frankie said. "All I did was shoot it, clearly it fell over and died of its own accord."

"I don't think breaking a vase counts as killing in any situation," Jim said. "But maybe you should..."

He stopped mid-sentence. Somewhere up ahead a door had opened. There was the sound of feet running towards them. Jim looked around quickly, but there was nowhere to hide at all. Nowhere to try and get the jump on whoever was approaching.

"Get your gun ready," Jim said, raising up his own and taking aim.

What seemed like forever passed in the space of a heartbeat. Eventually Jim got his first glimpse of whoever lived in this underground tunnel. A glimpse that was a little surprising.

"Is that a bloody leprechaun?" Frankie asked, sounding surprised.

It did look like a leprechaun to Jim also, but not the cute and friendly cartoon variety. More the small human with a slightly enlarged head type. He wore an emerald green uniform, a really shiny one, with some strange Celtic symbols emblazoned on the front of it. His beard was bright orange, but neatly trimmed, and made him looked like a tiny Amish person that had fallen into a bucket of paint. Twice. He came running down the corridor, slowing slightly after catching sight of the two crooks, and stopped at the broken vase.

"What do you pair think you're doing?" he asked, pointing a very chubby finger at them. "You shouldn't be in here!"

It can't be a leprechaun, Jim thought. *They aren't real.*

But as a rule Jim tended to believe the evidence of his eyes. Even if tonight his eyes were playing a sizeable amount of tricks on him. Keeping his gun trained on the short man, Jim glanced over at Frankie. His partner was staring at the person in front of them, clearly trying to make sense of things himself.

"Screw it," Jim said and pulled the trigger.

A dart shot out from the gun and hit the leprechaun-looking man in the chest. He looked down at it for a moment as it protruded out from his emerald green uniform, before his eyes rolled back in his head and he collapsed on the ground.

"Did you just shoot a leprechaun?" Frankie asked, staring at the fallen figure. "Do we bring it along with us? Get some wishes or something?"

Jim shook his head.

"Boss-man was very clear about this whole thing. We get in,

38

get the thing, and get out. No killing and I certainly ain't lugging around some midget just because we think it might be a leprechaun. We'd end up like the guys in that joke that get arrested for kidnapping a midget and keeping him under the stairs. Besides, for all we know this place is filled with those weirdos that dress up like elves and dwarves and what not. Prancing around the forest at the weekend pretending to be characters in a fantasy story. Freaks if you ask me."

Frankie looked from Jim to the tiny man and back again.

"But...is he wearing a green suit or is it a really shiny silver kind of deal? If it's green that definitely means he's a..."

"So I take it the cat drink didn't give you colour vision."

Jim sometimes forgot that Frankie saw the world in black and white. Not in the moral sense, there was enough grey in the crook's view of the world to allow him to steal for a living. More black and white in the canine sense of things when it came to seeing colours, or the lack thereof. It accounted for some of the hideous clothes he had worn over the years. Everything matched if you could not tell what the colour was.

"Yes," Jim said. "The guy is wearing a green suit, but that doesn't mean he is a bloody leprechaun. Just that he thinks he is. Don't go letting the fact that we drank a strange concoction, walked through a magically appearing doorway and are clearly in some wizard's castle under the park make you run to wild and magical conclusions. Okay?"

Frankie pointed at the possible leprechaun, a pleading look in his eyes.

"Just come on for God's sake," Jim said, stepping over the slumbering individual. "I want to get this job over with before it gets any weirder."

He did not wait to see what Frankie did. It was way past Jim's bedtime and this place was giving him the creeps. He just wanted to get the goods and get the hell back to normality, with a small stomach pumping afterwards to make sure that normality contained the exact number of hallucinations it was meant to. From now on he was going to stick to the simple jobs, like robbing apartments for T. V's and the likes.

At least that sort of job had no strange dietary conditions.

Chapter Three

The coffee was good.

There was no denying it, the coffee was great. If it had been socially acceptable to have an Irish Coffee at nine in the morning it would have been fantastic, but society frowned on things that made life fantastic. Society always frowned on the minority having fun.

Thankfully some bright spark had come up with flavoured syrups that made coffee even better. Filthy Henry sipped at his hazelnut latte as he walked back to the office, (his third since breakfast) and thought about the accompanying muffin he had purchased with it to eat back at his desk.

That was the problem with being half-human half-fairy, all the fun of being able to perform magic but none of the benefits. Any spell required something in the magical tank and the magical tank needed to be filled up by eating and drinking, no matter how small the spell. A fairy had an innate ability to naturally create the magical energy required for spell casting, an ability that the average human body lacked. Not that humans knew about this evolutionary defect, but for a half-breed it was a problem. In order to refill the mana reserves, the pool of mystical energy which allowed him to perform magic, large amounts of food had to be consumed. More food than normal, so that the excess could be converted into mana. It was either that or allow the fat stores in the body to be used as a source of energy.

A process that was best avoided unless a drastic amount of weight loss was required.

Filthy Henry liked to keep his reserve of magic always full, just in case. The job from last night had used very little energy but it was enough of an excuse to justify having an unhealthy mid-morning snack.

The fairy detective turned onto the upper end of Middle Abbey Street. Most of the shops were opening their doors, awaiting the first customer of the day to walk in. A Luas, Dublin City's wonderful light weight rail system, trundled down the middle of the street with a slight screech of metal wheels on metal tracks. The light rail system, or fancy tram as Filthy Henry liked to think of it, was Dublin's answer to a cheap mode of transport to get from one end of the city to the next and even some outlying suburbs.

Filthy Henry's office was located half-way down the street, the front door sandwiched between a Christian bookshop on one side and a derelict newsagents on the other. It was ideally situated, for a number of reasons. The primary one being that he had been able to buy both floors in the building, turning the top one into his apartment and the bottom into a place of work. Thus giving him the world's shortest commute in existence. One he was so proud of that Filthy Henry had considered giving Guinness Book of World records a call about it sometime.

The fairy detective pulled out the front door key with his free hand as he neared the door, then spotted something outside the building that soured his mood.

Even though it was early, Middle Abbey Street was not totally devoid of people. Dublin was like every city in the world. People that lived there had a requirement to work, it helped to pay the bills at the end of each month. So the suits trudged along, heading this way and that, all running late because it was already past nine. None of them cast a second glance towards Filthy Henry, they never did. He was just another face in the crowd, one the crowd as a whole generally deemed unworthy of their attention. Not that this bothered him. What did tug at his annoyance strings was that everyone was also avoiding the same spot in the middle of the street, whether they knew it or not.

Standing in this reverse-Bermuda Triangle was somebody that nobody else in the area could see except for the fairy detective.

What they were all subconsciously ignoring was a leprechaun; a full blooded fairy. Using natural fairy magic and the innate human ability to disregard that which they did not understand, the leprechaun was able to stand in the middle of the path unheeded. In a stereotypical sense of fashion the leprechaun was wearing an emerald green suit with matching shoes and had a neatly trimmed ginger beard along the edges of his face. He was leaning nonchalantly on a golden cane, examining the dirt under his fingernails.

"Lé Precon," Filthy Henry said, walking up to stand beside the leprechaun. "I've still got a month left to pay, so clear off."

A snot nosed runt in a two piece suit walked past them and gave Filthy Henry a funny look. To the runt it would have appeared as if the fairy detective was talking to himself. Filthy Henry considered using some magic to make the suit wearing yuppie's day a little less pleasant, but he was hungry enough as it was. Wasting magic on petty revenge would have required a couple more muffins than he currently possessed.

"Still fitting in so well, half-breed," Lé Precon said, walking over to the front door of Filthy Henry's building. "We need to have a conversation." He tapped on the door with the top of his cane, gesturing for the fairy detective to open it.

Filthy Henry took a mouthful from his coffee and glared at the leprechaun.

The problem with Lé Precon, if you could narrow the list down to just one thing, was that the short arse was used to getting his own way. Worse still was that Lé Precon was the de-facto King of the Leprechauns. Nobody had pushed him from the throne for the past three hundred years. In that time he had gathered around him enough people to make sure that whoever did try to push him fell down themselves.

Hard. Repeatedly. Onto something very sharp and probably poisoned.

Plus, like all of his big headed race, he was a loan-shark to the fairy world and even certain financial institutes in the human one. Owing money to a leprechaun was like selling your soul to the Devil, you got a good deal at the start but you paid for it through the nose in the end. Owing money to Lé Precon was worse still, it was selling your soul to a devil that the actual Devil feared.

Right now Filthy Henry owed the pint size loan-shark more money than he had earned in the last five years and get rich quick schemes were running out fast. The fact that Lé Precon was here, out in public, even if he was magically invisible to every non-fairy in the area, meant nothing but bad things were in the fairy detective's not-so-distant future.

Better just get this over with, Filthy Henry thought. *And today had been going so well.*

With a forlorn sigh he walked over, unlocked the door, opened it so that Lé Precon could enter the building, then followed quickly behind. As he closed the door Filthy Henry caught a glimpse of a woman wearing a long black coat standing on the opposite side of the street, watching them. He took note of her, left the door on the latch, then walked past Lé Precon without saying a word. The fairy detective climbed up the rickety old staircase to the first floor and tried to figure out why the King of the Leprechauns had decided to drop around.

At the top of the stairs was a small landing with a chair standing up against the wall, its cushion having clearly rested more than its fair share of bums over time. An office door with a frosted window pane set into it stood opposite the chair. Written on the glass in cursive script were the words, "Filthy Henry - Fairy Detective." Another set of stairs led up to the next floor, or home as Filthy Henry lovingly referred to it. Other than that the landing was empty, the only source of light coming from a single bulb that hung from the ceiling without a shade over it.

The fairy detective unlocked and opened the office door, then went inside. He walked around his desk, placed the coffee cup and muffin down on a pile of papers, and dropped into his chair in front of the window. Early morning sunlight filtered through the wooden blinds, giving the office a slightly yellow tint. Thankfully the poor light helped hide the fact that every filing cabinet, box and piece of furniture in the place had a thick layer of dust over them.

Lé Precon came up the stairs and looked around in disgust. He walked into the office, making sure not to touch anything, and stood in front of the desk.

"Why do you work in a place like this?" the leprechaun asked.

"Surely you're not suggesting that I use my powers to further my standing in the human world," Filthy Henry said, snidely. "After all, wouldn't that break some of The Rules?"

"Don't get lippy with me, half-breed," Lé Precon said. "You being alive this long is a massive violation of The Rules! Just remember how much you owe me and what the cost of not paying on time is."

Half-breed. Even after all these years of not caring the fairy world still threw that phrase at him to try and hurt his feelings. It probably irked them all that he described himself as a "Fairy Detective", which helped cushion the derogatory insults fairy folk used against him.

The leprechaun clicked his fingers and a red leather armchair appeared in the room, right in front of Filthy Henry's desk. Magic sparks in the shape of shamrocks ran along the edges of the armchair as it formed. A few multi-coloured shamrocks floated into the air and faded from sight.

For a moment Filthy Henry felt a pang of jealousy. If he had tried to do something like that it would have drained him completely of magical energy and then some. So badly, in fact, that he would have wound up in a week long coma. Not to mention the chair would not have looked nearly as nice, or remained around longer than a month. Yet this pint sized prince of pain-in-the-arse was able to just conjure up whatever he wanted, no problem.

Oh to be a real fairy, Filthy Henry thought.

Lé Precon, trying his best not to look smug at the expression on Filthy Henry's face and failing miserably, rested his golden cane against the arm of the newly created chair. He climbed up into it with a comedic wiggle of his bum and sat down. Pressing his hands together in front of his face he stared across his finger tips at Filthy Henry.

The fairy detective stared right back.

"Spit it out Lé Precon, I don't have all day. Have you come to collect early or what?"

"Such a foul mood when all I do is come offering a gift," Lé Precon said, feigning shock. He looked directly into Filthy Henry's eyes. "The Balance has been broken," he said, coldly.

"Not my problem," Filthy Henry said, picking up his coffee to take a drink. "So what if one fairy race has done something to another, you lot sort that out amongst yourselves. I only deal with the ones that start making trouble for humans, you know that."

Lé Precon leaned forward in his seat, which made his oversized head seem even bigger than his body. But his expression was serious, hinting that jokes were probably not going to be appreciated during the conversation.

"Listen you freak of nature, this isn't some game! The Little People were robbed last night. The Mothercrock was stolen from us. The Rules have been broken but not only that they were broken by two humans."

Filthy Henry stopped mid-sip.

Most of the tales about fairies were true, although it was a truth that had been distilled in such a way that humanity did not ask too many questions. As the centuries passed these truths became tales, finally becoming fairy tales and morphing into something unrecognisable from the truth. But like most myths and legends they still had to start somewhere, that spark of fact had to be there to get conjured into a believable lie. Otherwise nobody would ever believe the lie.

One true thing about the leprechaun race was the part about their crocks of gold. The magical little pot that never emptied of gold and could be found at the end of a rainbow guarded by a wise and friendly leprechaun. Except they never sat at the end of a rainbow, waiting for some stupid mortal out on a rainy day walk to stumble by and get filthy rich. That was a clear example of truth being transformed into tall tale.

The rainbow was a magical alarm system protecting the crock from being touched by anybody but the leprechaun who owned it. After all, it was not just humankind that sought riches and wealth. Fairies did as well.

Each crock of gold derived its endless source of wealth from the Mothercrock. A singular crock that powered every other, kept by the King of the Leprechauns. If it ever left his possession for more than a week rumour had it every crock in the world would lose its gold producing powers. Until it was returned to the King the other crocks were just big pots with finite amounts of gold in them.

It had become an urban legend amongst fairy kind, something that sounded plausible but could in no way actually exist. The fact that Lé Precon was mentioning it to Filthy Henry meant that the situation was serious. The Mothercrock was hidden, like all the crocks were, and protected by the most powerful of rainbows. For a human to have somehow figured out a way around all of that ... it was an impossible thing to even consider.

"Hang on," Filthy Henry said, turning in his chair so that he could look Lé Precon directly in the eye. "You're trying to tell me that two humans managed to locate and loot your hidden fort, getting around the rainbow alarm in the process? Seriously? Even I couldn't manage that and I am the most powerful magic wielding half-mortal around."

"Do I look like I am here to entertain you or something?" Lé Precon said. "Two humans broke into my little humble fort the other night and stole the Mothercrock. Humans, without any magical skills at all. Beyond being able to see things they shouldn't be able to see, of course."

Filthy Henry leaned back in his seat and whistle appreciatively.

That was impressive. If he ever met the brave sods that had pulled the heist he would buy them a drink. Actually he would make them buy him a drink, since they now had an infinite amount of wealth to dispose of.

"I'm still not entirely sure why you here, short arse," Filthy Henry said. "Looks to me like you need to hire some better security. When you find the Mothercrock that is."

Lé Precon sighed, tugging thoughtfully on the end of his beard.

"I'm here to hire you," the leprechaun said, sounding as cheery about that statement as if he was at a party in a cemetery. "The

Rules are clear on this. It wasn't a fairy that robbed me so we can't go after them. We need a mediator and unluckily you're the only one alive..."

"No thanks to your kind," Filthy Henry interrupted.

"Not my kind, half-breed," Lé Precon protested. "But let's not rake over those coals. It has been decided that we need to hire you to find the thieves and get back what's mine."

It really should not have, but this conversation made Filthy Henry feel really good. Generally his dealings with the fairy world involved sorting out trouble maker fairies who were terrorizing a human somewhere. Fairies breaking The Rules, potentially exposing the fairy world to mortals. The odd time he managed to convince a fairy to help him pull off a con on some gullible American tourists, splitting the take fifty-fifty. Those little scams helped pay the bills most months. So to have an important fairy, especially Lé Precon, show up on his doorstep looking for help, well that was a dear diary moment right there.

"I presume," Filthy Henry said, sipping at his coffee, ", that there will be some form of payment for this job. Compensation. Expenses. That sort of thing."

"You're a rat bastard half-breed, anyone ever tell you that?"

"Only your kind, every chance they get," Filthy Henry said, taking a mouthful of his drink.

"Well yes, there is payment for the job. One I think you will like," Lé Precon smiled. "How about I wipe your debt clean?"

Filthy Henry spat out his mouthful of coffee, spraying the far wall. He wiped his chin on the back of his hand, checking to make sure no drops were waiting to stain his clothes.

"Define clean?" he asked.

"We're both speaking English here you idiot, clean is clean. You won't owe me anything at all. Judging from your lovely place of work here I don't think you were coming close to getting the cash together anyway. Nice to see you invested what you borrowed so well."

"I don't come to you for financial advice," Filthy Henry said.

"No, you just come for the financing part. The advice I give for free."

It was a good offer, there was no denying that. The debt was sizeable, the terms of defaulting undesirable. Lé Precon was the most ruthless leprechaun around, hence why he had lasted so long as the big cheese. An opportunity to get squared away with him was too good for Filthy Henry to turn down and Lé Precon knew it.

But the fact that the short arse had come out to see him, rather than summon Filthy Henry, suggested that they did not just want his help. He needed it. The fairy world needed it.

Which meant that the payment terms could be improved. There was room for negotiation.

"That's a nice offer," Filthy Henry said, nodding his head with approval. "But I think you can sweeten the pot a little."

Lé Precon's eyes opened wide with surprise.

"Sweeten...? Do you know how many people have ever had the offer of their debt being wiped by me? I'll give you a hint: there are a lot of the same digit in the amount you owe me."

"Yea, I'm guessing you can count them out on no fingers as well, so what? No, I think that if I were to take on the case I'd want a little extra. Nothing too major, nothing crazy. Just one, small, extra little thing. Tiny, in fact. You wouldn't even miss it."

The fairy detective continued to drink his coffee, which had started to go cold, and said no more. It would give Lé Precon time to consider his options, which Filthy Henry figured were very low. The Rules were The Rules after all. If a human was somehow involved in this then they needed a half-breed's help in tracking them down. Sending a full blood fairy to do the job would have resulted in more Rules being broken.

Which meant the fairy detective was not so much a last resort as he was the only option. Making his request more of a veiled ultimatum with two options: agree or sod off.

"What's the extra?" Le Precon asked through gritted teeth.

Filthy Henry tossed his empty coffee cup into the waste paper basket at the end of the desk and smiled.

"I want one wish," he said. "To be granted by you."

Something snapped in Lé Precon's head, some muscle attached to his eye lid. It was the only explanation as to why his left eye started to twitch so violently all of a sudden. He just sat there, silently, with his eye lid doing a little jig on its own.

Technically the legend about capturing a leprechaun and getting three wishes was untrue. But that did not mean they did not have the ability to grant wishes. Filthy Henry figured asking for more than one wish would have been pushing his luck. Besides, he would no doubt have only wasted the second one on something stupid. As it stood he had already decided what he wanted to use the one wish on.

The same thing he had wished for his entire life. The only thing that no amount of magic, full blood or not, could grant him. To get it he needed the reality bending abilities of a wish, something only a leprechaun could do. Something none of them did lightly.

Lé Precon took a deep breath and closed his eyes.

"You'll abide by the Rules of Wishes?" he asked.

"You can trust me," Filthy Henry said, grinning.

"No I bloody well can't half-breed," the leprechaun said. "But this is one of those times where it's better to make a deal with the half-blood you know."

So I am their only option, Filthy Henry thought.

"Fine," Lé Precon said, reaching over the table with his hand. "You have a deal, but the extra is going to mean I want this done inside of the week. I don't want any of the other crocks to stop making gold. No other leprechaun is to know that I lost possession of the Mothercrock or it will be the end of me."

Filthy Henry grabbed the leprechaun's hand and shook it three times, sealing the deal between them. Two sparks leapt up, one from each of their hands, and danced together in the air for a heartbeat before vanishing. The deal was a magical contract now.

"Done," Filthy Henry said.

Two humans with an endless supply of gold were not going to be difficult to find, let alone deal with. Humans were nothing if not predictable. That wish would be as good as his by the end of the day.

Lé Precon let go of the fairy detective's hand and climbed down from the leather armchair. He took out a light green hankie from his suit pocket and vigorously wiped the hand which Filthy Henry had shook.

"You'll no doubt be interacting with our world a lot more than usual," the leprechaun said. "So I'll try to make sure every race knows to offer you assistance. I'll be in touch."

With that Lé Precon turned and left the office, walking back down the stairs and left Filthy Henry alone with his thoughts.

The fairy detective heard the stairs creaking followed by the street door opening. He reached over and picked up the muffin. It looked extra tasty this morning for some reason.

"Breakfast of champions," he said.

Filthy Henry bit into the muffin, enjoying the taste the moment it hit his tongue. The downside to having magic did have one upside, it had to be said. Being able to eat whatever the hell you wanted and use a little magic to burn off the calories was the best gym or diet regime in existence. No monthly membership fees. No irritating sweaty people clustered around you on a treadmill. You ordered a pizza, ate the entire thing, then let the fatty goodness get converted into mana.

The meeting with Lé Precon had unnerved Filthy Henry a little more than he was willing to admit. If a human, any human, had figured out that the fairy world was a real thing it meant trouble. That a human had managed to steal from a fairy meant a new word had to be created in the English language to describe an even bigger level of trouble.

A knock on the glass panel of the office door drew Filthy Henry back from his mouth-watering muffin meditations.

Standing in the doorway was the woman from the street.

She was a good looking woman, which was a rare thing when it came to the usual female visitors of Filthy Henry's workplace. Her hair was long, a chestnut-brown colour, and she had a dazzling pair of blue eyes. There was a nice shape to every part of her body, all the bits looking exactly as eye pleasing as they should.

"I'm closed for the next half hour," he said, taking another bite from his breakfast. She may have been attractive but he was in the middle of breakfast after all. Certain standards of living had to be adhered to.

"I was told you're a private investigator. One that dealt in...special...cases," the woman said, her hands fidgeting as she spoke.

"I am," Filthy Henry said, chewing on another mouthful of muffin.

"Well I want to hire you to find my cat," she said. "She's a very special cat and..."

Filthy Henry held up his hand, indicating that the woman should stop talking. He looked her over once again but would never have guessed that she was a crazy cat lady. They generally frequented his office as well, but clearly all of them subscribed to the same fashion magazines. Magazines which said the current, yesteryear and future look for a woman obsessed with cats was wild straw like hair, one crazy roving eye, smoke stained teeth and clothes that had not seen the light of day since 1950.

"Look," he said, disappointed that this was some new attractive breed of crazy cat lady before him. "I'm not some sort of pet detective. You say you lost your cat? I'm going to save you my considerable fee and solve the case for you now in two minutes. Pussy has either ran away and found itself a new owner that feeds it some treats it prefers or there is a red stain on the road somewhere near your house that wasn't there the day before. Thanks and tell your friends, I could use the business."

He smiled at her, then took another bite from the muffin.

The woman looked hurt by what Filthy Henry had just said, tears welling up in her eyes.

"I'm sorry to have wasted your time then," she said, gruffly. "Obviously the short man with the golden cane has given you a case worth a lot more than finding my cat. Goodbye."

She turned and went back down the stairs.

Filthy Henry stared after her, mouth opened wide.

Fairy folk could not be seen my normal people. Full stop. Well more semi-colon, but it was still an extremely rare thing.

People that had slight mental problems saw fairies. But society had a great way of dealing with these people and kept them all locked up in one nice location. To help them get better, of course. Drunkards sometimes caught sight of fairy folk, but in the cold light of sobriety after a night of binge drinking it was easily swept under the logic carpet as a great night of fun with the only question being 'Why were the girls on that hens night dressed up like pixies?'

But that woman had not been young enough to have imaginary friends. She was definitely sober and did not seem to be a nut job, cat thing pushed momentarily to the side. Which meant that a normal human had seen Lé Precon dealing with Filthy Henry in the middle of the street.

Coincidences were things that the fairy detective believed happened to other people. He wolfed down the last morsel of his breakfast and ran after the woman. In the world of magic coincidences just meant things were more intertwined that one would expect.

Chapter Four

After what they had seen under The Phoenix Park Jim and Frankie both decided against dropping the goods off straight away. Things had to be re-evaluated. Stimulants removed from the body. Possible medical examinations booked both for their organs and in a mental capacity.

"Was that a rainbow?" Frankie asked, staring at the road ahead of them with glazed eyes. "I could only see a dome of brightness spinning around. Like a grey-white sort of..."

"We said we wouldn't talk about that again!" Jim shouted as he looked for a place to park the car.

It was coming up on noon and they both figured that whatever had been in those vials was finally out of their system. The greasy breakfast they had gotten straight after the job had also helped a good bit. Jim had used the simple logic of a man who had been on a bender the night before. Find the first café that smelt like it was cooking up a fry and order the biggest artery clogging dish you could. Soak-age for whatever had been drunk the night before.

By sheer fluke, or unintended brilliance, it had worked. Half an hour after the last grease covered slice of toast had been eaten both Jim and Frankie had started to see clearly once more. The odd looking people that walked the streets of Dublin had faded away, leaving behind the expected normal people in their stead.

With his mind clear enough to risk driving again, Jim had decided they should head to the drop off point down by the docklands. At this stage Jim just wanted to finish the job and enjoy an extended holiday. Maybe speak to a career guidance counsellor about different jobs he could take. After the antics of last night thieving had completely lost its appeal to him.

Whatever happened to just giving a guy a crowbar and pointing him at a window that needed opening?

The docklands were a part of the city located, ironically enough, down near the docks. Once upon a time there had been numerous warehouses sprawled throughout the area, home to various containers for storage and what not. Nowadays all that stuff was kept up in the actual docks and the warehouses had become derelict buildings with only a handful of them still used for actual storage.

As they drove past one of the warehouses that had long since been abandoned Jim saw a car up ahead pulling out from a parking spot. Indicating, Jim steered the car towards the spot and parked, bumping the kerb with the front wheel.

"Maybe I should have drove," Frankie said, unbuckling his belt.

"You've no license," Jim said.

"True, but it's less illegal to drive a car without a license if you don't have the learner plates up. Least then if the cops do stop you they can only do you for forgetting your license, not driving when you have signs on your car to tell people you are only learning to drive. "

Jim turned off the engine and opened the driver door.

"Stop thinking so much and just help me get this bloody thing into the warehouse," he said.

Frankie climbed out the other side of the car. They walked down to the boot, opened it up, and looked at the goods from the night before. If 'goods' was an accurate description for what they had been asked to steal. Gun to his head Jim would have said it was a worthless heap of shite that could have been left where it was. Even if it had been beneath a strange light show, one that only Frankie was able to walk through for some reason.

"Do you reckon it is worth its weight in gold or something?" Frankie asked as he reached into the boot and pulled out the crock.

It looked no better in the daylight that was sure. Jim wondered if the thing was some sort of antique. Rich employers loved their antiques. They would hire a whole squad of crooks, thieves, lowlifes and robbers to steal one spoon from an old widow living on a hill in the Galway countryside. All because the spoon had once been used to make a cup of tea for some king that visited the area a million years before.

Rich folk were just weird like that. More money than sense, a condition they all suffered with.

Frankie placed the crock on the ground and slammed the car boot shut.

The crock looked like it had been beaten into shape by a blind blacksmith. One who had heard a poor description of what a crock should look like. It was made from some sort of iron, blackened from years of dirt and grime. There were no handles on it at all, which made carrying it somewhat awkward, and aside from a few random symbols that had been etched onto the outer surface it was totally plain. A small child could have easily sat it in, but that would have been the only use Jim could see for the ugly thing.

"Maybe it makes things you put into it turn into gold," Frankie said, picking the crock up once again and stepping onto the pavement. Jim snorted, laughing at the idea. Except somewhere in his mind a penny dropped. A dull penny that was nice and shiny by the time it bounced of the mental floor of his mind.

He reached into his pocket and pulled out the car keys. Ordinary, simple, inexpensive car keys. Then tossed them into the crock. They clanged against the inside, causing the crock to ring like an obese bell. Jim counted to ten, then reached in and pulled the keys back out.

They were unchanged.

"Guess it doesn't change things to gold then," he said.

Frankie stared at him.

"I was only joking," he said. "You know, because of all the crazy crap we saw last night."

Jim reached over quickly and flicked Frankie's left ear, hard. He looked up and down the street, checking that nobody was paying them any real attention.

"Just bring the damn thing into the warehouse will you," he said, pocketing the car keys once again.

They walked down the street, stopping at a warehouse with a red wooden door. According to the instructions given to them by their employer this was the drop point. It looked disused, abandoned. The windows had wooden boards up, covering them completely. Graffiti was sprayed along every inch of the walls, the typical dyslexic spellings of names and phrases. One section had what looked like a stick-man army, each brandishing an anatomically impossible penis.

"Kids these days," Jim said, stepping up to the warehouse door and banging on it.

From inside came the sound of locks being opened, chains pulled back and bolts moved. The small door, set into the larger wooden barrier, opened slightly on creaking hinges. Nobody appeared. It was as if the door had opened a little by itself. Jim pushed against it, opening it fully, and motioned with his head for Frankie to step inside with the crock.

"Why is it always a stupid warehouse?" Frankie asked,

stepping inside with the crock in his arms.

Jim scanned the street one more time, double checking that no by-standards were going to spontaneously turn into witnesses, and followed Frankie inside.

The interior of the warehouse was gloomy, dark. A yellowish light streamed in from some dirt encrusted panels in the roof. Somewhere there came the rustle of feathery wings, followed by the cooing of pigeons who were no doubt squatting in the rafters above. There were large wooden crates stacked all over the place, like a game of Tetris that had gone incredibly wrong. Standing in the middle of the warehouse floor was a large wooden desk and chair, positioned out of any direct sunlight. A lamp was turned on, standing to the right hand side of the desk.

Seated in the chair behind the desk was their employer, partially hidden by shadows.

"I trust everything went smoothly," he said as the thieves entered. "Please ensure the door is locked behind you Jim. Thanks ever so much."

Jim closed the door to the street and slid everything back into place, sealing them inside with their employer.

"Everything went fine boss," Frankie said, strolling towards the desk and showing off the crock.

Their employer leaned forward, the bottom of his chin coming into the light cast by the lamp. His hands slid across the desk, reaching out towards the stolen goods.

Jim noticed that they were strangely pale, but passed it off as just the poor lighting in the warehouse. They had never seen their employer during the daytime, or outside even. Not that it mattered, most of their employers tended to hire them over the phone or in some back alley pub late at night. It was just how things were done.

"Yea," Jim said, walking back down the warehouse floor and standing beside Frankie. "Everything went smoothly. Aside from the crap you made us drink. You make everyone who works for you drink that stuff? That's bound to be an illegal substance on some country's drug list."

Their employer laughed.

"No, Jim," he said. "That potion is only for a special sort of person under my employ. You should feel honoured that you had a glimpse into things most mortals never fully understand."

"Mortals?" Frankie repeated the word, looking at Jim for an explanation of its meaning.

Above them something moved along the rafters, disturbing the pigeons. Wings flapped rapidly as the birds scattered. Jim looked up but could not make out anything. A shiver ran down his spine. Something about this little meeting was giving him the creeps but he could not quite figure out what. His gut feeling was that things were not all as they should be and generally he trusted his gut completely.

"Frankie, if you would be so good as to place the crock on the desk for me," their employer asked politely.

Frankie walked over and dropped the crock down on the desk, causing the lamp to rock slightly.

Their employer dragged the black metal container closer, turning it around slowly as he examined it in the light.

"Gentlemen you have done very well," he said. "You will go down in history for this one, an impossible crime pulled off perfectly. The alarm system proved to be no issue for you?"

"Well," Jim said. "It took a few minutes to get around alright, some pretty fancy stuff. They get that in from Japan or something? I've never seen anything like it. I couldn't get past it at all but Frankie was able to just stroll right on through. Not really sure why that was, maybe you could explain that one?"

Their employer said nothing. He simply sat there and his little finger around the edge of the crock. Silence reigned supreme in the warehouse for a couple of minutes.

"So can we get paid now?" Frankie asked, showing signs of agitation. "Because both of us are pretty wrecked after last night and I just want to crawl home to my bed."

"Yes, yes I can imagine so," their employer said as he continued to look the crock over. "I'd say that you both saw things last night which made you think you were dreaming all along. Your own little visit to Wonderland. You have earned a nice long rest."

Jim was not sure why, but something about that last sentence did not sit well with him. It was one of those statements you would hear a politician make. A string of words that could mean a number of things depending on how you interpreted them. He was never one for book-reading or paying attention in school, but the thief knew enough about telling lies to spot one being told to him directly.

There was a sudden rush of wind to his left, nearly knocking Jim over, and Frankie disappeared from sight. All that was left of his partner was a single shoe wobbling on the warehouse floor by the desk.

"What the hell was that? Where's Frankie?!" Jim said, looking around rapidly with his fists at the ready to punch at something.

Their employer had retreated back into the shadows, bringing the crock with him. All that could be seen of him was a gloomy outline seated behind the desk. He was drumming his fingers along the crock, a hollow metallic ringing filling the air.

"Well, I figured that you both wanted to get a little rest after pulling off the job," their employer said. "So I merely accommodated him. Don't worry you can get some rest soon as well. The most peaceful rest you've ever had."

Up above the birds were disturbed once more as something moved amongst the rafters like a ninja.

Jim could feel his heart pounding in his chest, panic setting in. Panic that he had not experienced in a long time. Right now he was in a situation that had not been anticipated. Frankie had vanished into thin air, taken by a gust of wind that haunted the warehouse. There were shadow ninjas roaming the roof above, no doubt waiting to drop down and take him away. It was like being in some old horror movie, right before the killer sprung his most terrifying trap.

"Listen here you," Jim said, putting on a brave face and waving his fist at their employer. "I'm not scared of some parlour tricks pulled in a spooky ass warehouse. I've knocked bigger men than you out before and I can do it to you no problem."

There was another rush of air, toppling over the desk and knocking the lamp to the ground. Their employer was no longer in his seat, as if the wind had picked him up just like it had with Frankie. Jim took a cautious step toward the desk, fists at the ready. He craned his neck to get a look over the desk at the floor.
There was nobody there.

"Oh this is getting..."

"Creepy?" their employer whispered, directly into his ear.

Jim whirled around, throwing a right hook with the intention of punching their employer in the head. He put his entire weight behind the punch, wanting nothing less than four teeth to be embedded in his knuckles.

If it had not happened right before his eyes Jim would have sworn that there had been some sort of computer effects involved. As he turned their employer looked at Jim's approaching fist. There was a blur of motion and Jim's hand passed through air,

63

connecting with nothing. As his momentum carried him on another blur happened and their employer returned to the same spot he had been standing in.

He smiled at Jim. A smile which revealed a set of elongated canines that had no right being in a human mouth.

"My turn," their former-employer said as his canines grew in length.

Jim screamed.

Chapter Five

It never ceased to amaze Filthy Henry how fast a woman scorned could walk. Nothing on Earth could move as fast. If such a power source could be harnessed for the good of all mankind the world would be a better place. Cars designed like ones from The Flintstones would become the norm and all those oil rich countries would not be able to give away their produce.

The fairy detective came out onto Middle Abbey Street, pulling the front door closed behind him, and spotted the woman just as she turned to go down Upper Liffey Street. He had to run in order to catch up with her. Even then she did not change her pace, forcing him to jog along beside her.

"So," he said, trying to come up with some charm offensive on the spot. "You saw the short arse did you?"

"What do you want?" she said, eyes fixed straight ahead. "You made it perfectly clear that you weren't going to take on my case. You said you weren't a pet-detective, remember?"

Filthy Henry cursed how the female mind worked. Ask them to remember easy directions from one place to another they would get lost before leaving the house and some how end up in India. Say something that they found to be slightly insulting and they could call it up verbatim until the end of time. Then again not all men were great at directions either. The problem was that men forgot the wording of an insult in the time it took to throw a punch, meaning they had a lot less to recall in their favour when it came to bringing up old arguments.

The fairy detective rolled his eyes. It was too early for this. He could use some magic to make the conversation go a little smoother, but that would only have made her talk until the spell expired. Not tell him the truth or engage in a proper conversation. Making her feet stop working was another option, although there was the problem of momentum then. If her feet suddenly ceased responding to her she would topple forward and hit the street. Which would no doubt make her even less inclined to have a conversation. Bloody noses and missing teeth tended to annoy people.

He decided to try something that had not worked for him in years. "What's your name?" Filthy Henry asked.

She stopped walking and looked at him, confused. A truck drove by, trundling down the narrow street.

"My name? Shelly..."

The truck driver blew on his horn at two teenagers who had decided to run out in front of him in order to cross the road. Filthy Henry was unable to make out Shelly's surname over the noise and glared at the back of the truck as it continued on its way. The teenagers, safely across the road, gave the truck obscene gestures as they continued at a stroll down the street.

"Well, Shelly," he said, surprised that it had been that simple to get her to stop and talk with him. "You caught me at a bad time earlier. The short arse who was in my office rubs me up the wrong way sometimes. Plus I owe him far too much money, but that will all be sorted by the end of the week I reckon. Not that you needed to know that last bit, of course, but I figure it might explain why I was being short with you. How about we get a cup of coffee and talk about your cat?"

"Why?" Shelly said. "You've already made it perfectly clear that cats aren't important. Plus I don't have as much money as the small gentleman clearly does. Who can afford a solid gold cane like that? Anyway if that is the class of client you work with normally I won't be able to pay you a huge fee."

"Let's start again," the fairy detective said, flashing his

winning smile at her. "You only get one chance to make a second impression after all. I'm Filthy Henry, Fairy Detective."

He held out his hand. Shelly looked at it, then back at him.

"Where are we going for this coffee that your buying?" she said, her hands kept firmly in her coat pockets.

#

The café on Moore Street was pretty busy considering how early it was. There was a steady trail of suit wearing yuppies coming in for their morning caffeine fix on the way to work. Practically every single one of them had those ridiculous smartphones out, pretending to be hip and check their emails. No doubt they were just updating their social network statuses to inform the world that coffee was being bought.

Filthy Henry detested each and every one of them. Mainly because he did not see the point in having a phone you could edit a full feature film on while looking at porn. His phone could make calls and send text messages. What more could you need a mobile phone to do? He collected his drinks order from the pimpely-faced youth behind the counter and brought them over to a table by the window where Shelly sat. Placing one of the mugs in front of her the fairy detective sat down in the chair opposite.

She had seen Lé Precon, showing up in his office right after the little green midget had given him a job to do. Somehow, some way, something about Shelly was connected with the case. Sometimes the Forces of Magic just worked liked that, ensuring people were in the wrong place at the right time. All Filthy Henry had to do was get her to talk.

"So," he said, smiling to ease the tension. "You came to me about your missing pussy."

"Cat," Shelly said, bringing her coffee mug up to take a sip.

"Not pussy, cat. Pussy is a word used by dirty minded individuals trying to be funny."

Cross sense of humour off the list then, Filthy Henry thought.

"Cat it is. But why did you come to me?"

Shelly looked around the coffee shop, as if she was embarrassed. Her gaze fell for a couple of seconds on a nearby empty table, before she shook her head and looked away. She lowered her mug back to the table and stared out the window at some people passing by. Whatever she wanted to say must have been fairly strange, at least to her normal view of the world.

"If it helps at all," Filthy Henry said, "there is a detective-client confidentiality clause. Kind of like with a doctor. Whatever gets said stays between us. You won't find it on a website in ten seconds time."

He could see her weigh up what had been said, finally taking a deep breath and relaxing a little.

"Her name is Kitty Purry," Shelly said, tapping her thumbnails on the handle of her coffee mug.

"That's...original," he said. "Where did you come up with that name?"

"I didn't," Shelly said, eyes still focused on the street outside the window. "She told me that was her name."

The human body is a remarkable thing. It can do things all on its own, without any input from the actual human that owns the body. Filthy Henry often used this to his advantage when working a case. You could tell a person was lying based on the movement of their eyes. A nervous twitch would become more evident the closer you got to the truth. But blushing, blushing was just hilarious to watch. Right then Shelly was as red in the face as a Red-man.

"I'm sorry," Filthy Henry said. "Did you just say your cat told you she was called Kitty Purry?"

"Forget it," Shelly said, pushing back her seat from the table and taking her coat off the back of the chair. "I knew you'd just think I was some crazy cat lady that has no friends."

"No, not at all, just sit back down there will you."

She looked at him, one arm in her coat the other still out. "Why?"

To her a talking cat was a source of ridicule, something her friends no doubt would mock her about. But people usually just put up lost cat posters when a pet disappeared. A talking cat though, you would want to find that animal before anybody else did. Whoever found that cat had something that could earn them a sizeable amount of money. So you would go and hire a person to find the cat, because the animal was your friend.

Now a normal person would consider a talking cat to be some sort of mental problem. Easily disregarded as a good reason why better pills should be prescribed to the person having fantastic feline conversations. Yet Shelly did not appear crazy. Plus she had seen Lé Precon, which meant that there was a much more magical explanation for why her cat apparently spoke to her. Also for the briefest of moments she had looked at the two fairy folk seated in the table beside them having coffee. A table that to the non-fairy world should have seemed completely empty.

"What do you work as?" Filthy Henry asked, taking a mouthful of coffee.

"I'm an artist," Shelly said, still standing up. "I do paintings and sculptures. What does that have to do with Kitty?"
Creative sort, Filthy Henry thought. *With a highly developed imagination she's probably seen glimpses of the other side forever and not even realised it. Merely painted what she saw after her mind just stored the information for later use.*

69

"Did you have an imaginary friend when you were younger?" Filthy Henry asked. "Maybe see people that weren't there when you looked again?"

Shelly's eyes opened wide as Filthy Henry spoke. She glanced once again at the fairy folk beside them, then slowly took her coat back off and sat down once more.

"Yes," she said in little more than a whisper. "How did you...?"

The metaphorical nail had been hit on top of the cranium.

"I'm going to talk here for a few minutes and you can stop me when things start sounding familiar, okay?"

All she did was nod.

"Excellent," Filthy Henry said, settling back into his chair and folding his arms. "You see things that others can't see. Nearly all the time, more so when you were younger, but not for very long. A fleeting glance and then it's gone. They weren't imaginary friends as such, but they would interact with you like they were. Not all of your young toddler friends saw what you did, but there were a few. As you grew up your friends started to see these things less and less, but you still could if you really tried. You started drawing from an early age, capturing what you saw on paper. The years continued to roll on by and you too started to see them less and less, but you still could remember them clearly. You worked them into your paintings and sculptures. Sometimes you would be sitting in the middle of a field or a shopping centre, your mind wandering, and you would catch a glimpse of something that wasn't there. Only a glimpse. But enough to make you go home and create something new. On very rare occasions you would find yourself walking down the street and apologising for nearly walking into somebody, even though nobody was in front of you. Any of this sound familiar yet?"

Shelly stared at him with her mouth wide open. If her chest had not been moving it would have been hard to tell whether or not she was breathing. But her reaction was all Filthy Henry needed to confirm his theory was right. This woman was one of the rarest sort of people, still slightly in touch with her younger self. Still able to believe that magic might just exist in the world. Enough so that she acknowledged, even if it was on a deeply subconscious level, that the world as she saw it was not all there was to see. She was able to peep behind the curtain once in a while. She could catch a glimpse of the fairy world.

"Now," Filthy Henry said. "How could I know that, short of reading your journal? Which you do not keep because you didn't want to chronicle down these things just in case people thought you should be locked up."

Shelly shook her head slowly from left to right. Her shoulders moved slightly, as if she was trying to shrug but had forgotten how to.

"Well," the fairy detective continued. "It's because I believe you really did get told by your cat what her name was. Although the twist is your cat is not a cat as you know it."

"What is she?" Shelly asked, swallowing before she spoke.

Filthy Henry pushed his chair back from the table and stood up. He checked around, making sure nothing was left behind, then walked around and stood behind Shelly's chair. Taking hold of the back of it, he slid her out from the table too, then picked up her coat. He held it open so that she could drop her arms into it.

"I'm going to tell you," he said, "but not in here. We don't want to go making a scene."

#

Shelly had fond memories of Moore Street, going back to when her grandfather was still alive. Every weekend he would come out by bus and collect her from her parents' house, bringing her into the city for a few hours. Without fail they would always come here to get the fruit and vegetables for the coming week. He always had a list, provided by her grandmother, on what exactly was needed.

So instead of just going to the local shop, which was two doors down from his house, Shelly's grandfather would make a forty minute trip on the bus so that he could shop on Moore Street. As far as he was concerned this was the place to get the freshest fruits and vegetables of all.

"Everything in a store is covered in chemicals," he would tell Shelly as they strolled down the cobble stone street between the stalls. "You don't want to eat chemicals, you want what the chemicals can't give you. Here's the only place you can get that. These people are proper Dublin, they get proper fruit and veg around here. Put that down, you've no idea where that syringe was before you."

Shelly loved Moore Street because it always brought back those memories of her grandfather and how he had been before he died. "You okay?"

The fairy detective's question brought her back to the present, leaving memory lane for another time. They were both standing in the middle of Moore Street, people passing them by. Around them stall owners shouted out various things for sale at fantastic prices. The smell of fruit and vegetables wafted on the breeze.

"Why are we here?" she asked him, watching a young girl buying some apples from a fruit stall nearby.

"Your cat," Filthy Henry said. "I reckon it really did talk to you, although it shouldn't have. It was breaking The Rules. But you can never trust a Cat Síth to follow the rules. They're as bad as actual cats like that. Worse, in fact, because the little feline fecks should know better."

"Kitty Purry was a cat," Shelly said. "I don't know what that other thing is you mentioned. A Sith Lord?"

"A Cat Síth? I'll explain in a minute," Filthy Henry said, walking over to a fruit stall and picking up two bananas. "Good source of potassium these."

He paid for them, peeled one and started eating it.

"I'm going to show you something now, something that most people never get to see in their adult years. But I reckon it will be easier to show you than most people. Hell it's the only reason I am bothering to show you full stop."

Shelly took a step back and looked the fairy detective up and down.

"You're not going to show me your thing are you? Like some pervert?"

"I charge a bit more than a bunch of bananas for that sorta thing love," Filthy Henry said with a dirty smile. He finished off the fruit, dropping the skin into a nearby bin, and walked over to Shelly. "Now, this won't hurt a bit and can be undone in a minute if you want. But once I do it, you can control it yourself. Follow me?"

She had no idea what he was talking about and was beginning to wonder why she had even come to him in the first place. An advert in the newspaper suggested that he was the sort of detective she needed. How many people lost talking cats after all? Plus the ad did say that he worked for no mental health institutions, which was a tick in the pro column. Men in white coats generally got called when people spoke about talking cats. Filthy Henry raised both his hands up and lightly touched her temples.
"What are you...?"

"Just relax, it will be bright for a few seconds," he said.

Sparks were running around Filthy Henry's hands, little bright blue ones that moved like glowing ants. Each one raced along his skin towards his fingers tips. There was a slight tingling sensation at the side of her head, then Shelly could see nothing but electric blue. Her eyes were still working, she could move them, but everywhere she looked all that could be seen was blue.

She felt Filthy Henry take his hands away from her face. The blueness of her vision lasted a second longer before everything returned to normal.

"What was that?" Shelly asked, rubbing at her eyes. "How did you...?"

"Magic," Filthy Henry said, calmly, " is real. It always was and always will be. The only thing is most of the world doesn't know it, can't get in touch with it. Logic pushes it out of your mind, makes you see the world like everyone else does. Makes you 'normal'."

She shook her head, blinked a few times. Everything seemed to be just as it was before.

"The thing is," Filthy Henry continued, stepping beside her and taking her gently by the arm. "Just because you don't believe in magic doesn't mean it stops being real."

He guided her down the street, strolling slowly past the stalls. Whatever he had done was not making her feel sick, she felt fine in fact. So if it turned out he really was some sort of sick pervert Shelly was confident she would be healthy enough to introduce her knee to his groin.

"All it takes is for somebody to help you see things a little better," Filthy Henry said, stopping and turning so that they faced two stalls. "So long as you could see things a little on your own to begin with."

Shelly looked at both stalls. There was nothing particularly special about them. One was selling knock-off handbags, quite good replicas it had to be said, and the other had a selection of chocolates on offer. Neither stall owner was looking at the other, both facing opposite ends of the street and shouting out their wares. People were walked past, some stopped to look, others ignored them completely.

"What?" Shelly said, shrugging.

The fairy detective pointed at the empty space between the two stalls. It was large enough to fit another stall in there easily. In fact Shelly was wondering why there was such a large open space unused by some other stall owner. Generally they fought tooth and nail with each other to try and keep their spot.

As she looked at the empty space Shelly blinked, which caused something to happen.

It was like watching a mirage form. A wavy image appeared, blurry at first but rapidly getting sharper and coming into focus. Where once was empty space there now stood a third stall. This one was not manned by somebody who looked like the other stall owners on the street. Instead this seller was a tall, slender, woman with pointed ears. She just sat on her stool, watching the people walk by. Nobody seemed to notice her, or even look at her, but she was the most strikingly beautiful woman that Shelly had ever seen.

"What...how?" she said.

"She's a fairy," Filthy Henry said. "I amplified your innate ability so that it worked fully. Simple spell, only cost me a banana to cast as well. That's a bargain really."

The pointy-eared woman cast a glance at Shelly, head tilted to the side.

"See something you like, dear?" the pointy-eared woman asked, waving a slender hand over the objects she had for sale.

"Don't bother," Filthy Henry said to the pointy-eared woman, grabbing Shelly by the arm and leading her away. "We're just browsing." He dragged Shelly back down Moore Street towards Henry Street.

But this was not the same Moore Street they had just walked down only a moment before. All around them new stalls had appeared, each one selling something strange and different compared to the others that had been there before. Spaces that were once empty now were occupied, ignored by the other stall owners. Even the shoppers had increased in both number and variety. There were still the normal people that had been there before, but now there were others. Tall and thin, short and strangely dressed. Small people with wings or coloured all in red.

It was like a fairy tale reunion was happening right in the middle of Dublin, but nobody seemed to care. Nobody even seemed to notice the strange creatures all around them, as if they were all invisible.

Back on Henry Street the fairy detective let go of her arm. Shelly looked around her as more of the magical beings just strolled on past, the other shoppers oblivious entirely.

"How? What?" she said, slightly panicked.

"You saw Lé Precon earlier," Filthy Henry said. "That sort of means you've seen things all your life, only you kept it to yourself and passed it off as fantasy. But you're an artist, which means that you're more in tune to the impossible than most people. All I did was boosted how you see the world. It's easier to do if you can sort of do it already anyway. I can do it with most people but they would only have the ability for an hour or so. Plus, since you already told me you had seen Lé Precon, I am not technically breaking The Rules by allowing you to see the Fairy World. More like...bending them."

Shelly stared at Filthy Henry. He had a strange blue glow

coming off him, outlining his entire body like little flames. It had definitely not been there before. All around her the world had changed, literally in the blink of an eye.

Fairies flew by on tiny wings. A group of leprechauns walked past sipping coffee. New, exotic, shop fronts existed where no shops had been before.
"Is it permanent?" she asked.
Filthy Henry shook his head.

"No. Like I said I can undo it if you want, or you can just make it turn off and on at will. Whichever. But if you don't want me to get rid of it you will be able to use this new sight whenever you want."

She thought about it. It was weird, but in a wonderful way. It would be a shame to get rid of it rather than try to control it. At least without trying first.

"You can really take it back? This isn't some sort of trick is it? You didn't spike my coffee did you?"

"I can really take it back," Filthy Henry said. "No it isn't a trick and trust me, I don't need to spike a person's drink. I've much better ways of altering a person's mind to make them do what I want."

Shelly sighed and closed her eyes. She took a deep breath and focused her thoughts away from anything to do with magic, thinking back to how she had previously seen the world. When she opened her eyes again the blue outline had gone from Filthy Henry and the street was only half as busy as before. No fairy folk were in sight. Everything had returned back to normal. At least what had once passed for normal.

A swan came flying down Henry Street, swooping over their heads. It banked left, circled lower, and landed ungracefully on the ground. Folding its enormous wings, the bird shudder all over and then waddled up to Shelly and Filthy Henry.

The fairy detective looked down at the swan and groaned.

"Why couldn't they have sent somebody else?"

The swan honked a couple of times at him.

"Fine, fine," Filthy Henry said. "But it wasn't my idea. You know you can't drink and glide."

Another honk from the swan and the bird took the skies once more, flying away from them and up over the buildings. Some people on the street ducked as the bird flew over their heads.

"Tell him I am on my way!" Filthy Henry shouted after the bird. "What the hell was that? You can talk to animals as well?" Shelly asked, watching the swan fly away.

"No, I can't talk with animals. That would be just stupid," Filthy Henry said.

"Well then what was that? Was I just loosing my mind? You've done something to my brain with your little magic trick haven't you?"

The fairy detective smiled at her.

"Well for starters it wasn't a swan, it was a Leerling. If you'd been using your newly acquired fairy vision you would have seen a glow coming from him and even heard him speaking. But I can explain more of that on the way. That's assuming of course that you still want to hire me to find your talking cat."

Without waiting for any more of the conversation to develop Filthy Henry started walking away from her.

Shelly stood in the middle of the street, very confused. This was not how she had imagined her day would go. All she had wanted to do was hire somebody to find her cat and now it was as if she was a character in some urban fantasy novel. A fantasy novel where the main source of information was an annoying twat that had just walked away.

"Here," she said, following Filthy Henry down the street. "What the hell is a Leerling?"

Chapter Six

Leerlings were the most useful of the fairy folk as far as Filthy Henry was concerned. He had problems with most of them on a personality level, but in so far as magical abilities went they were very handy. As a race they caused him the least amount of bother, another one in the plus column for them.

It stemmed from the fact that they only had one trick. A Leerling was able to change from human into swan form and back again at will. That was all they could do. This meant that you had a lot less mess to clean up if a Leerling was involved, unless it had done some droppings while in swan form of course.

They were one of the few races that any human could see, without magical aid. Mainly because there was nothing the brain found strange about them. In swan form they looked, acted and sounded like a normal swan. As a human they were just another face in the crowd. Most of them even had the common sense to transform from one form to another out of sight. The few times they had been seen changing out in the open had led to an old Celtic legend being created, with the usual over-embellishments from the bard to make the story seem more fantastical than it was.

Fiction just had to be stranger than truth.

Since Leerlings could so easily integrate into human society they had become unofficial spies in the human world, working mainly in the areas of emergency services. They had integrated quite well into An Garda Síochána, Ireland's unarmed police force, given how efficient they were at stopping crime. Being able to glide over the streets instead of patrol them on foot resulted in Leerlings being the most efficient members of the force. Every Garda Station in Ireland had at least one Leerling working there; as did most hospitals and health centres. Whenever an incident was reported or a crime committed that had a hint of fairy involvement a Leerling would inform the fairy world that something had happened. That way fairy kind could work on containing the story before it spread through the land and ruined things for them.

Filthy Henry explained this concept to Shelly as they walked towards the docklands. Surprisingly she was adapting to the giant shift in her view of the world quite well. He had never shown a person the world beside the world before, figuring it would lead to madness. Yet here was Shelly, taking it all in her stride and asking enough questions to make him regret giving her the enhanced sight in the first place.

"So how many swans are Leerlings then?" Shelly asked, eyeing a swan that was bobbing up and down on the river Liffey. "Because I've been in the park on a summer's day with a boyfriend in the past and I'd hate to think that..."

"Good lord!" Filthy Henry said. "They are people, like you and me, not perverts. Just because they can hide in plain sight doesn't mean they go watching you with some guy's hand up your shirt. Besides, that's an ambiguous question. You might as well ask how many people are Leerlings, since they can look like either. They don't class themselves as birds or people by default."

That seemed to satisfy her enough to leave the paranoid questioning alone. She stopped walking and leaned against the stone wall that separated the pavement from a drop into the murky waters of the Liffey. The river itself began in the Wicklow mountains and meandered its way through three counties, fresh and clean and bubbling with natural beauty, before entering the Irish Sea at Dublin Bay, bringing with it a sizeable portion of pollution from the city. The general rule of thumb for health conscience swimmers was to never dip a toe in the Liffey within the city limits, unless you enjoyed large doses of penicillin.

Filthy Henry watched Shelly as she closed her eyes, took a few deep breaths, then opened them and stared intently at the swan on the water.

"It's a swan," he said, knowing exactly what she was doing.

"I just wanted to check is all," Shelly said, closing her eyes again. "This is all sort of new to me remember, not as old hat as it is for you."

"Trust me," the fairy detective said as they started walking again. "It becomes mundane pretty quickly. The novelty will wear off."

"So where are we going anyway?" Shelly said, falling back into step beside him. "You never did say, you just told me that a talking swan had dropped off a message and then walked away. What about my case? What about Kitty Purry?"

Filthy Henry groaned.

"I'll help you find the magical talking cat, alright! But the Leerling requested I look into something for him and it sort of supersedes your missing pet problem at the minute."

"Oh really," Shelly said with a sneer. "What could be so important that you need to look into it straight away?"

"There were two bodies found in an abandoned warehouse this morning by an old man out for a morning stroll," Filthy Henry said. "The Leerling heard the call come in over the radio and passed on the information to those that needed to know, me being one of them."

"But two bodies being found doesn't really suggest fairy, does it?"

"It does when they have no blood in them," Filthy Henry said.

"No blood? What, you're trying to tell me now that vampires are real as well and that they are classed as fairies?" Shelly said, laughing.

Filthy Henry stared blankly at her.

"Only the Irish ones," he said. "Besides, after what you've seen so far today are really going to question whether or not another magical creature is real? Think about it, the stories have to come from somewhere."

"Oh..." Shelly said. "But why call you in?"

"The bodies are human, which makes it a crime that fairy folk can't solve alone. I've a foot in both worlds so I am the one that gets dragged in. Whether I want to or not. Just let me get up to speed on this problem and then we can talk more about your case, alright?"

They continued walking in silence after that. Filthy Henry kept catching Shelly closing her eyes tightly and then opening them again, whipping her head forward in the process as if she needed to nudge the fairy-vision into place. She would look at somebody that walked past them, then close her eyes and turn the fairy-vision off again.

Filthy Henry started thinking about the double murder they were heading towards.

It was possible that there was no fairy involvement at all, just some sick twisted human that took blood as a trophy of his victims. Such a thing was not only heard of in the realms of a Hollywood B-movie. The world was full of people, it stood to reason that a few of them would be missing an entire Meccano set of screws in their grey matter. There was only so much sanity to go round after all and the global population grew every day.

But that did not rule out a fairy entirely. They had different ways of dealing with each other, making sure justice was given in a Biblical fashion. The whole 'eye for an eye' thing made much more sense to them.

A Garda roadblock had been put in place, preventing anyone from approaching the crime scene. It was the standard affair when something happened in Ireland. Block off as much space as possible, just in case the perpetrators left some handy clue nearby, and cause mild pandemonium for a couple of hours while things were examined. Some younger members of the force had been assigned to traffic duty, standing in a line and redirecting cars away from the street. This was met with the usual helpful characteristic of most city drivers, outrage and horn blowing as to why they could not just go where they wanted. As a result there was an impromptu car-park forming in the area as drivers argued with officers, stopping their cars and causing every car behind to be stuck in place.

It warmed Filthy Henry's heart no end.

"Why are you smiling?" Shelly asked him as they approached the Garda barrier spread across the path.

"Oh nothing. I just like to see drivers get annoyed is all. It's my guilty pleasure. They all think they own the roads and we all know that really only the taxi drivers actually own the roads. Taxi drivers just drive wherever and however they want, no questions answered."

A young Garda, clearly fresh from the training college judging by the oversized yellow hi-visibility jacket he was wearing, approached the pair of them. He looked like he was trying to puff out his chest. His jaw was set firmly. All he needed was a big sign that read 'I am a figure of authority. You will respect!'

This should be fun, the fairy detective thought.

"Just keep quiet for a minute and wait here," Filthy Henry said to Shelly.

She nodded and stopped a few feet from the barrier.

The fairy detective stuck his hands into his coat pocket and marched forward with purpose, heading directly for the young Garda. He nudged the barrier aside with his foot and kept on going.

"Here," the young Garda said, holding up his hand and pointing at the moved barrier. "You can't do that. This is an official crime scene and I..."

"Where is Officer Downy?!" Filthy Henry shouted, cutting the power tripping youngster off before he had a chance to build up steam. "I told him to meet me here first thing with a status report on the situation and here I am instead talking to you? Who the hell are you? Don't you know who I am?"

This trick would not have worked on a longer serving Garda, but a fresh recruit had no street experience. Nobody walked into a crime scene without first showing identification, let alone began shouting out demands. It was just not done. The uniform demanded some respect, but the new officer had not been around long enough to know that. Meaning he was now caught off guard by the man who had just walked in requesting another officer by name. A name that was probably important but somehow unknown to the young officer.

Filthy Henry could see the Garda think things over in his head, his position of power wavering slightly. Something had just happened, but he was not sure what, and this man before him seemed like he could be a person to not cross. Demotion in your first year on the force was something every rookie wanted to avoid. More so when the only rank below you meant being a trainee again. The fairy detective had pulled this stunt a hundred times, he knew exactly what to do next to reinforce his position and be allowed to see the bodies.

"Right, officer..." Filthy Henry said, indicating with a circular motion of his hand that a name would be required from the young man before him.

"Um...," the young Garda said, his sure footing a lot less sure.

"Officer Um," the fairy detective said. "Go find me Downy now and bring him back here. I don't want to be walking around this crime scene getting accused of being with the press or anything. MOVE UM!"

The young Garda visible jumped back a step as Filthy Henry shouted at him. He saluted with his right hand, then his left, then with both at the same time, before turning around and running down the street towards the parked Garda cars with flashing blue lights.

He waited for the rookie to be a fair distance away before Filthy Henry motioned for Shelly to come over to him.

"Officer Downy?" she asked.

"Yea, what's wrong with that?"

"You could have come up with a better fake name than Downy, it sounds made up."

"Well you can tell him that when you see him. I'll be busy examining dead bodies and making sure that the fairy kind haven't crossed some lines," Filthy Henry said.

He started walking down the street in the same direction that the young Garda had gone.

#

Shelly waited for a heartbeat of indecision, then followed him.

This was rapidly becoming one of the strangest days of her life. Ignoring the fact that she now had a new party trick, she was intruding on a crime scene with a man she barely knew. Yet something about his manner suggested this was not the first time he had done this. He was too cocky, too self-assured. If she had met him on a night out she would have marked him as an arsehole

86

that was full of himself and thrown her drink over him.

Either that or gone home with him. It would have depended greatly on how bad a week she had had. "Just don't say anything and look like you belong," Filthy Henry told her. "The trick is to not appear like you shouldn't be here. We get in, have a look at the bodies, and get out before causing too much trouble. With any luck people will just think I am a higher up on the force and you are my assistant."

"Your assistant!" she said, a little too loud.

Some Garda looked up from whatever they were doing and gave them both a curious look. The fairy detective stopped and turned on the spot, staring directly into her eyes.

"Sorry," Shelly said. She felt her cheeks go red.

"I have a few more tricks up my sleeve than just opening your field of vision," he said in a low voice. "So either keep quiet and play along of your own accord or find out what a puppet feels like. A silent one."

She did not like the sound of his not-so-veiled threat.

"Fine," Shelly said, begrudgingly. "But I'll only play along if you agree to take my case!"

"Hardly blackmail but fine," Filthy Henry said after a moment of thought. "You keep quiet here and I will take on The Great Case of the Missing Kitty. Happy?"

Shelly smiled at him and nodded her head. He nodded once in agreement then started walking towards the parked Garda cars with Shelly close behind.

A plain-clothes officer watched them approach as he leaned on the bonnet of a squad car. He waved a notepad in the air to get their attention, motioning that they were to come over. Shelly could not help herself. Right now her eyes were like a new toy on

Christmas morning. She closed them, concentrated for a moment, then opened them to see the fairy-enhanced world.

The Guard had a bright yellow glow coming off him, spreading out into the air like fire. Little flecks drifted away, vanishing as they left his body. Every second fleck looked like a tiny feather, right before it faded out of sight. The glow around the Guard was a lot brighter than the glow Filthy Henry gave off. None of the other Garda gave off a similar magical outline, this one seemed to be the only fairy in the area.

"What kept you?" the officer said as Filthy Henry and Shelly came closer. "I'm having a hell of a time containing all of this."

"Well we don't all have wings concealed in a convenient location to help us get around, Downy." Filthy Henry said, looking at the assembled Garda around the street.

"You're a Leerling?" Shelly asked, her curiosity getting the better of her. "Oh 'Downy', like with a downy feather pillow. I get it now, ha."

Filthy Henry and Downy both looked at her like two teachers who had just been interrupted while they decided what punishment to dish out to a student.

"Didn't know you were on a date," Downy said to the fairy detective, grinning.

"It's not like that, she's another case I'm working on. How much time can you give me in there?" Filthy Henry said.

Downy pulled back the sleeve of his coat, checking his watch.

"For you, half-breed, I can give you fifteen minutes. But you either have to run after that or risk getting pinched by one of these normals. It is a crime scene with two human bodies after all. Plus you're the only spell-caster in the area so any magic is up to you."

"Can't you help him out?" Shelly asked.

Filthy Henry groaned.

"What did I tell you about shutting up?" he said. "No, a Leerling can only go from feathered fowl to unfeathered fool. That's the only magic they have."

"Oh," Shelly said, feeling abashed. "Right. You did mention that before. I was listening, honest."

"How'd you hear about it?" Filthy Henry asked the Leerling.

"One of the lads, my lads, was bobbing up and down on the river waiting for somebody to come along and throw bread in. Can't beat a bit of soggy bread after your morning cup of coffee. I tell you, it's the only thing humans do right in this world. No offence."

"None taken...I guess," Shelly said.

"Anyway," Downy continued. "There he was, bobbing away and minding his own business, when somebody screamed inside the warehouse. Being as he was actually meant to be working he shifted back into human form and took a look inside. Called it in when he found the bodies, then flew off once we got here to make sure you were in the know."

"Wait...if you can enjoy things like coffee why would you hang around all day waiting for soggy bread lumps to be tossed at you like some common swan?" Shelly asked.

Downy chuckled and went back to writing in his notepad.

"You've got fifteen from now, half-breed," he said. "Nobody is in there at the minute, since we are waiting for the state pathologist to get over here. He doesn't like the Crime Scene guys to go in without him. Watched too many of those poxy American cop shows if you ask me. Just get what you need and get out unseen, got it?"

"Cheers," Filthy Henry said, grabbing Shelly by the arm and leading her towards the warehouse entrance.

She heard him muttering something under his breath as they walked. His outline intensified as tentacles of blue light spread outwards from him. Any Garda that looked at them attracted one of the tentacles. It lashed out and touched the Guard on their head, after which they seemed to lose all interest in Shelly and Filthy Henry.

At the warehouse door Filthy Henry stopped and looked at her over his shoulder.

"I'll understand if you want to go back and wait behind the barrier," he said, letting go of her arm and placing a hand on the door.

"There's no blood, right?" she said, considering his offer.

"Apparently not," he said. "Ready?"

Shelly nodded. Filthy Henry pushed opened the warehouse door, which creaked ominously on its hinges as it revealed the dark interior beyond.

"Well that was a little clichéd," Shelly said.

"You'll get used to it," Filthy Henry replied, carefully stepping inside.

Chapter Seven

Each fairy race gave off a magical smell, a scent specific to that kind of creature regardless of whether or not they could cast spells. Leerlings, for example, always smelled like damp feathers, even when in human form. Leprechauns gave off a strange hair smell, like a barber shop after a busy day. When magic was cast in an area it too left behind an odour, albeit just a stronger version of the normal fairy scent.

Humans could not smell the fairy scents, they were as invisible to them as the rest of the fairy world. But Filthy Henry did not have this limitation. His fairy side picked up the scents easily, allowing his human nose to sniff in an entirely different spectrum. It was like having a very small bloodhound attached to your face, one trained to sniff out magical foxes.

As Filthy Henry stepped inside the warehouse he took a good, long, whiff of the air and smelled...nothing.

"Well now that's odd," he said, walking into the gloomy interior.

Shelly jumped in after him, bumping into his back as the wooden door closed behind them.

"What's odd?" Shelly asked, peering over his shoulder at the disused warehouse.

"Well," the fairy detective said, walking across the warehouse floor, "there doesn't seem to be any fairy smells around at all."

"You can smell really good as well?" Shelly asked. "It's a bit dark in here isn't it, did you bring a flash light."

"Ha," Filthy Henry laughed. "Where I go I don't need flash lights."

He held up his left hand, fingers spread out wide.

"*Solas liathróid*," Filthy Henry said.

A bright glowing orb of white light appeared in his hand, illuminating the inside of the warehouse like a floodlight at a football pitch. It pushed back the darkness, bullying its way throughout the building and making shadows run before it. The fairy detective tossed the glowing orb up into the rafters. There it floated in the air, suspended on invisible strings.

Shelly stared up at the glowing ball.

"Did you just say 'light football' in Irish?"

"Maybe," Filthy Henry said. "Magic for me works like it does in those fantasy books, except I don't get to speak broken Latin."

"No," Shelly said. "But pigeon Irish, that's just to be expected?"

"Come on," Filthy Henry said. "I think I see one of the bodies."

They headed down amongst the rows of cargo crates that lined the warehouse floor. When they reached the body Shelly gasped, covering her mouth with her hands and rapidly averting her gaze to stare intently at the nearest crate. Filthy Henry thought he heard the unmistakeable sound of some vomit being swallowed back down.

"You've never seen a dead body I take it," he said.

Shelly shook her head quickly.

"So what part of the 'let's go and check out the dead bodies in the warehouse' bit did you not understand then?"

"What happened to him?" she asked in scarce more than a whisper.

Filthy Henry reached over and gave her a reassuring pat on the shoulder. She did not seem in need of any more attention, at least as far as he could tell. Her face was drained completely of all colour, but that just meant she was more alive than the body at their feet. The fairy detective knelt down and examined the corpse.

The victim had been completely drained of blood, probably even all bodily fluids. There was nothing left behind but a dried out husk, making it impossible to tell how old the person had been. Even telling how much they had weighed would have been an impressive trick, given the state of the body. They had been discarded on the warehouse floor, like an empty fast food container.

Filthy Henry leaned in closer. It looked like they had put up some sort of a fight. The victim's clothes were torn and ripped all over. One finger was bent out of shape.

"What did those?" Shelly asked, edging a foot nearer to the body and staring intently at the neck area.

Filthy Henry looked up and could see the blue glow coming from her eyes. She was using the fairy-vision. Her hands were cupped around her eyes, like children would do to pretend they had binoculars. The fairy detective figured she must have been using them as blinkers, to somehow shield out the entire body from her field of vision. All that she wanted to see were the little marks on the victim's neck.

The fairy detective turned up his own magically enhanced sight and looked at the neck. Immediately two small circular marks on the victim's skin appeared, little wisps of red energy drifting up from them like smoke.

"Bloody Stokers," Filthy Henry said, prodding the dried skin around the wound.

"Stokers?" Shelly asked crouching down closer to the body

and gingerly reaching out with her hand towards the red smoke.

"Vampires," Filthy Henry explained. "Any of the ones in Ireland are usually referred to as 'Stokers', after Bram Stoker wrote that book. It sort of helps to differentiate between the fairy kind of vampire and the sort you get roaming around Europe."

"So then a ... Stoker ... did this. You're sure?"

Filthy Henry nodded and pointed at the puncture wounds.

"See the trails coming up from the holes? That's fairy power, it will be gone in another couple of hours. A normal vampire wouldn't leave that behind, so that means we are dealing with a Stoker. Meaning it is something that I have to look into. But why would one risk the trouble of breaking The Rules?"

The fairy detective stood upright once more. He looked around, searching by the light of the glowing orb for anything else in the warehouse that was worth look at. At the end of a row of crates he spotted a foot. In his experience feet were generally attached to a body, or missing from one. Either way it merited his attention.

He walked toward the foot, Shelly scurrying after him, and found the second body. It was like the first, a dried out husk. Two identical marks were on the victim's neck. Identifying either of them was going to be impossible, too much damage had been done. But there was something different about this body.

With a gesture Filthy Henry brought the floating orb down from the rafters, moving it so that it hovered just above their heads. As the light hit the dried up body the fairy detective frowned. Covering victim number two was a layer of dust, unevenly distributed. Neither body had been there long enough for normal dust to gather in such a large quantity. The pattern of dust was also interesting. Some parts of the body had no dust, others a thin layer, with a large collection spread over the victim's legs.

Filthy Henry reached into his trench-coat pockets and pulled out a small, empty, sandwich bag. He bent down and scooped some of the dust into the bag, sealing it shut and holding it up to the light. He had an idea about what the dust was, but it would have wrapped things up in too neat a package. Pocketing the bag he looked over the body once more.

"Should you be doing that?" Shelly said. "It's like stealing evidence, isn't it?"

He went to answer her when something between two nearby crates caught his attention. Something that his gut told him would be best for Shelly not to see, just to be on the safe side. Filthy Henry generally trusted gut feelings completely. They tended to be spot on.

"Keep an eye out for anybody entering the warehouse," Filthy Henry instructed Shelly. "We're probably out of time at this stage."

"I'm not your bloody assistant you know. In fact I'm your employer, you can't just go ordering me..."

"Will you just go before I get my Union Representative onto you. You've met him before. Surly bastard who makes fun of women with talking cats, look practically the same as me."

Shelly drew a deep breath to speak then seemingly thought better of it. She looked back at the entrance to the warehouse, saw the coast was clear, then ran over and crouched behind some boxes. Once he was sure that her attention was fixed on the warehouse door, Filthy Henry reached in between the two crates.

His fingertips brushed against fur.

"Crap," Filthy Henry said.

He double checked that Shelly was not looking at him before grabbing the furry thing and bringing it closer. Using the dried up body to hide it from Shelly's sight, Filthy Henry laid the furry object on the ground beside the victim's body

It was the body of a Cat Síth and Filthy Henry, betting man that he was, would have given good odds that the fairy had gone by the name of Kitty Purry as well. Sometimes coincidences wanted to play with you, just for the fun of it. Telling Shelly would have been the right thing to do, but he wanted to be certain first. After all, Dublin had a lot of cats in it, both fairy and normal, so it was possible this was some other talking cat that had just died in the warehouse. A warehouse that just happened to be the scene of another fairy related crime.

The Cat Síth was too big to hide in one of his pockets. Filthy Henry figured it would be better to tell Shelly once they had gotten out of the warehouse, just in case she became emotional and started to cry or some such girly thing . Which only left one option open to him to get the fairy body out of the warehouse

"Time to work off some of that breakfast I guess," Filthy Henry said to himself as he placed both his hands over the deceased Cat Síth.

He closed his eyes and focused his thoughts on a box back in his office on Middle Abbey Street. A box that was empty and big enough to hide something like a dead cat body. Once the mental image was clear in his mind the fairy detective cast his spell.

"*Suíomh bogadh*," he said.

There was no bright glow or lingering spell effects this time. One second the Cat Síth body was there beneath his hands, the next it had vanished with a strange plopping sound. As if something had been dropped into water. For a split second the warehouse floor beneath him rippled, then returned to normal.

"Henry!" Shelly hissed.

Clicking his fingers, Filthy Henry extinguished the glowing orb above the corpse and plunged the warehouse once more into gloomy darkness. He waved for Shelly to come over to him. She peered around the corner of her hiding place then darted across the floor towards him, keeping as low as she possibly could.

"Leave your fairy sight on," Filthy Henry said as his eyes adjusted to the gloom and the world took on a slightly blue tinge in the darkness..

"Three Garda just came into the warehouse with some medical types," Shelly said. "I don't think they saw your globe."

Downy had no doubt given them as much time as he could. Which was nice of him, but still a little warning that they were running out would have been even nicer. How hard could it have been to 'accidentally' test a megaphone or something? Now they were both sitting beside a corpse with no valid reason for being there and the only way into the warehouse was blocked by people that liked to arrest things.

Filthy Henry looked around them, trying to see if there was any way out.

The warehouse was like all buildings of its type. Big and wide interior with only a few windows set up high near the roof. Meaning it was going to be nigh impossible to sneak out a back door or use a convenient window to get away without being caught.

To make matters worse Shelly had started to panic. She was breathing faster than before. Obviously the thought of getting nicked for murder was not an appealing one to her. Truth be told it did not roll all that well with Filthy Henry either, but he had been in situations like this before.

"Can't you just magic us out of here?" Shelly asked, pressing up against a crate as if it made her invisible to the naked eye. "Make us see through or use that thing you did coming into the warehouse to begin with? The thing with the trails of blue light?"

"No," Filthy Henry said. "Making two of us invisible would take a lot of energy and I don't have that after...making the ball of light. I haven't had a proper breakfast yet and have been doing too much magic as it is on an nearly empty stomach."

"You were eating a muffin with coffee when I was in your office forty minutes ago!"

"I know, usually I have that while waiting for my porridge to heat up."

"Well bloody well come up with something to get us out of here will you?" Shelly said, peeking down at the medical team who had reached the first body and were starting to examine it.

Filthy Henry groaned inwardly. Yet another reason not to have a partner was making itself abundantly clear. When you worked alone you only had to worry about getting yourself out of situations like this. With a partner things got a lot more complicated, what with having to save two people.

"Come on," he said, taking Shelly by the hand and leading her further into the warehouse and away from the Garda.

#

Since meeting this man Shelly had developed the ability to see things that were not really there, or were there but just not meant to be seen. Entered a Garda crime scene, through the front door nonetheless, while an investigation was going on. Aided in the theft of evidence from said crime scene and was now running from the very same crime scene and the law itself. All because she had wanted him to find her cat

At that moment she felt like a cat herself, figuring that her curiosity was most definitely going to kill her.

"Where are we going?" she asked him in a whisper.

"Just keep up and make sure you don't get seen," Filthy Henry hissed.

They kept moving quickly amongst crates and boxes, the alleyways of the warehouse. Filthy Henry clearly had no idea where the hell he was going, stopping at every corner and looking around for a moment before running off in another direction. All that he seemed to be doing was putting distance between themselves and the Garda by the dried up bodies.

"I thought you worked with them," Shelly said.

"Would you stop yapping and look for...perfect."

He let go off her hand and ran over to a small office cabin set into the back corner of the warehouse, as far from the front door as possible. It was your typical office cabin, faded white paint all over the walls, small windows set into it so the warehouse floor could be observed from within. The fairy detective pushed open the office door and peered inside. He looked back at Shelly, a big grin on his face.

"Got to love warehouse offices that have windows on all the walls," Filthy Henry said. "Come on, we have a way out."

She looked around, made sure that no Garda had spotted them, then crept over to the office. Inside everything was dirty and covered with trash, the office clearly as unused as the warehouse had been. There was a large collection of crushed beer cans littering the floor, an indication that somebody had used this spot for some quiet under-age drinking at some stage. Filthy Henry was over at one of the windows, pushing it up and open. Once it locked into place he popped his head through, out into the alley that ran beside the warehouse. Without a word he climbed onto the window ledge and then dropped to the ground outside.

Shelly went over to the window.

"Christ!" she shouted as Filthy Henry's head appeared in front of her, startling her.

"Oh that was just brilliant," he said. "I come back to help you out, being all gentleman like, and you go and shout. Come on, before they get here."

He helped her climb out of the window, into the alley beside the warehouse.

"Now what?" she asked.

"Well," Filthy Henry said, looking back at the street. "How about we go get lunch after our run."

"Run?"

The fairy detective nodded his head towards the street, then turned and started running down the alley in the opposite direction. Shelly looked back, saw the newly recruited Garda that Filthy Henry had tricked earlier on watching them, and decided that a little light exercise would be a great idea.

Work up an appetite for lunch and all that.

#

On Kildare Street there stands a building that has been home to a strange collection of people for many years. Not that this is common knowledge, since the inhabitants of the building keep to themselves.

The occupants had, over the decades, become very good at discouraging people from prying into their affairs. There was nothing like an unexplained disappearance or ten to make people want to avoid a place. Coupled with a masterful game of 'Chinese Whisper', where the word 'empty' somehow got mixed up with 'mass murderer', and the building became the world's best hideout.

The former employer of Jim looked at his assembled henchmen and smiled.

Everything was going nearly to plan. The Mothercrock had been stolen. All three of the gullible employees disposed of. All without anybody catching wind of what was really going on. If only that Garda Leerling had not shown up when Jim and Frankie were being retired from active living; then the caper would have easily fallen into the category of a 'perfect crime'. But there was no time to dwell on that. With any luck the two bodies would keep the Garda force busy for days to come. Which meant it was time to move onto phase two.

He reached inside the empty crock and pulled out a fistful of Euro notes. A slight magical light came off the notes as The Mothercrock's energies completed their creation. Clean and crisp and freshly minted through magical means. That was another of the wonderful properties that a leprechaun crock had. If you listened to the fairy tales all the crock could do was make gold, but gold had to be converted into cash somehow. You could not just walk into a shop and hand over a gold coin, expecting to get the right amount of change back. Chances were that the coin you gave the shopkeeper would be enough to buy the shop itself.

No, the real beauty of the crocks was they could make any currency in any denomination. Not many people outside of the fairy world knew that fact. If you wanted gold you could conjure gold, but if you needed a few Euro for the bus you could make that as well.

Jim's former employer held the Euro up for all the henchmen to see."You are all going to be involved in making history," he told the assembled group. "Each and every one of you. I cannot tell you how much this will mean to me, after decades of waiting my time has finally arrived. Then again, to paraphrase a great author, time is on my side."

This got the desired chuckle from those in the room. A little bit of species-specific humour never failed with fairy folk.

"I want to let you all know that I could not have done this without you," he continued, pulling more money out of The Mothercrock. "Literally I would not be here today if it were not for you. I will not forget this when we succeed, have no fear. Can you bring that over to me?"

This last sentence was directed to the nearest henchman who had a large bag in his hands. He stepped closer and spilled the contents of the bag on the ground. Jim's former employer reached down and picked up a brown leather wallet from the pile of wallets, stuffing it with money.

"A small token of my undying," more laughter from the crowd, "appreciation. Each one has been hand stitched by busty virgins in some sun soaked land. Afterwards you will get to meet them, have a drink on them if the mood takes you. But first I want each of you to go forth with your new wallet and complete the final stage of the plan."

A hand was raised in the back of the room. It did not annoy Jim's former employer, but he was confused. Surely nobody could have questions at this stage, everything was so simple and straightforward. All the hard work had been done already.

"Um," the questioner said. "Can we wait until evening? Just it's a little bit bright outside."

Jim's former employer looked over at the blacked out windows to his left. He had forgotten the time, lost in the excitement of his brilliant plan coming to fruition.

"Yes," he said, " valid point that. Take your new wallets and wait until dusk. You know the rest. Although if somebody has a spare bottle of factor sixty sunblock handy I wouldn't mind borrowing it. I'll pay you back, honest."

Yet another laugh. With an audience like this it would be easy for a man to believe he was funny. Jim's former employer tossed the full wallet towards the nearest henchman. He then bent down, picked up another one and started to fill it from The Mothercrock.

Soon, so very soon, Jim's former employer knew he was going to get the recognition that he deserved.

Chapter Eight

Shelly watched, slightly disgusted, as Filthy Henry shovelled food into his mouth. It almost seemed like he was afraid somebody would steal the food from his plate. One hand always had a utensil at the ready, as if to stab any approaching hands that attempted to steal a morsel from him.

"You sure you ordered enough?" she asked.

Before the fairy detective stood three plates. One was stacked with what could only be described as a mountain of chips, complete with a ketchup-capped summit. Another had two cheese burgers on it, with the remains of a third. The last had been home to a slice of apple tart with cream that Filthy Henry had ordered and eaten while waiting for the chips and burgers to arrive. Shelly's tea and club sandwich had been added to his order almost as an after thought.

"Yea," Filthy Henry said, mouth full of chewed burger. "This should get me back up to normal levels. Why?"

"No reason," she said.

It was getting easier to turn on and off the fairy vision. Shelly found she had started to do it now without even thinking about it, all in a literal blink of an eye. One second the world was normal, the next everything was covered with magic. Even this small café had hints of magic around the place. There were a dozen empty tables, but nobody who entered from the street seemed to pay them any attention. When she looked with her fairy vision Shelly saw the tables were in fact occupied by faeries, enjoying a cup of coffee and a chat like it was the most normal thing in the world.

"Human mind fills in the gaps with cold hard reason," Filthy

Henry said, as if reading her thoughts. "It's part of the magic. Two worlds occupying the same space, you have to make sure things don't collide by accident. So even though they can't see people sitting at the table, their sub conscious can. But the logical part of their brain makes them not try and sit at the table because they don't feel like it."

Shelly turned her fairy gaze on Filthy Henry. The blue glow returned, outlining his entire body.

"So what are you then? You a Leerling as well? Why did that Garda keep calling you 'half-breed'?"

The fairy detective stopped chewing, chin jutting downwards, and stared across the table at her. If looks could kill Shelly reckoned herself and anybody directly behind her would have been dead ten times over. It was like being caught in the headlamp of an oncoming train. Around them the café seemed to grow darker, like all the light was being sucked out of the world.

Just as fast Filthy Henry's mood returned to normal. He slowly continued chewing on his food. The dimmer switch of the world was turned back up.

"It's just a derogative term that the fairy folk have for me," he said, swallowing. "I'm the only one of my kind. Nobody else like me. Unique in every sense of the word."

"So, about my cat," she said, taking a sip from her tea and hoping to change the subject.

Picking up his napkin, Filthy Henry wiped around his mouth and cleaned his fingers. He pushed the plates away and settled back in his chair, seemingly content with his feed.

"Right," Filthy Henry said. "Your cat wasn't a cat, like I told you already. It was a Cat Síth, a fairy cat. To be more precise it was a fairy that looked like a cat. She was black as the ace of clubs, right?"

Shelly nodded.

"The talking, well that is something she should have known better," continued Filthy Henry. "But that's the problem with Cat Síth, they get to a certain age and they just want to settle down and play house-cat. So they find themselves somebody that will take in an ageing stray. With you though she lucked out, being an artist you could hear her actual voice without any magical assistance. Meaning she could converse with you and your mind accepted it. Truth be told it isn't the worst crime that a fairy could commit but it is breaking The Rules. I bet you had her for...five months....before she spoke to you for the first time."

It had been four months to the day as it happened, but Shelly did not see the benefit in correcting him on that. What was the point in sitting on your high horse if it turned out what you thought was a horse all along was actually a unicorn? She closed her eyes, turning off the fairy-vision in the process, and sighed.

"Yes," she answered.

"Yea, figured as much. See Kitty was probably seeing what sort of human you were. Would you be the kind that went blabbing your mouth or have a break down when an animal started talking to you. Once she figured out that you would be too embarrassed to admit your cat was talking she knew you were going to be her retirement home. Slightly selfish to be sure, but most Cat Síth are like that."

The metaphorical rug was quickly yanked from beneath Shelly's feet.

"Listen," Filthy Henry said, reaching over and taking one of her hands in his. "I'm not saying that Kitty Purry didn't like you for you, she did. But as a race they are worse than real cats, because they have intelligence. Intelligence isn't what separates animals from humans and fairies. It's what makes us worse than them. We can think up ways of being a bastard and then do it. But she did pick you for your qualities. If you want I can make you forget all about this, I'm fully recharged now, ha ha."

It was a tempting offer. To go back to normal, forget that fairy tales were real and all around her drinking coffee. Forget about a magical talking cat that had been her friend for the past two years. It would be so easy. Yet Shelly knew, deep down, that even if she did forget she would never be able to live with herself. Kitty Purry deserved to be found, after all that was what friends were for. They did not come to bail you out from jail after a night on the town, they were sitting right there in the cell beside you.

She looked up at Filthy Henry. He was giving her a sad little smile.

"No thanks," Shelly said. "I would rather find her than never remember her. She is my friend. I'm sure wherever she is, she is scared out of her little fairy cat head."

Filthy Henry's eyes opened wide as she spoke. He slowly pulled his hands back across the table.

"Sure," he said. "Sure, sure. Sure she is. Scared. Petrified you might say. Dead stiff. With fear!"

"Okay," Shelly said, frowning. "So how do we go about doing this then? I'll pay you obviously but I sort of want to help as well. There is a whole new world to explore and you're the only tour guide in town it seems."

He rose from his seat, leaving some money down on the table to cover the cost of the meal.

"Well then," Filthy Henry said. "First thing we have to do is get you up to speed. You've got some homework to do. Come on."

#

Like most cities in the world Dublin had a collection of book shops, both big and small. There were the usual brand chains, small chains, big names and family run affairs dotted everywhere.

Stores of the written word. Bazaars of the bound book. Places for people to go so that they were enveloped in an atmosphere of writing and imagination.

Over the years Filthy Henry had frequented many book stores, but there was only one that he classed as a proper book store.

It stood on Parnell Street, around the corner from the Rotunda Hospital, and was what all other book stores strove to be in his opinion. Nothing could compare to it. It was a large building with two levels, the lower for new books and the upper for used ones. Once you entered entire days could be lost as you navigated the labyrinthine array of shelves and displays. He always thought that they should hand out free maps of the store upon entry, so that you could find your way back out again.

For him it was more magical than anything in the fairy world.

"Chapters?" Shelly said. "You brought me to Chapters?"

Filthy Henry looked at her, his arms spread out wide in benediction as he stood in front of the building. It had been intended to be a dramatic revelation, this temple of worded wonder. Yet Shelly was looking at the building like it was just another book store.

"Yes, Chapters," he said, defeated a little. "Why, what were you expecting?"

Shelly shrugged.

"I dunno, maybe something a bit more magical. You go and show me that things are not as they seem with the world and then bring me to a normal bog standard book store like it is something special."

"It is," Filthy Henry said, gesticulating wildly at the building front. "How can you not be impressed by this place? Look at it, it's awesome. What did you want? Some sort of back alley behind a pub that magically transformed into a street filled with wonderful stores?"

"Well..."

"Oh for the love of Dagda!"

The fairy detective marched through the open store door, not waiting to see if Shelly followed. As always the store was fairly busy with the usual mixture of browsers, shoppers and people treating it like a free library. On more than one occasion Filthy Henry had seen a person reading a book in the store, mark their page, then bury the book at the very back of the shelf before leaving. One of his guilty pleasures was finding such books and moving the bookmark, just for fun.

He quickly looked around the ground floor, failed to spot anything that caught his attention, then headed to the second hand section upstairs.

Layout wise the upper level was a mirror image of downstairs, the only exception being that the stairs on this floor led down instead of up. People came to this level with old books that they felt no longer deserved a place on their shelves at home. Cash strapped university students in need of beer money were the usual regulars to this section. They would bring in piles of books, usually still in the cellophane wrapping they had been bought in, and exchange them for some beer tokens. An age old tradition that none of their parents ever found out about.

The black market of higher level education.

Filthy Henry always stopped by the second hand section, because you never knew what little gems had been carelessly sold to the store without a real understanding of their worth. For today's excursion, however, he bypassed all of the shelves and displays, making a beeline directly for the folklore section at the back. He slowly browsed the shelves, moving some books around as he searched.

"Can I help at all?" a shop assistant said, strolling down the aisle with a stack of books in her hands. "No thanks," Filthy Henry said. "I've got two eyes in my head."

She shot him a dirty look and continued on her way.

"So you're just a charmer to everyone you meet, aren't you?" Shelly said as she came up to stand beside the fairy detective, the shop assistant passing by her. She looked around at the books. "What are you looking for?"

"Ah," Filthy Henry said, picking up a battered and worn book from a middle shelf and handing it to her. "Your homework for the rest of the day."

She took the book and looked at the cover of it.

"'The Big Ass Book Of Faeries'," Filthy Henry said. "Basically everything in there more or less explains the fairy world to you. The only thing is that they come across as if they are fairy tales for children. But it is as good a guide as you can get in the mortal world. Generally fairy kind like to keep to themselves and their doings secret from humans. Any material that goes into too much detail never stays in circulation long. But they let fairy tale books slide because not everything in them is true."

Turning the book over in her hands Shelly looked at him.

"I'm guessing there isn't an 'Idiots Guide To Fairy-folk' then," she said.

"You're holding it," Filthy Henry replied, walking down the aisle towards the cashier desk. "Most of it is based on hearsay, some of it on facts and the rest is plain made up. You'll have to decide what's what yourself."

At the cashier desk the fairy detective took back the book from Shelly and gave it to the girl behind the cash register.

"I take it your eyes found everything you were looking for," the girl at the desk said, ringing up the sale and putting the book into a paper bag.

"I did," he said. "Although I think the pole I was looking for is still lodged in your arse. Pay the girl will you Shelly?"

Shelly frowned.

"Why am I buying it? You want me to read it."

"This is the School of Filthy Henry," the fairy detective said. "You don't get education for free in Ireland, everyone knows that. First lesson: buy your damn course work and meet me outside."

He smiled at Shelly, winked at the cashier girl, then headed down stairs and back out the front door of the store.

It was true that sometimes he let his mouth work without first engaging his brain, but Filthy Henry figured that the world owed him a sizeable amount at this stage. All his life he had worked alone, with no praise or thanks from anybody, and yet people expected him to always be nice and polite and helpful. If only they knew how many times he had saved the world from magical destruction.

The fairy detective looked at the people walking along Parnell Street

The city was getting busier now. More shoppers were on the street than before and the lunch time crowd was moving along like a herd of lemmings, searching for the cheapest meal they could find that was still within walking distance of the office. Cars drove past, some with that special brand of driver who seemed to think the horn should be blown every time some other car actually obeyed the rules of the road to the letter. Even the fairy numbers on the street had increased.

It was turning into a nice day though. The sun hung in the sky, high over the buildings, warming all below and pushing away the clouds that had been there that morning. Some young boys had taken off their shirts and were strolling along topless. This was a strange and, in Filthy Henry's opinion, idiotic tradition that most of the youth in Dublin City did any time there was sunshine for more than two seconds. As if the people of the world needed to see pasty white skin outside of a beach. Filthy Henry decided to teach them a lesson they would no doubt forget and cast a small spell on each of them, one that would result in a nice sun burn before the day was out.

Maybe then they would keep their shirts on during the infrequent spells of good weather.

Shelly came out of the store, book bag in hand, and stood beside him.

"You know you can be a bit of an ass when you get going," she said.

He shrugged. It was not the first time somebody had pointed that out to him and something told him it would not be the last either.

"Oh, there sure is a lot of them," Shelly said, looking up and down the street.

Filthy Henry could see the blue glow coming from her eyes.

"Yea, as crazy as it might sound but they have things to do as well. Just like your average Dubliner. Well now, look who it is."

A man was walking down the street. He had on a black suit, long black coat and matching top hat. In his left hand was an old, brown, leather briefcase while his right had an umbrella in it. Despite the fact that it was not raining the man had the umbrella up and opened, with his coat collar turned up. At this distance it was hard to see the man's face, but Filthy Henry knew who it was.

There was only one person that walked around Dublin dressed

like that. One fairy to be precise.

"You do much reading?" Filthy Henry asked Shelly, keeping his eye on the approaching man. "The classics in particular."

"I do a bit, why?"

"Well I figure you might want to meet this guy," he said, indicating with a nod of his head at the umbrella carrying man.

Shelly looked down the street at the man, then back at Filthy Henry.

"Who is he? What's with the umbrella, it's a lovely day?"

The fairy detective just smiled. Explaining that little character quirk was going to make a lot more sense to her after she had been introduced.

"Well now, Henry the fairy detective," the man said with a voice as smooth as a gravestone. He came up and stopped beside the two of them. "I don't believe I've seen you in a while. How have you been keeping?"

"Not too bad Abe, not too bad," Filthy Henry said. "Don't usually see you out during daylight hours. What's with the get up?"

Abe tugged at his coat collar, making sure it was covering as much of his person as was possible, and looked around the street. Filthy Henry had always gotten on well with this particular fairy person because he too was technically a half-breed. Even if it was a half-breed that had been created using the standard fairy methods. "Well, you know, have to keep going with the old project," Abe said, smiling a little and showing the tips of his very elongated canines. "I don't believe I've met your associate before."

"Oh this is Shelly...Godfrey," Filthy Henry said, waving for her to step forward. "Shelly Godfrey, Abraham St. Oker."

112

"My surname isn't Godfrey," Shelly hissed as she stepped forward. To Abe she said, "Pleased to meet you."

"He doesn't know your surname?" Abe asked, putting down his briefcase and offering her a gloved hand to shake. "Well then that must mean that you are one of his clients. What fairy trouble are you having then, since you're obviously not one of The People?"

"Oh you're a ... Well I need him to find my talking cat," she said. "Otherwise I think I would still be walking around not knowing any of this other stuff existed."

At the mention of her cat Abe's eyes glanced left. It was such a quick reaction that Filthy Henry was not entirely sure he had even seen it happen. Abe had always been easily scared ever since the Stokers had done their thing to him. Like Shelly, he was relatively new to the whole fairy-world side of things. Even if that relativity nearly reached a full one hundred years.

"Well you have the right man for the job with young Henry here," Abe said, patting the fairy detective on the shoulder. He reached down and picked up his briefcase again. "Now if you will both excuse me, I really must run in and make my purchase before my sun screen wears off. We don't want that happening in public now, do we? It was a pleasure to meet you Shelly. Good-day."

He smiled at both of them and went into the book store, folding down his umbrella once inside.

Shelly looked at Filthy Henry and shrugged.

"Why did I want to meet him exactly? Is he some sort of important fairy? Like the short green guy?"

"No," Filthy Henry said. "He would have been a fairly important human though, before the Stokers turned him into one of their own as a sort of thank you for writing a book about them."

"He wrote a book about vampires?" Shelly asked, craning her neck to watch Abe through the store windows. "Was it any good?"

"You might have heard about it, depends how much reading you do. Think they made it into a movie at some point as well. Speaking of which I have a few things to do. We can pick up on your case tomorrow after you have looked over your homework."

He turned and started to walk down the street, towards a pedestrian crossing at the bottom of Moore Street. Shelly had not noticed him walking away, but he knew the question she was going to ask before she even said it.

Curiosity was not just for cats.

"What was the book?" Shelly asked, still watching Abe through the window.

Filthy Henry pushed the button on the pedestrian crossing and waited for the green man to appear.

"He wrote 'Dracula'," Filthy Henry told her as the crossing started to beep loudly, indicating he was good to go. "You just met Bram Stoker."

Chapter Nine

Filthy Henry climbed up the tiny staircase to his office, opened the glass paned door, and went inside. He took off his coat, tossing it in the rough direction of the coat rack, missing said rack entirely, and walked around to his seat behind the desk.

Lé Precon's fancy leather chair was still there, some residual magic fading into the air. The fairy detective gave some consideration to setting fire to the chair with a little spell, but the amount of energy it would cost him was not worth it. Besides, there was always a bored teenager somewhere in Dublin looking to set fire to something. All he had to do was leave the chair in a place it could be easily procured by the miscreants.

Sometimes you did not even need to leave it outside your property for them to get their hands on it.

Filthy Henry took a pad and pen out from a desk drawer, setting them down in front of him.

This morning's little crime scene visit and seemingly random meeting with Shelly needed to be documented. Everything noted down, cross-referenced, assigned a little category in the puzzle that was the case so that the picture could start to appear. Solving a case was exactly like doing a jigsaw puzzle, Filthy Henry always thought. You had to lay out everything neatly before you started and make sure you had all the bits. It was hard to finish a thousand piece jigsaw of clear blue sky if all you had were red tiles.

He flipped open the notepad and with the pen drew three lines length-ways down the page, creating three columns. Along the top of the page he wrote 'Lé Precon', 'Missing Cat' and 'Bloodless Bodies', one in each column.

Filling out Lé Precon's list of clues was easy. For starters he knew what had been stolen and guessing the motive would hardly tax the brain. If you wanted an endless supply of riches you steal something that creates an endless supply of riches. The fact that it was The Mothercrock, however, did raise questions. Any leprechaun crock would have done the job, but The Mothercrock was a different target entirely. Stealing it brought down the whole financial system of fairy kind like an unregulated banking system would have for the human world.

This could of course mean that the real motive behind the theft was not just riches, it may have been intended as an attack directly at Lé Precon himself. A way to steal power out from under him, bring his reign as Leprechaun King into question. After all, how could you be King of the Leprechauns without your own crock of gold? Filthy Henry wrote the word 'Personal' at the end of Lé Precon's list and underlined it twice. There may be more to the theft than just plain old fashioned greed and despite not liking the short arse the fairy detective felt he should look at all possible angles.

He moved over to the final column, the one that was for the two stiffs in the empty warehouse. This one was going to be a little more delicate, require a bit more finesse to solve. Two humans had been killed by what looked to be a Stoker that had decided The Rules were only guidelines and could be ignored. Normally the vampires were not a problem. Since the advent of blood donations and blood banks the Stoker's had become a lot more civilized about the whole 'drinking blood' thing. The problem with drinking human blood was that you got all the infections that came with it. As the human population grew it became a bloody game of Russian Roulette as to whether or not you drank from somebody who was carrying something. If you did become infected you suffered with the symptoms forever, or until a wooden stake was driven through your heart.

Which made blood banks a much safer option. Screened

claret with a nice labelling system so you could sample your A-positive or O-negatives depending on your mood. How could anybody turn their fangs up to that?

So why one, or more, had decided to go directly to the source was just as interesting as finding out who the vampire had been. More to the point why had they drained the bodies so completely? A general rule of blood-sucking thumb was that you never completely drained a victim of their blood when feeding, something to do with the last beat of a heart being a dangerous thing to a Stoker.

This case was going to require some dealing with the Stoker community in Dublin. Generally they were the better self-policed fairy element in Ireland, because they lasted longer than most of the other races combined. If one stepped out of line it drew suspicion on the rest of the race. History was one thing a Stoker did not forget, they were better than elephants that way. Flaming pitchforks and giant toothpicks to the heart nurtured a strong survival instinct. So they liked to make sure that everyone followed The Rules, even more stringently than the other fairy-folk had to.

Filthy Henry frowned and scribbled down 'Renegade?' at the top of the list. He tapped the pad with his pen and stared at the central column.

"Already bloody solved," Filthy Henry said to himself, throwing down his pen and leaning back in the chair.

He had very little doubt in his mind that the body of the Cat Síth from the warehouse was Shelly's pal. An educated guess was hardly required to join the dots. She had hired him to find a fairy cat and less than two hours later a dead fairy cat had been found. When magic was involved coincidences were a lot more common than one would suspect.

But for the first time in his life, Filthy Henry found himself

117

wanting to be proved entirely wrong.

On the top of his filing cabinet Filthy Henry spied the box that currently contained one dead Cat Síth. He got up, walked over to it, and popped open the lid.

The furry corpse inside looked like a cat that was just sleeping in a funny position. A funny and presumably uncomfortable position. Reaching inside Filthy Henry raised up the animal and checked for a collar, finding it straight away. There was a little bronze name tag, in the shape of a fish, attached to the leather loop. Stamped on the metal surface in bold black letters were the words 'Kitty Purry'.

"Ah crap," Filthy Henry said, placing the head back down.

He cast a preservation spell and tossed the ball of energy at the box, to prevent the body decaying for a few weeks. There was no point in telling Shelly just yet, but a dead cat would stink the office up something fierce until the fairy detective did tell her.

Filthy Henry looked out the window, up at the little scrap of sky that he could see between the buildings, and let his mind wander like a child in a toy store.

A visit to Lé Precon's fort would probably be a good idea. No doubt the leprechaun had sealed off the whole area using a mixture of magic and misdirection to ensure that neither human nor fairy could contaminate the scene, just in case. In that respect the short arse was better than the entire Garda force at crime scene maintenance.

Filthy Henry closed the notepad, stuck the pen into the spiral loop, and put the pad in his pocket. It was time for another crime scene visit.

#

Getting to Conyngham Road took a lot longer than it should have from the office. This was not a reflection on the poor state of public transport in the city, the public transport was always poor in Dublin when you really needed to rely on it for getting about the place. Instead of the usual sixteen minute journey it had taken the better part of an hour. It literally would have been quicker to walk, a thought that Filthy Henry ignored as he sat on the bus in the middle of traffic. Traffic that had built up because gas leak that had been detected, resulting in the entire area around Conyngham Road being evacuated and sealed off. As generally seemed to happen in Dublin when there was a single disturbance in the flow of traffic everything was diverted all over the city, with no real plan in mind aside from causing endless tailbacks and mild pandemonium.

Finally though the bus had gotten close enough to The Phoenix Park that the fairy detective was able to jump out at a red light and make his way towards Conygnham Road.

A large contingent of safety works had descended on the street at six in the morning, placing metal barriers across the road. All the residents had been moved from their abodes and any businesses had been notified and told to not bother opening for the day. Only the bus depot had been left alone, although the lack of activity happening inside would have made a person think otherwise. Most of the drivers were standing at the main gate watching the theatre of the street that was happening right before them.

There were large white vans parked everywhere, bright orange lights twirling around on the roof to attract the attention of passers-by like moths to a highly combustible flame. Some Garda patrolled along the metal barriers, making sure people stayed on the side deemed to be safe.

It was all very exciting stuff.

Filthy Henry stood a little back from the crowd and observed.

To the normal person nothing was out of place. Everything

was being done perfectly. A news crew had taken up station at the end of Park Gate Street, cameras rolling and reporters reporting. A throng of people were crowded around the barrier, most of them clearly with nothing better to do with their day other than gaping at the safety crew at work.

It all brought a smile to the fairy detective's face as he turned up his magical vision and examined everything again.

The Garda were real but under a spell, judging from the yellow clouds around their heads that convinced them they had been assigned this duty. None of their radios were turned on, preventing any questions from their station as to what they hell they were doing all day and why they had not reported in recently. When everything was done they would return to a serious reprimanding from the higher ups, made all the worse because of the magical amnesia they would have preventing answers being given. The white vans with lights were all real as well, but not one of the safety workers was. Each barrier had a van parked at the end of it, all very normal looking. Except that the vans were acting like a giant projector screen for the people standing on the 'safe' side of the barrier. None of the safety workers ever approached the vans at all. Rather they all worked in the distance, away from prying eyes. It was the sort of magic that made a three-dimensional movie seem like child's play.

Magic like this required a lot of energy, probably even a good few fairies, to maintain all day. Filthy Henry guessed that the vans were not only acting as a limit for the spell but also home to a dozen or so leprechauns.

He walked up to the left most barrier, wondering what spell would be required to get past the Garda, when the officer waved at him.

"Sir," the Garda said. "We've been expecting you, chief said to just go straight on through."

The Garda pulled the barrier aside so that Filthy Henry could go around it, then pushed it back in place and continued to watch the crowd.

"Cheers," the fairy detective said, walking past the vans and onto the very empty street beyond. He looked back at the crowd.

From this side the illusion was distorted, out of focus. Like watching a television while sitting right beside it. Some of the safety workers overlapped, because the spell only catered for perspective from one side and not both.

The side door on the nearest van opened. A leprechaun popped his head out.

"You're alright to walk around on this side half-breed," he said. "There's a *Gcuirfidh* spell in place over the whole street. This is all just to stop people wondering what's going on."

"So I can walk around freely without being spotted by a human? You're sure?"

The leprechaun laughed.

"Duh. Unless you look in a mirror. Or half a mirror, ha ha," he said, sliding the door closed once more.

Filthy Henry groaned. Just once it would have been nice to work with the fairy folk and not be reminded about his past. The majority of them despised him but acknowledged that he was just a necessary evil. Like exams in summer time or taxes, you would rather they did not exist but understood they had to. It was hardly like he had asked to be born, let alone born a freak of magical and natural nature.

"Should have just told him to sod off," Filthy Henry said to himself, walking down the street towards the entrance to Lé Precon's fort.

The entrance into the underground fort was open, unsealed

and unhidden. Usually it was totally invisible and locked down, even from other fairy kind. Nobody could get in or out without Lé Precon's say so. The only reason Filthy Henry knew its location was because the smarmy King of the Leprechauns had negotiated the terms of his loan there. It had been a well choreographed scene, purely so Lé Precon could display his wealth and power to the fairy detective.

Filthy Henry entered the fort and started to walk down the corridor. No guards were posted, no spells were in place. Seemingly with the removal of the only valuable thing in the fort Lé Precon saw no reason to protect anything else.

"Took your bloody time," Lé Precon said as Filthy Henry entered the main chamber of the underground fort. The leprechaun was sitting on a little golden throne directly opposite the entrance. "I mean you'd swear you have more important things to do with your time other than work for me. Do I need to remind you about how much you owe me?"

Filthy Henry stopped just inside the doorway and smiled at the leprechaun King.

"Downy got in touch, couple of drained corpses needed my attention. Rogue Stoker most likely."

Lé Precon was clearly surprised by this little bit of news, but remained silent on the topic.

The fairy detective looked around the room.

There was only one way in or out of it and that was the way he had just came. Most people would have kept something as valuable as a crock of gold hidden deep in the centre of a maze, or locked up in a vault of some kind. But that was not how fairy folk worked. While the corridor from the street was a straight line to the chamber it was only that way because Lé Precon permitted it to be at that moment in time. Using the rainbow as the crow flies could be the longest distance between two points, a trick all leprechauns used. In the centre of the room was a slightly raised platform, circular in shape, with a shallow groove in the middle. This was where The Mothercrock had stood for centuries, although not always underground. Once, long ago, Ireland had been populated with nothing but the fairy folk. Back then there was no need to hide from sight and exist in a world that was slightly out of phase with the rest.

How times change, Filthy Henry thought.

He strolled around the room, looking for anything that might be a clue.

Fairy folk did not use any sort of CCTV, since a spell was better at preventing something being stolen than simply watching the crime happen after the fact. So chances of seeing how the two humans had pulled off the caper would be out of the question. There were no magical burn marks on the wall, not even a whiff of a spell in the air. It was almost as if no magic had been used to stop the theft at all, or commit the act for that matter.

Filthy Henry stopped beside the throne and put his hands in his pockets.

It looked like they had just walked in and picked the crock up.

"How did they disable the rainbow?" Filthy Henry asked.

"They didn't," Lé Precon said. "It was still on after they left."

The fairy detective found that hard to believe. Rainbows were part of the legend of leprechauns. If you found the end of a rainbow you got your hands on the pot of gold. Every small child heard the tale, every adult knew it. Nobody ever pulled it off, obviously, because you never could get to the end of a rainbow. But that was also because no mortal knew the truth behind the tale.

Each crock of gold was protected by a combination of magical spells that prevented practically everything in the world, and some things not in it, from touching or interacting with the crock, save for the leprechaun who owned it. Such a gathering of energy culminated in a literal rainbow that glistened over the crock, spinning around it rapidly like a multi-coloured dome. Nothing could get past it, not even magic. It was completely protected.

In terms of The Mothercrock there were a team of leprechauns that worked for Lé Precon, his Rainbow Guard. Each one focused on powering one colour of the spectrum, since The Mothercrock was the most important of them all. It was an honour to serve in the Rainbow Guard and only the best and strongest ever made it into the ranks. For the spell to still be in place after the theft had occurred, well it made no sense at all. It would mean that a human had somehow figured out a way around a millennium old spell. A problem that no fairy had even managed to scratch the surface of.

"So where are your midget Power Rangers then?" Filthy Henry asked. "Surely they must have seen something happening. Sensed a disturbance in The Force."

"You're watching too many of those moving pictures," Lé Precon said. "There was only one of them that encountered the two humans and he was knocked out."

"Knocked out?" Filthy Henry. "This is just getting better and better. How did that happen exactly? Aren't the Rainbow Guard trained for everything?"

Lé Precon shifted on his throne, his stubby legs moving like two fat sausages trying to run back to market. He glared at the fairy detective.

"Look I didn't get you involved in this to take the mickey out of it! I got you involved because The Rules are plain and simple. Humans were involved and you have to figure out the how and why. Now just do your job half-breed so that I don't have to listen to you any longer."

Filthy Henry clenched his jaw and stared at the Leprechaun King. People could not pick their parents, but that did not seem to matter when a cheap insult was available. If the payment for solving the case had not been so good the fairy detective would have told the stubby arse-wipe exactly where to go.

But The Rules were The Rules and Filthy Henry really wanted to get paid for this case. If nothing else it would finally put an end to all of the half-breed crap forever more.

"Where is the guard that was knocked out?" he asked.

"Out front being punished. You won't miss him, he will be there for another month. Longer if The Mothercrock doesn't get found."

Filthy Henry decided there was nothing else to learn in the chamber and left, going in search of the Rainbow Guard witness.

#

Back on the street nothing had changed save for the size of the crowd at the barriers.

Filthy Henry walked out into the middle of the empty street, safe in the knowledge that the illusion spell would keep him hidden from sight, and looked for the unfortunate Rainbow Guard.

Knowing Lé Precon's penchant for punishment chances were the Mighty Midget Power Ranger had been transformed into something. An unfitting punishment of course, but the Leprechaun King would always put in two clauses to get you out of the spell's effects. You could either wait until his mood changed and whatever crime had been done was undone or you could solve the problem yourself. The only problem with the second clause was Lé Precon liked to transform people into stationary objects, making it sort of hard to move around and figure things out.

A quick glance revealed the victim of the Leprechaun King's wrath had been stuffed into the shape of an ornate light fixture, attached to the wall of an office building. Even without magical vision it would have been easy to spot the Rainbow Guard, since the light matched nothing else on the building. For a start it was the only fixture that was on any of the walls in the area.

"Maybe you can illuminate the events of last night for me," Filthy Henry said, walking over and looking up at the light.

One thing that could be said about Lé Precon, he had an artistic temper. Whenever he punished somebody with a transformation they were always turned into something exquisite when examined up close. This light fixture was made from polished bronze, the arm curling in on itself in a spiral. Where it was attached to the wall tiny metal leaves could be seen, almost as if they had sprouted from a living plant. The bulb was housed in a small cup with a little detailed face adorning the part that pointed towards the street.

A face that had a little beard on it and moving features.

"Very funny, Filthy," the face said as two tiny metal eyes focused on Filthy Henry. "Do I have to listen to a truck load of your puntastic wit now or are we going to get on with this?"

"Hey I'm here to brighten up your day," the fairy detective said, smiling.

The transformed Rainbow Guard groaned.

"Dagda why did it have to be you! Go on then, ask your hilariously phrased questions."

"Well how about describing what happened to me, since you're the only eye witness. Where were all the other Rainbow Guard?"

It is hard for a light fixture to look sheepish, but the Rainbow

Guard somehow managed it. He saw something very interesting on the ground and decided to stare at it until the moment had passed.

"Let me guess," Filthy Henry said, scratching his chin thoughtfully. "You lot drew straws to see who would stay sober and the rest of them were away from their posts enjoying one or twelve? That about right."

The little bronze face wiggled its eyebrows up and down, the best nod that could be managed without a neck.

"Well let's just keep that from Lé Precon for the minute," the fairy detective said. "So go on, shed some light on the events for me already."

"Well the fort entrance opened up of its own accord, which it can only do if one of us Rainbow Guard approach it or Lé Precon himself commands it. So I figured I better go see what was going on, just in case I needed to run interference for the lads. Anyway I go running along and these two humans are strolling down the main corridor like they own the place, shooting at pots. There was clay everywhere!"

"Anything unusual about them? Magically enhanced at all?"

"No nothing," the Rainbow Guard said. "That was the strange thing. They had masks on but I could see their eyes and they didn't have a glow or nothing. Besides that only works if they have potential and neither of them had any. Two magically brain-dead men is what they were. Even Lé Precon couldn't have given them a second sight if he wanted to, at least not without using a wish to alter reality a little."

Filthy Henry looked back across the street at the open entrance into the underground fort.

"They had to have had something," he said, staring at the opening in the wall of the Phoenix Park. "Otherwise they wouldn't have been able to see the doorway to begin with. Plus they needed something to make it open, a spell of some kind or an enchanted rock at the least."

"There was something coming from them," the bronze face said. "But I brushed it off as being the one drink that I had had going straight to my head."

"Well?"

"They both had the aura of a Cat Síth coming off them. Only faint, mind. But still I'm sure of it. Then again what do I know really? I'm a bloody talking lamp."

The words drift over Filthy Henry's head as his mind latched onto the one phrase that it deemed interesting.

Both of the humans had a faint Cat Síth aura coming from them.

Filthy Henry would still not have bet the rent money on anything but the coincidences were starting to stack up like dominoes. It was looking more and more likely that Shelly's case and this one were linked by one magical talking cat.

As he mulled over what the Rainbow Guard had told him, Filthy Henry spotted something on the ground at the foot of a nearby flower bed. It was a crushed up can, one of those energy drinks that people loved so much because they did not appreciate the joys of a well brewed cup of coffee. Normally trash would not attract the fairy detective's attention all that much, considering how littered the streets of Dublin were most of the time, but this was not just trash. At a crime scene like this it was a potential clue. The levels of potential increased due to the fact it had traces of magic coming from it. Little tendrils of magical energy swirled out the top of the can.

Pulling out an empty sandwich bag from his pocket Filthy Henry walked over to the can, bent down, and picked the can up with the bag. He sealed it and looked around for anything else that had magic coming from it.

"What's that?" the transformed Rainbow Guard asked.

"Not sure," Filthy Henry said.

The fairy detective looked around the flower bed some more, lifting up branches and pushing apart bushes. After a minute Filthy Henry found clue number two. Buried under some leaves and petals were two glass vials that glowed like sticks at a rave party. With care he opened up the sandwich bag again and added the two glass vials to its contents.

"Are you serious?" the Rainbow Guard said. "I've been here for hours and my possible salvation was right beside me. What did you find, tell me so I can take credit for it?"

Filthy Henry pocketed the items and started walking towards the white vans. "Possibly nothing, possibly something. I reckon it might illuminate matters a little further. "

"Rat bastard. You and your puns. You think that's punny don't you!" the bronze face shouted after him.

Chapter Ten

Shelly had been reading the book of fairy tales that Filthy Henry had made her buy for four straight hours. She had decided that reading it in one sitting would make it less embarrassing, although who she was going to be embarrassed in front of was the real question. Over the years her list of friends had dwindled down to a handful in total. Even then they rarely made the first move to get in contact with her. Chances were nobody was going to suddenly barge into her apartment while she lay curled up on the couch reading about leprechauns and talking cats.

She had always worried about becoming a cat lady, one of those old spinsters that you would see spending more time with animals than people. Talking to the cats as if they could respond. That was until Kitty Purry had actual spoken back to her. At first she was sure she had lost her mind, but then the cat had definitely spoke about things that Shelly knew nothing about.

The only downside was that with her lack of other friends to contact Shelly was never sure if Kitty actually did speak, that it was not all some elaborate hoax her subconscious was playing. After all it would not be impossible for a cat to start talking about things you had no idea about, because having no idea about them meant you would not be able to verify the truth of what was being said.

The Catch-22 of a singleton.

But, questions of sanity pushed to the side, Kitty Purry was Shelly's friend and she felt she owed it to the cat to find her. Even it that meant her understanding of the world was flipped upside-down like a character in a fantasy novel.

So she read the book and took notes along the way to see if

she could come up with a spotters guide to surviving in a world with fairy folk.

The problem was how to separate fact from fiction. Filthy Henry, the ignorant private dick, had not told her anything before leaving her on the street earlier that day. He had not even said goodbye. One second he was telling her that Bram Stoker had just walked by, the next he was gone. Whatever else he was, Filthy Henry had clearly been dragged up by his parents and learned no manners along the way. Without guidance Shelly figured taking everything with a pinch of salt was the best course of action. Some of the information was easily ignored, like the one about leprechauns and rainbows. That had to be pure fantasy, embellishment on the part of the author. Others were a lot harder to disregard. Like the one about babies being swapped with a Changeling. It sounded so far fetched that it quite possibly had come back from the other side of falsehood and was true.

As she read the book it became obvious why fairies kept their world invisible to humans, assuming a tenth of what she read was factually accurate. If a human ever captured one of the really magical fairies they could force them into doing whatever they wanted, use magic to gain an unfair advantage over the world. Then again with all the magic that fairies had in the stories it was a wonder they had not just taken over the world already. Nothing could stop them, little groups of super powered midgets firing fireballs around the place and wreaking havoc. Who would want to stand in the way of that?

Shelly turned the page, opening up the section on magical fairy animals and read about the kind of fairy that Kitty Purry was. She read the stories three times, one after another, and at the end could not fathom why somebody would steal a talking cat.

They had no magical powers at all, other than being able to speak, and the Internet was full of videos of talking animals. In this day and age it was not impossible to make it seem like an animal was speaking. Hell some of them even managed to bark and meow sounds that could be human words. Plus you could not make a Cat Síth do anything it did not want, they were like normal cats in that regard. So all you wound up with was an animal that would refuse to talk. Hardly a money making scam.

Shelly closed the story book and rubbed at her eyes, wiping away some tears that had formed.

Kitty Purry had been catnapped, or worse, Shelly knew deep down. The cat had been missing for three days now and Shelly's only hope of finding her was a bad mannered detective who could guide her...

A thought occurred to Shelly, one she was surprised had taken her so long to think up. Filthy Henry had given her fairy vision, or enhanced an ability that she never knew she had apparently. He was no longer needed to guide her around the city. With her new power Shelly could go out and find another fairy that might be a bit more helpful, maybe even find Kitty herself. Wiping her eyes Shelly grabbed a note pad and pen, pulled on her coat, and left the apartment.

#

Alcohol has many uses.

In times past it had been used in a medicinal fashion, helping to wash out gunshot wounds so as to prevent infection and as extremely cheap pain relief while said gunshot was being operated on. As the times changed so did the uses. Alcohol was drunk in large quantities to help erase painful memories, or get the courage to talk smoothly to a member of the opposite sex. After all, who could resist a chat up line that ended with vomit covering your shoes?

Some folk liked to use alcoholic drinks, such as beer, as a method to improve how they thought, a sort of mental lubrication. Something to get the gears in the brain turning fast so that a solution to a particular problem presented itself in a timely manner. Preferably before the courage to chat up the blonde at the end of bar appeared, thus erasing all memories of a solution in the process.

A beverage with many forms that had survived the ages and attempts to suppress it.

Filthy Henry hated it, or to be more precise he hated human alcohol.

Due to his magical nature normal alcoholic drinks had no effect on him whatsoever. In his youth, Filthy Henry had partaken in the honourable tradition of getting some age-appropriate stranger to purchase the cheapest cider possible for himself and his friends. The purchased paint-thinner was then drank in a field somewhere, out of sight of prying parental eyes. Everyone else got skulled out of their minds. The fairy detective never even felt light headed.

He experimented throughout the years, drinking more and more potent combinations. Each one resulted in what seemed like a level above being sober. Super sobriety almost. Filthy Henry soon became the only person that could be a designated driver and still drink the Stag under the table at the end of the night.

Then came the day Filthy Henry learned about fairy-alcohol. Brewed by the magical folk for consumption by themselves. Drinks that had never before passed the lips of a mortal. When he had finally gotten a handle on his powers and what he actually was the fairy detective had walked into a fairy tavern on Pearse Street and ordered his first proper drink. The funny thing was that even the strongest fairy beverage did not have him end up on his ear, lying in a pool of his own saliva while he tried to say the alphabet in a spiral fashion. But it did enough to make drinking seem like a worthy past time, it just took a lot more for him to get into a merry drunken state.

The tavern in question was a well known fairy tavern, Bunty Doolays' Bar, and had become Filthy Henry's local watering hole over the years.

Here all the races of fairy could mix and mingle, drinking until the small hours of the morning, without ever being made to feel unwelcome. Most of the fairy-folk got along with the other races, but there were always one or two groups that just had a deep hatred for one another. A grudge that had happened centuries ago still being carried on, even though nobody alive remembered the original insult that had sparked the whole thing off. But in Bunty Doolays' Bar none of that mattered, the hatchet was left well and truly at the door. If it was not then whosoever started the violence wound up with said hatchet embedded deeply in their anatomy.

This was neutral ground, where people came to gather and partake in that aged old tradition of brain cell killing. Safe in the knowledge that the only violence which might occur would be as a result of knocking over somebody's drink.

Filthy Henry loved it. It was the only place in the world where he did not feel like such an outsider.

He had taken up his regular spot at the end of the bar, farthest from the main door but nicely situated beside the emergency fire escape. Nobody was sitting near him, which meant Filthy Henry could leave his notepad out on the bar counter and work on the cases while drinking a chilled glass of fairy ale.

"I hear you've gone and given somebody The Sight," a female voice said to the fairy detective.

Looking up from his scribbles Filthy Henry saw the proprietor of the pub, Bunty Doolay, standing in front of him as she wiped down the counter top with a cloth. A cloth which was moving of its own accord, guided by her magic. Bunty Doolay was best described as a *sidhe*, a sort of elf creature with incredible magical abilities. She came from Northern Ireland and nobody knew when she had actually moved to Dublin. Her race was one that they aged so slowly it was impossible to tell how old they were. In simple human terms they were the sort of person that was constantly asked for identification when in an off-license, even if they spent an hour looking for a nice bottle of wine, a trait shown by all under-age drinkers, and were really in their mid-twenties.

She was like all female *sídhe,* physically beautiful in every way and able to have her pick of males. Her eyes were completely blue, no iris to be seen, with long, light coloured, hair that matched her soft white skin. Most patrons of the bar had tried their luck to woo her at some stage, each getting shot down in the most pleasant of ways imaginable. Except for one brave soul who had pushed his chances a little too far and gotten a knee to the groin as a reward for his efforts.

Filthy Henry could not help but smile at the sight of her.

"Huh?" he said, getting lost in a day dream that he knew should never be spoken out loud in her presence.

"I said that I heard you let some mortal see the fairy world," Bunty said, leaning against the bar counter. "What is it with you? Do you just want to go looking for trouble?"

"Nah," Filthy Henry said with a shrug. "It generally has a good idea of where I am. I think there is a smart-phone app or something."

Bunty Doolay smiled at him, shaking her head slightly.

"Smart arse. So what's going on then?"

The fairy detective explained the three cases that he had on the go. About the bodies drained of blood, Shelly's missing pet and that a crock had been stolen. He left out the minor detail that the crock was in fact Lé Precon's, since that information did not need to enter the public domain just yet. Finding out that the basis of your financial institution had just been robbed was something nobody needed to hear. It would be like a bailout being forced on a small country because they let their banks fail miserably.

"...bringing me here," Filthy Henry said, taking a mouthful of fairy ale and savouring the taste. "What better way to look at the bigger picture and try to come up with a solution? Besides I thought you might have heard about anyone messing with rainbow alarms recently? Trying to crack them."

Bunty gestured with her hand and the dust cloth glided along the counter top towards her. She reached out and grabbed it, absent-mindedly dusting the counter between herself and the fairy detective.

"No. Sure it's impossible. Nobody can get around a leprechaun rainbow, it's been tried too many times. Mostly by other leprechauns so that just shows how fool proof they are."

"Yet," Filthy Henry said ", somebody has managed it. I just can't figure out the 'how' of it yet. Then there is the drained bodies thing as well."

"Dagda above, Henry," Bunty said. "You're looking for a rogue Stoker. How is that not jumping right out at you like being slapped in the face with a fish?"

Filthy Henry frowned. Northern fairies had some strange saying, ones that had somehow made it into the human phrase-book as well. But they never made sense in Dublin.

"What does that even mean? I know I am looking for a Stoker. Besides I think I found him already."

He reached into his coat pocket and pulled out the little bag of ash he had taken from the crime scene. As doggy bags went it ranked fairly low down the list, but a clue was a clue and a true detective never turned his nose up at one. Carefully Filthy Henry placed the bag on the counter between himself and Bunty. Folding his arms he nodded at the bag of ash.

"You rat bastard," Bunty Doolay said, looking at the bag. "I thought you just wanted to bend my ear."

"I did," Filthy Henry said, nudging the bag towards her with his hand. "But you know I haven't got enough magic in me to do the spell correctly. Besides you're the only one I would trust with something like this."

She snatched the bag off the counter and stuffed it into her pocket before turning around and storming down the bar.

"I'll be in touch," Bunty said to him as she walked away. "Now get the hell out! Before you're barred you rotten half-breed."

Insults were like wasp stings, Filthy Henry found. Small ones were annoying, depending on where they came from. But if a friend insulted you, and meant it, it was like the entire nest had decided to play pin-the-tail-on-the-human. Insults from friends hurt so much more.

Filthy Henry gathered up his belongings, downed the remains of his drink, and left.

#

Shelly walked down Parnell Street, bathed in the light of a hundred street lamps, amazed at what she was seeing.

Everywhere she looked there were fairy-folk doing fairy-folk things, while normal people walked right by them oblivious to it entirely. It was fascinating to watch. Nobody ever accidentally interacted with anybody else. While there were a lot less fairies on the street, the ones that were there walked about without being careful. People, normal people if that was not too racist a phrase to use, would suddenly go around them, or stop and look at the time all the while avoiding a collision.

What was more interesting was that since gaining her fairy vision the magical people seemed to notice her now. Whereas they walked by humans without giving them a second glance, most of the fairy-folk would nod polity at Shelly as they crossed paths.

Two worlds inhabiting the same place. It was simply amazing.

As she came near the book store Shelly spotted a familiar fairy face. Abraham St. Oker had just stepped out, a bag of books in his hand. She smiled at the sight of him. He had seemed pleasant enough when they had met earlier and Shelly hoped that maybe the vampire would be willing to help her find Kitty.

"Sorry, Mr. St. Oker," Shelly shouted, running up to him and waving her left hand in the air to get his attention.

"We meet again, Ms. Godfrey," he said, turning around to look at her.

"Um...yeah. That still isn't my surname."

"Apologies," Abe said. "I tend to trust the words from Henry a little too much. How are you?"

"Well actually I was wondering if I could ask you a favour," Shelly said.

In the book store window hung a digital display. It was the best sellers list for the month, compiled using information gathered across the country from practically every book-store in Ireland. Most book stores did something like this, to try and draw business in from the street. People who read knew what they wanted to read, generally ignoring such lists. But there was always somebody going on a sun holiday who wanted 'something to read beside the pool' and would buy whatever was on the list. It caught Shelly's attention for a split second, before she looked back at Mr. St. Oker.

He was also looking at the list, although it seemed as if he was studying it very intently.

"Well I would be happy to help, young lady," Abe said,

frowning as he read the top ten titles. "But sadly it would seem that I have more work to do. Perhaps when I am finished we can continue our conversation and I can lend you some assistance. Good evening."

With that the vampire author continued on his way, walking quickly down the night-time street.

Shelly watched him go, feeling a little disheartened. He was the only other person she knew in this new world, so it appeared her only options for finding Kitty Purry were to go it alone or continue searching with the fairy detective.

Turning to go she caught sight of the book list again and read the title of the tenth book. It seemed that 'Dracula' by Bram Stoker had made it back onto the list. Yet St. Oker had not seemed happy about this. Shelly found that a little odd but thought no more about it and headed home.

Chapter Eleven

"Kick him again! Make sure he is awake."

Pain exploded through every part of his body, dancing a little tap-dance number along his nervous system. There was a rumble in his stomach that had nothing to do with hunger and everything to do with trying to disperse the pain quickly. He curled up into the foetal position and tried to breath. The last few minutes had been a crazy blur of activity, similar to an unwanted acid trip. Sleep had been rudely turned into waking as he had been dragged out of bed and down the hall to the front room by hands unseen.

Without any time to at least get a pair of pants on.

"Go get him a glass of water or something. Something bland!"

Footsteps walked away, heading off in the direction of the kitchen at the back of the apartment. There was a faint smell of magic in the air as a spell was cast.

"Sit up, half-breed," Lé Precon said. "You know I am not one of those leprechauns that has to look down on people who are vertically advantageous to me."

Hands grabbed Filthy Henry by his shoulders and pushed him up so that he was sitting on the floor. He rested his back against the leg of the coffee table. Found breathing a little easier. You never appreciated the little things, like filling your lungs with oxygen, until it became difficult to do so.

"You know most people just drop over with breakfast," Filthy Henry said, looking about. "A cup of coffee and an apple Danish would be my first choice."

"Most people do what they're told without me needing to

140

chase them up about it," Lé Precon said. "I mean really! Why haven't you found my bloody Mothercrock yet? Do you realise the gravity of the situation here?"

Lé Precon was standing just inside the doorway to the room, leaning on his golden cane. Beside Filthy Henry stood another leprechaun, one of the Rainbow Guard judging by his bright blue uniform. Another brightly dressed one, wearing a yellow outfit, came back into the room and handed a glass of water to Filthy Henry. The fairy detective could see Lé Precon was taking no chances here. There was absolutely no magical recharging energies in a glass of water unless it had been conjured from magic. The Leprechaun King was clearly hoping that Filthy Henry had very little magical reserves. Not that Filthy Henry had a plan of action. He was not in mortal peril, aside from getting a few bruised ribs possibly, and even if he had a plan there were three full fledged leprechauns in his apartment. Any spells he would use against them would be a distraction at best. Unless he cast one really big one and then raced to the kitchen to eat the entire contents of his fridge.

Contents which, he was pretty sure, consisted of an out of date loaf of bread and a mouldy pepper.

"What do you want from me?" Filthy Henry asked as he took small sips of water, pondering possibilities. "You hired me yesterday to find your magical piss pot and expected me to what exactly? Have it before tea time?"

Lé Precon looked at the fairy detective and waved a hand nonchalantly in the air.

"Well...yes," he said.

Filthy Henry rolled his eyes.

It was the typical rich client attitude to a case. He had seen it a hundred times in the past. Why was it not possible to solve things sooner? How much time could it really take to get rid of a puca infestation? What do you mean the priceless heirloom has left the country and you have to track it down? Is there not one of those apps on those intelligent phones to help with that?

For some reason the fairy detective found it refreshing to see that even leprechauns could behave like moronic wealthy humans.

"I have exactly one clue to work with and you expected me to find your Mothercrock in a day? That's the height of stupidity, you do realise...OW!"

The blue-uniformed Rainbow Guard had kicked Filthy Henry in the side. Hard.

"No need for heightist remarks like that, half-breed," he said with a sneer.

"I don't think it was a heightist remark, Syril," Lé Precon said. "But the kick was appreciated." He turned his attention back to Filthy Henry. "So, do I get a report at least?"

The fairy detective rubbed at his side to ease the pain. He glared up at Lé Precon, who was creating another of those fancy leather chairs to sit on, making himself right at home.

"I'm sitting here in my underwear at half six in the morning, do you really want me to answer that?"

Another kick landed firmly against his body, smashing into the same spot as before.

"It's seven you filthy scum," Syril, the blue Rainbow Guard, said.

"Actually it is half six, Syril. I thought we had sent you to go learn how to tell time recently," Lé Precon said.

"Well this has been lovely," Filthy Henry said, pushing himself up from the floor.

142

A hand was placed on either shoulder, forcing him back down. Manners, it would seem, were another thing that Syril had to go on a course to learn. The fairy detective wondered if maybe his yellow costume cretin could join him on that particular day as well.

"I'm working on it Lé Precon," Filthy Henry said through gritted teeth. "I can't work miracles you know. It will take a bit of time to track it down. Besides, how the hell did you get in here? It's magically sealed against everything except me. Took me a week to cast and I had a migraine for a fortnight while I ate food to recharge."

Lé Precon chuckled, wiping an imaginary tear away from his eye.

"Please, half-breed," he said. "Your spell is pretty good, very good in fact considering what you had to work with. But what sort of loan-shark would I be if I couldn't get into the home of people that owe me money? How else can legs be broken? Once you make a deal with me your magic ain't worth squat until you pay me back in full. Meaning...?"

Filthy Henry sighed, defeated.

"Meaning the sooner I get your bloody Mothercrock back the better for my accommodation."

Lé Precon grinned and hopped down from his magically made leather chair.

"See, you're not as stupid as we all think. Just wrap this up by Friday, I'm growing impatient if you hadn't guessed. I want many names Filthy. Many names! Or you and me will have another conversation similar to this one. Only with more of my men along for the fun."

The room gained a very psychedelic colour scheme as all three leprechauns used their magic to teleport away. Rainbows of

143

colour covered everything, swirling like oil on water. It was a trippy thing to watch, even with knowledge of magic and how it worked. Filthy Henry closed his eyes, seeing the ghost image on his eyelids. After a few seconds the colours intensified, then vanished completely. The fairy detective opened his eyes and looked around at the now empty room.

Empty save for the newly conjured red leather chair that Lé Precon had left behind. Showing off with magic just to show off, a horrible trait to have.

A trait that Filthy Henry was envious off and if everything went according to plan, a trait he could soon have himself.

He pushed himself up from the floor and walked down the hall, back to his bedroom.

The bedroom looked like the training ground for a terrorist organisation. The floor was home to every item of clothing Filthy Henry owned, in varying states of cleanliness. There was a leaning tower of dirty dishes at the foot of his bed. The bed itself was only partially made, mainly because he fell asleep on top of it and was too lazy to crawl under the blankets. It was the typical bachelor bedroom.

After rummaging around for five minutes to find a clean suit, socks and underwear, the fairy detective started getting dressed.

Working on a case was never a straight forward thing. They always differed from each other, even if on the surface they looked to be the exact same. Almost like each case was a fingerprint, unique in some small subtle way to other cases. While one Red Man might be happy to have a plate of freshly washed clothes left out every night to keep the peace, another might not like that bargain one bit.

Lé Precon's lack of understanding of this basic concept had just ruined Filthy Henry's day. In order to get the thing solved by Friday the fairy detective would have to ignore all other cases.

Meaning Downy's drained bodies would have to wait until next week before getting properly looked into.

Not that they were likely to re-humidify in the meantime. That was one of the nice things about working on cases that involved dead things. Unless it was a Stoker the deceased tended to stay in one place.

Much like Kitty Purry.

As he put on his tie Filthy Henry thought about Shelly. It was probably the wiser course of action to just tell her that he had found the Cat Síth and be done with it. There was no reason he had to try and be nice about that case, they were not friends. No feelings could be hurt. But somewhere deep down Filthy Henry felt like he had to spare her feelings somehow, even if he was not sure why.

"Fecking women," Filthy Henry said, pulling on his trench-coat.

This was why private detectives worked alone, he was sure of it. Women only served to muddle things up. Either that or they turned out to be some sort of *femme fatale* that the detective should have stayed away from the moment they first met. Right now Shelly was muddling things up for him. He had never cared about a client's feelings before, why should she be any different.

Filthy Henry went out to the hallway, picked his keys up from the table by the front door, and left in search of an early breakfast.

#

St. Oker's reaction to being back on the best seller list was still puzzling Shelly. One would have thought that getting back onto a list when you had not written anything in a few decades, not to mention were presumed dead, would have been considered a good thing. Yet the vampire author had seemed unhappy about it all.

It just seemed a little...strange.

Since she had no commissions that needed finishing any time soon, a handy job perk of self employed artists, Shelly had decided to go and see if Filthy Henry had any leads on Kitty Purry.

It was all very exciting, like being in an old private detective movie. Less cloak and dagger more pixies and magic, but still beggars could not be choosers. Besides, despite his appalling attitude problem and complete lack of manners there was something about the fairy detective that Shelly found attractive. Much to her annoyance.

The first man that had talked to her for more than ten minutes in years and he turned out to be a magical prat.

Even still, as she stood outside the door to his building Shelly could not deny that she was looking forward to seeing him. Plus she figured it might be worth mentioning the strange reaction from St. Oker. Maybe Filthy Henry could go around and act like a friend to another creature, congratulating the vampire writer for getting back onto the top seller list.

"You're up early?" Filthy Henry said.

Shelly looked left and saw the fairy detective walking down the street with a tray holding two coffees and carrying a small white bag in his hand.

"Oh...um...hi," Shelly said, caught a little unawares. "I was just...you know...passing by."

He looked at her, arching an eyebrow.

"At half nine in the morning you just happened to be passing by my office on Middle Abbey Street despite not living in this neck of the woods at all? Really?"

She was no good at lying, it was definitely not her niche market. Under the cool gaze of Filthy Henry her mind went

146

completely blank. If he had smiled right there and then Shelly reckoned her knees would have started shaking. But for the life of her she could not figure out exactly *what* it was about the smug git that she found so appealing.

Filthy Henry walked past her and up the steps to the front door, unlocking it and going inside, leaving the door open behind him but not saying a word.

Ignorant shite, Shelly thought as she followed him, closing the front door behind her and climbing up the rickety staircase.

By the time she reached the first floor the fairy detective had already gone into his office and was seated behind his desk, taking out two pastries from the white bag and placing them down on a sheet of paper; the bachelors version of a clean plate. He looked up at Shelly as she walked into the room and begrudgingly offered her one of the two coffee cups.

"Milk and sugar already in it," he said as she took the cup from him and sat down in the big red leather armchair.

"Thanks," Shelly said. "I saw St. Oker again yesterday. Outside the book-store."

Filthy Henry chuckled, munching on a mouthful of pastry.
"That guy," he said, spraying pastries crumbs everywhere.
"Gets the gift of immortality and what does he do with it, huh?"
"Was he always a...you know," Shelly asked, taking a sip of her coffee.

There were more than two sugars in it, that was for sure. She could feel her teeth rotting just from the small sip she had taken. Shelly placed the cup down on the floor by her feet, hoping it was far enough away to stop the sugary damage reaching her mouth.

"A vampire?" Filthy Henry asked. "No, he was turned like any human. It's possible, just like the stories tell you. The Stokers in Ireland changed him as a thank you for writing 'Dracula'. See he

147

came up with the idea for the story without knowing that there were fairies all around him. When it was published the Stokers liked how he had not made them into moody vampires that run around in sunny fields with diamonds sparklingly all over them. He kept in the blood and guts and threw out all that romantic crap. Even though there is a romantic side to the tale, I suppose. They wanted to thank him by making him a vampire. Calling them 'Stokers' sort of happened as a result. But just look at how he spends his time, hilarious."

"I'm missing something here, aren't I?"

Filthy Henry finished off the first pastry, washing it down with some of his coffee. He tilted back on his chair and planted his feet up on the desk.

"Well he has this goal. A dream if you will. He wants to see 'Dracula' as the top selling book of all time. So he spends his eternal rest of the undead buying copy after copy of it. Trying to bump it up the list. Most of the books he ends up donating to libraries and schools, since he can't store them indefinitely. But he doesn't make any money off it now, since nobody is going to believe he is still alive and kicking. It all goes to an estate under his name, but one that he has no control over. Plus he had to change his name, since Bram Stoker is one of those ones that sticks out in your mind when you hear it."

"He didn't change it all that much," Shelly pointed out.
"Well nobody said he was one hundred percent original."
"That doesn't really explain why he was so annoyed with the book rankings when they got posted up in the store," Shelly said. "If anything I'd have though he would be pleased to be back on the list."

Filthy Henry looked at her, coffee cup half way to his mouth.

"What book rankings?"

148

#

The former employer of Jim, or Mastermind as he had started to think of himself, had gathered up as many of his trusted supporters as he could find. They had been told to bring friends and family, to make a night of it. Fun for all involved. There were so many of them packed into the room that by all logical reasoning the walls should have started to bulge and tear under the pressure.

"My fellow Stokers," he said, the crowd growing silent as he spoke. "It would appear that our best efforts are not good enough. To use a deplorable cliché, I need you to now give me one hundred and ten percent."

At the back a hand was raised, the questioner's face hidden from sight.

"If you are going to ask me how can you give me something that is mathematically impossible be fair warned that I have in my possession enough holy water and wooden stakes to make each and every Stoker in this room nothing more than moist ash on the floor."

The hand vanished from sight. It did not go back down. One second it was in the air, the next it was not. All without the intervening step of moving. A slight disturbance in the crowd indicated that the questioner was relocating, just to be on the safe side.

The Mastermind did not smile. Under any other circumstances it would have been a smiling matter, but his great plan was not working. Short of turning the entire population of Dublin into Stokers and enlisting them to work for him there was very little he could do. He reached down and picked up a school bag from a pile of bags, holding it above his head.

"In here you will find thirty tubes of sunscreen, factor sixty.

The sort that ginger people love to use because, let's face it, they are only one evolutionary step away from being vampires themselves. You will use this to walk around during daylight hours and continue with the plan. Each school bag also has more funds than you were given before. These are to be used to speed up the purchasing process. I know that time is on our side, but I'm bloody sick and tired of waiting for infinity to get here."

He tossed the bag towards the nearest Stoker.

"Make me proud," he said. "Don't forget there is a 'me' in 'team' and you don't want to disappoint me."

Chapter Twelve

"Well I'll be," Filthy Henry said.

They were standing outside a book-store on O'Connell Street, the main thoroughfare in Dublin City. The fairy detective was staring at the digital screen in the front window, scanning through the titles. His gaze fell on the last entry. He just stared at it in disbelief, as if it was a heavy set cheerleader propping up the rest. There, for all the world to see, was 'Dracula'. Somehow back on the best selling list for the month.

Shelly looked at him.

"So this is important then?" she asked.

"Not really sure," Filthy Henry said, scratching at his chin thoughtfully. "I mean it doesn't really mean anything. Could be just a fluke. All the buzz around vampires these days could have sparked an interest in his book. Sometimes if a new vampire movie or show comes out people like to read the original tale."

"A fluke like me having a talking cat and needing to talk with the only fairy detective in Dublin to find her?"

Filthy Henry looked at Shelly from the corner of his eye.

There it was again, that feeling. The one that hinted that somehow unrelated things were connected in some way. Just not in an obvious 'hit you over the head with a hammer' sort of way. It was a hard one to ignore, but right then Filthy Henry was finding another feeling just as hard to ignore.

Guilt.

At the mention of Kitty Purry's name the fairy detective felt the weight of the world on his shoulders. He found something very interesting to look at in the store window, leaning in to avoid eye-contact with Shelly.

"About your cat," Filthy Henry said.

"Oh?"

"Yea...oh."

This feeling of guilt was extremely unusual for the fairy detective. Generally he did as he pleased and very rarely treated a client with the proper respect they deserved. To him clients were just walking money machines. Which was probably why most of the fairy and human world had a grudge with him in some shape or form. Yet just talking to Shelly was undoing all his years of being a proper bastard, making him want to tell her the truth. Even if the truth did run the risk of hurting her feelings.

Something else that the fairy detective was found interesting, the fact that he cared about somebody else's feelings beyond his own.

Filthy Henry took a deep breath to steady himself, stepped in between Shelly and the store window and looked directly into her eyes.

"Look I should have told you this sooner," he said, feeling his face go red. "I found Kitty Purry."

Shelly clapped her hands together with glee, her mouth forming the largest smile that Filthy Henry had ever seen. A smile of pure joy if ever there was one.

"Really?!" she screeched. "Where is she? How is she?"

The guilt was compounded even more.

"Well see...here's the thing...she isn't so much with the breathing any more."

It was the softest way he could think of to break the news to her. Filthy Henry rarely had to come up with a nice way to deliver bad news. His favoured approach was to just break the news and collect the fee for closing the case. Mainly because he knew what was about to happen next and generally tried to avoid it as much as possible.

Shelly's eyes started to water instantly, tears forming like emotional dew. Her bottom lip quavered. All colour had drained from her face.

"She's...dead?" It was said in scarcely more than a whisper.

Filthy Henry nodded once. He looked down at the toes of his shoes and stared hard at them.

"How long have you known?" Shelly asked, tears streaming down her face.

Men are the weaker sex in many respects, not that they would ever admit it. What they have in brute strength they lack in many other areas. One such weakness all men suffered from, no matter how tough they were, was the emotional questioning of a crying woman. Once the water works were turned on even the blackest of hearts could feel strings being plucked, knowing deep down the truth was required to make the tears stop.

What surprised Filthy Henry most was at that moment he could feel a lump forming in his throat at the sight of Shelly visibly upset. He wanted nothing more than to ease her pain, or at least make her stop crying in front of him. All the crying was making him feel like the worst person in the world, which he liked to think he was not. At least he tended to live in hope that there was somebody worse than him in the world.

Somewhere.

"Only a little while," Filthy Henry lied with practised ease, slowly looking up from his shoes to the tear filled eyes of Shelly. "I found her in the warehouse with those two bodies and the..."

The slap blind sided him completely, causing a bright light to flash across his vision and obscure the world for a few seconds. A ringing sound hummed away in his left ear. Filthy Henry was pretty sure one of his fillings had been knocked loose as well. It was the mother of all slaps, the most painful one he had ever gotten in his entire life. Which was saying something since women tended to reject his lurid ideas for activities in the bedroom with a slap to the face.

Nothing ended a chat-up in a pub like a slap to the chops.

Shelly stared at him for a couple of seconds before turning and marching away, pushing through the crowd.

Filthy Henry watched her go while he rubbed his cheek to help ease the stinging sensation. But the slap itself was not what was hurting him most. Deep down, in the pit of his stomach, the fairy detective knew that he had just hurt the first person he had ever considered a friend.

#

"You know you're an arsehole, right?

"It's been said before."

"But seriously. On the grand scale of arse and hole you are right at the top of both."

That was the problem with Bunty Doolay. For all her visually stunning eye appeal she spoke straight. No word play, no double meaning. If she thought you were acting like a moron she would tell you and leave no room for misinterpretation. Should misinterpretation occur it was entirely on the part of the listener and would no doubt lead to more direct attacks on a person's character.

But Bunty Doolay's was the only pub in Dublin open to serve real drink so early in the day. Meaning the not-so-friendly vocal sparing would have to be tolerated.

It was either that or be left alone with his thoughts, something Filthy Henry really wanted to avoid. Cast a spotlight on your own soul and you always ended up depressed at what you saw, because it generally matched what other people saw too.

"Can I just get another drink, please?" the fairy detective asked, pushing forward his empty glass. "It's been one of those mornings."

Bunty Doolay opened the bottle of fairy ale and slowly filled up the glass with a golden fluid.

"You're lucky I even let you back in here after your little stunt yesterday," the Sídhe said. "Have you any idea of how badly I slept last night?"

Filthy Henry rubbed a hand over his face, the sting from Shelly's slap earlier was still hanging around for good measure. He reached over and picked up the refilled glass, while Bunty was still pouring the drink out, and took a sip from it.

"I know! I'll owe you, alright," he said, gruffly. "It's the same with all you fairy races. I ask for help and end up being in debt somehow. Nobody ever seems to owe me favours for some reason."

"So you are just adding 'jackass' to the list of things you are becoming today, is that it?"

Filthy Henry downed the rest of his drink in one mouthful, wincing at the taste of it burning the back of his throat. He looked across the counter at Bunty through watering eyes. Alcohol induced tears, not some sort of emotional based ones. At least that is what he hoped.

"Well it's early yet," he said. "Don't rule anything out. So what did my little bag of dust tell you then?"

Bunty Doolay reached under the bar counter and pulled out a glass jam jar with a metal lid screwed onto it. Inside the jar a small blue ball of light pulsed, each pulse matching a gentle hum that seemed to be coming from the container itself. She placed it down on the bar counter beside his drink and walked away.

"You managed to make a wisp from it then?" he asked, looking at the light in the jar.

"Don't open that thing in here," she called back to him, ignoring his question completely. "The lunchtime rush is about to start and I don't want you depressing my clientèle."

Filthy Henry picked up the jar, put on his coat, then dropped the jar into his trench-coat pocket. He stood up and walked towards the front door, leaving the pub without saying a word.

#

Wisps fascinated Filthy Henry, mainly because the energies required to create one were way beyond anything he would ever be able to achieve himself. If somehow he got lucky enough to have the right amount of magic stored up to cast the creation spell the physical drain would have killed him. Meaning the overall benefit of creating a wisp in the first place was greatly outweighed by the negative factor of not being alive afterwards to use said wisp.

Which was why Bunty Doolay had been needed, even though she was less than happy about the fact. The fairy detective knew that he would have to buy her a present of some sort to thank her, which would in no way count to paying off his debt with her for performing the magic in the first place. But he had needed the wisp created and gun-to-his-head trusted nobody else to do the job for him. The problem with artificially created wisps was they did not last as long as the genuine article. A wisp spotted out in the wild was usually a soul that had not want to moved on, but had no idea how to take on a decent incorporeal form. They just drifted about forever, making alien-junkies believe that the bogs of Ireland were U.F.O hotspots. Wisps created from the remains

156

of a deceased creature had a much shorter life expectancy, making communicating with them all the more tricky. Every ounce of energy the wisp used to speak shortened the time it would remain in existence.

Filthy Henry sat on the couch in his apartment and tapped the side of the jar. The wisp inside flew around the glass like a trapped fly.

In this state, held forever in a little jam-jar prison, the magically created being could live for a couple of months. Although months of existence as something that could hardly be considered decent. Wisps were only vaguely aware that the world was around them and had a strange obsession with occupying trees. Filthy Henry knew the kinder thing to do would be open the jar and begin the questioning, expend the life force to allow the soul move on.

Even if it was a Stoker that had broken The Rules and did not deserve the bliss of the afterlife.

The fairy detective carefully placed the jar down on the coffee table and picked up a salt shaker he had brought in from the kitchen. With precisely no pomp and zero flare he sprinkled a circle of salt around the jar, making sure that there were no broken sections. Filthy Henry loved salt, the most universal seasoning ever. Useful for adding flavour to a dish or containing a spirit in one location. Every magical practitioner worth his NaCl crystals made sure they never ran out of the stuff.

With the circle completely drawn Filthy Henry unscrewed the jar lid, tossing it down onto the table.

Without waiting to be asked the wisp shot out from the mouth of the jar like an electric greyhound. It rose several inches before hitting an invisible wall, little white lines scattering through the air. The wisp dove towards the jar, banking to the left at the last moment and once again connected with the invisible barrier. On the table top the salt granules moved slightly, more white cracks ran through the air for a second.

The barrier held.

"I will drink your body clean of blood!" the wisp said as it flew off in another direction, once again hitting the unseen wall.

"Yea, that's sorta what I wanted to talk to you about," Filthy Henry said, settling back into the couch and putting his feet up on the table. He made sure that the salt circle was not disturbed. "You've been a bad little Stoker haven't you?"

The wisp raced around the invisible barrier, cracks appearing and vanishing in its wake.

"You're not going to get out of there any time soon so why not calm down, answer a few questions for me, and then I will break the barrier and let you move on."

Like a child coming down from a sugar rush, the wisp spun around and drifted towards the jar. It floated over the glass opening, pulsating with a blue light.

"Really?"

"You have my word," Filthy Henry said, holding up his hand and making the cub scout sign with three fingers. "Once you answer a few of my questions you will be free to move on."

Wisps lacked facial features but Filthy Henry imagined that the magical creature was giving him a look of disbelief. Trying its best to find a trick hidden in the offer but failing to. The problem now was time. All the attempts at escaping had burned up valuable energy that the wisp did not have to spare. Meaning a lot of questions were going to have to get bumped up the list of priority.

"How long have you been operating in Dublin and how many

people have you drained in defiance of The Rules?" Filthy Henry asked, staring directly at the floating orb of light. "Lying won't get you out of here any sooner, just to point that out."

The wisp bobbed up and down in the air.

"I've only been a vampire for two days and those idiots in the warehouse were my first kills. Initiation into the Brotherhood of Blood!"

Filthy Henry frowned. Stokers were known for having many interesting traits. Sleeping in coffins. Ordering garlic bread in a restaurant without the garlic. Wearing sunglasses while sitting in a nightclub that was so poorly light the bathroom signs were in Braille. Forming stupidly named groups was definitely not up there on the list. It was not even on the list. Stokers were like every other fairy race, they liked to keep their heads down. So to be told that there was a group of Stokers in Dublin operating under some ridiculous name was like getting told that the Internet could be downloaded onto an old three and a half inch floppy disc. In other words highly unlikely.

"So you had only been a vampire for a couple of days? What was the name of the one that turned you?"

The wisp raced around the barrier, cracks spreading through the air.

"I don't know. He was a posh sounding twat. Just came up to me in the pub one night and told me all about this vampire lark. I thought he was talking out his arse but then he showed me his fangs. Plus he moved so fast, like really fast. Said that all I had to do was one little job for him after he turned me. That was it, payment would have been made in full. All I had to do was drink those two guys dry of every drop of blood."

With a wobble the wisp stopped moving, hovering at eye level with the fairy detective.

"Um...can you see my feet?" the wisp asked in a concerned tone. "I think I have lost my feet. Not my shoes...just to be clear. But my actual feet. They should have ten toes, five on each foot."

Filthy Henry scratched his chin.

This was the problem with magically created wisps. Unlike the ones that formed naturally the type created from spells did not make the transition to incorporeal form smoothly. They still thought they had a body and were just as they had always been. Right up until the moment they winked out of the world.

"Don't worry I will help you find them before you move on," Filthy Henry said, thinking carefully about his next question.

So far he had found out that a posh vampire had turned some drunk in a pub into a Stoker, for the sole purpose of killing two random humans in a warehouse. The mere act of telling a human about Stokers was yet more Rule breaking. Aside from the knowledge that the killer had only recently been turned not a lot of new information had been uncovered. But why would a Stoker make a new vampire solely to break The Rules, that made no sense at all.

"Can you remember what the vampire who turned you looked like?"

The wisp pulsated, blue light illuminating the room for a moment.

"Nah...posh twat like I said. Spoke all proper like. I thought he was taking the mickey to be honest. Right up until he started necking on me. Seriously how have I lost my feet? Is that normal for vampires? Think he had on a hat, like that American President fella used to wear. Now are you going to help me with this foot situation I'm in?"

A strange idea popped into Filthy Henry's head, based on years of experience with Stokers and their dietary habits. One thing a Stoker never, ever, did was completely drain a body of all the blood. Something to do with causing the heart to melt and accidentally get sucked through the opening the vampire was drinking from. It was the Stoker equivalent of indigestion, literally getting heart burn. So before they started operating blood donation clinics a vampire would drink right up to the second last beat of the heart and then let the victim die naturally.

In so far as you could count death by massive blood loss natural.

So why would two nobodies in a warehouse have to be completely drained? Unless there was something in them that meant the blood was evidence. Something in the blood..

"What did the blood taste like?" Filthy Henry said, sitting up straight and leaning in closer to the wisp.

"Oh man...it was like nothing I've ever tasted. I thought it would be disgusting but once I got the scent of fresh, warm, human blood all my doubts disappeared."

The wisp started to glow brighter as the emotions attached to the memory burned up more energy. Filthy Henry noticed that there were tendrils of magical smoke drifting off the orb. It was using up more of its time.

"It tasted like cookie-dough ice-cream mixed with maple syrup. I couldn't wait to start on the second moron once the first one was empty. You know I think I even licked my lips afterwards, that's how tasty it was."

Suddenly the wisp shot straight up into the air and did a little flip of joy. More tendrils of smoke were coming off it, signifying that the energy binding it together was rapidly running out. It only had minutes left. But the fairy detective did not really care about this, because the wisp had given him a big clue. He had never tasted blood himself, but conversations with Stokers over the decades had enlightened his knowledge on the subject.

Human blood tasted nothing like cookie-dough ice-cream. Human blood tasted like the world's best brewed cup of coffee to vampires, that was why they enjoyed it so much. Never had a Stoker described the taste in any other way. It did not matter if it was O-positive or A-negative, it all tasted like coffee to them.

Which meant that whatever else had gone down in that warehouse, the two victims had something a little extra coursing through their veins. Something that someone did not want to become common knowledge. What better way to hide such strange blood than to have a creature drink every last drop of it from their bodies?

"Here," the wisp said as it floated down so it was eye-level with Filthy Henry once more. "I don't seem to have my hands either. I've lost my hands and feet. Who are you anyway?"

It was loosing its sense of self. At best the wisp had twenty seconds left in this world before it moved onto the next.

"I'm Filthy Henry," the fairy detective said, reaching over and brushing away some of the salt.

The wisp changed to a shade of blood red.

"The half-breed! He warned me about you. Said you are a con-artist, you trick vampires. I'll drain you dry!"

It rushed straight towards him, growing smaller as more and more magical smoke came off it. With the salt circle broken there was no barrier to prevent it from flying away from the table, directly at the fairy detective's head. He smiled as the ball of energy washed over his face, the last burst of magical power that had formed the wisp dissipating. As it passed over his head the light in the room returned to normal, minus the blue glow cast by the wisp.

"See," Filthy Henry said to the empty room, rising up from the couch. "Told you I would let you move on."

Chapter Thirteen

Everyone in the café kept looking over at her when they thought she would not notice. But as always in that sort of situation she did notice, right when they looked at her. Causing that uncomfortable cycle of sly eye-contact, embarrassed look, looking at something else, and more sly eye-contact.

Shelly knew full well why people kept staring at her. Since entering the café she had not stopped crying. She had just taken up a small table by the window, ordered a coffee, and sat there as tears streamed down her face.

To make things worse Shelly was not entirely sure what was upsetting her more. That Kitty Purry was dead or that Filthy Henry had hidden the truth from her.

Sure you could argue that he had some misguided sense of chivalry, but what right did he have for not telling her? True the fairy detective had brought her into a magical and wonderful world, but that did not allow him to lie to her. It was not like she was some little orphan kid that had just found out she had magical powers and was destined to fight the worst evil the world had ever seen. That sort of stuff only happened in fairy tales.

Quickly Shelly flicked on her fairy vision, just to not get caught off guard if a fairy did suddenly appear in front of her. The café was fairly busy, packed with young college students and late night shoppers, but apparently magical creature free. She left her enhanced sight turned on and looked out the window.

It certainly felt like Filthy Henry had betrayed her, regardless of what he may or may not have intended. After all if they were not friends, or at least acquaintances, then there was the small fact that she had hired him to find her lost cat. She was his employer, he should have told her the moment he found Kitty Purry.

Although why Kitty had been in the warehouse along with two dead men? Kitty had been old, rarely going for walks on her own that took longer than half an hour. The warehouse had been down in the docklands, at least an hour from home by car. Who knows how long it would have taken a cat to walk there.

Across the street three fairy-folk were coming out of the Eason's book-store. Each of them had two large shopping bags in their hands, bulging with books. They came down the steps and crossed the road to the median, walking along with the rest of the shoppers. But they had come close enough for Shelly to see that the three were not just fairy-folk. They were Stokers. Even through her tear brimmed eyes that much was obvious.

She watched them walk down the street until they passed from sight, then turned back and stared at the empty chair across from her.

Buying books in bulk was not something strange, people did it all the time. One of Shelly's ex-boyfriends had once blown an entire wage packet for a week in a book-store without even realising it. Then tried to pass off the 'Big Book of Serial Killers' as a present he had intended to get her for her birthday. Not that he had forgotten her birthday, nothing like that, he just knew how much she 'loved' serial killers. Presumably fairy-folk enjoyed reading books just like humans did. But still, there was something odd about three Stokers walking around the city carrying big bags of books that seemed a little strange to Shelly.

Not that a lot of what she had seen over the past few days was normal. She was just developing different shades of normal. A gradient of oddness.

Purely on a whim Shelly gathered up her belongings and left the café, heading across the street and walking into the book-store.

It was not as nicely laid out as Chapters, but like every book-store there were shelves along every wall overladen with books. Given it was Thursday, which meant late night shopping in the city, the store was still quite busy, eager readers judging books by their covers before purchasing them. Shelly passed by all the displays and special offer stands, searching for one particular item that she knew had to be in the store somewhere. On the ground floor, just behind the escalators, Shelly found what she was looking for. The list of current best sellers, displayed on a computer screen like in every other store. She scanned the titles quickly and spotted what she sought straight away, her hunch becoming a full blown theory in the process.

Sitting happily at number five on the list was 'Dracula' by Bram Stoker.

"I've got to go tell that poxy fairy detective," Shelly said to herself. "Something isn't making sense here."

She turned around to leave the store and collided into somebody who had been standing behind her.

"Apologies my dear," a smooth toned voice said as a strong hand caught Shelly by her elbow, preventing her from falling over.

"Sorry," Shelly said, " should have looked where I was...going..."

Cold blue eyes stared at her from beneath a black top hat. Abe St. Oker smiled his fang filled smiled, releasing his grip on Shelly's elbow when it was clear she was steady on her feet once more. In his other hand he held a stack of books, each one identical to the others in the pile.

"You sure do like your work," Shelly said, smiling nervously and indicating the multiple copies of 'Dracula' with a nod of her head.

165

"Oh this...my little hobby," St. Oker said, his gaze drifting up to the list of best sellers.

As he read down through the titles St. Oker's smile grew, showing more teeth.

"Well isn't that something," he said, seemingly to himself. "Still not there just yet. But..."

He did not finish the sentence, just left the word hanging in the air as he looked at the display of best sellers.

Shelly looked over her shoulder with the fairy-vision, relieved to see that the shop was filled with humans. Something about St. Oker's manner was making her want to be somewhere else at that moment. Somewhere that had lots of holy water mixed with crushed garlic contained in crucifix shaped bottles.

"I'll leave you to your shopping," Shelly said, looking back at Abe St. Oker and smiling. "It was nice bumping into you, ha ha." It was a nervous laugh, but that was the best she could manage at that moment. She walked away from the vampire-author, towards the side entrance of the store that led out to Middle Abbey Street. Pushing on the glass door she ran down the steps quickly and looked about. Shelly could see some fairy folk walking about, but nobody was paying her any attention. She turned right and ran down the pavement towards Filthy Henry's office.

#

Pounding on a front door generally means only one thing. That the person doing the pounding really wants to enter the building upon which they are door pounding. This is an obvious enough conclusion to come to. Doors have been knocked on since they were invented, otherwise occupants would sit inside all day and wonder why they had no friends visiting them. However, while a knock suggested a person would like to be let inside eventually, pounding implied urgency. It hinted that the pounder was really interested in no longer being on their side of the door,

166

wanting to be very much on the other side.

In Filthy Henry's experience people who pounded on doors rarely had the occupant's best interests at heart. He walked out from his office and leaned over the bannisters, looking down the rickety staircase to the front door on street level.

"Open! Up! You! Lying! Toe! Rag!" the pounder shouted, each word getting a bang on the door to really emphasis it.

"Shelly?" he shouted down.

"Why?! Have you lied to any other women in the last twenty-four hours?"

Filthy Henry would never have admitted it, even under torture, but he was happy to know that Shelly was outside. He ran down the stairs, pulled back the bolts, unlocked the door, which Shelly was still pounding upon like a woodpecker on steroids, and opened it.

The bottom of a fist came hurtling towards his face. Filthy Henry fell backwards, landing awkwardly on the stairs and staring up at Shelly.
"Oh..." she said, her fist still in the air. "I didn't think you were going to open the door."
"Well it's open now," he said.

Shelly did not wait for any further conversation. She darted inside, spun around, slammed the door shut and slid the bolts into place. He noticed she was panting, clearly she had been running. But why? Unless his whole white lie with a hint of black had really annoyed her to the point where she wanted to cause him physical harm.

"Right..." she said, resting her back against the door. "No more crap from you. Got it?"

Filthy Henry simply nodded, moving so that he was sitting on the bottom step of the stairs.

"What's wrong?"

Shelly stared intently at him, making him squirm a little on the step. It was one of those stares that teachers used until a naughty child cracked and admitted to putting a thumb-tac on their chair.

"I want you to tell me the truth from here on out," Shelly said. "For a start what is your last name? Nobody is just called Filthy Henry."

The fairy detective grimaced and scratched absent-mindedly at his ear.

"Ask me anything else," he said. "I'll tell you the truth, honest. Just I never tell anybody my last name."

"Why not?" she asked, crossing her arms and staring even harder if such a thing were possible.

The fairy detective sighed. Despite being somebody that dealt with matters of a private nature for others he had never enjoyed sharing his own private matters.

"I'm a half-breed," Filthy Henry said, rubbing his hands together. "Something that the fairy world does not like to exist. If people knew my surname they could track my family. Basically I don't tell anybody my full name so that it is harder to find out where I came from. Alright?"

Shelly shrugged.
"Fair enough. Then how about this, what sort of fairy are you? Then I'm going to tell you a little theory I have been working on about those two bodies in the warehouse. Got it?"

The fairy detective nodded once again, purely because he figured doing anything else would have been the worst course of action to take.

168

#

A common misconception of vampires is they can blend into shadows. Abe St. Oker had only learned after his transformation that this was one ability the blood suckers did not have. It was a myth created by humans to explain how a vampire could so easily disappear from sight. The reality was that a vampire was simply very good at hiding right out in the open. People stood out less when doing exactly the same as those around them. When you stood in a doorway, trying to hide in a shadow, that was when you drew attention to yourself. If you just walked down the street, casually, without doing anything out of the ordinary, you blended right in.

Which was how Abe St. Oker was able to watch Shelly from across the street as she banged on the door to Henry's office. Filthy Henry as the other fairy-folk called him.

The vampire-author walked along with the crowd of late night shoppers, a little slower than those around him, and cast a glance over at the woman. He saw her banging, shouting, the door opening and her running inside. All without being seen. All by hiding in plain sight.

It was unfortunate that Shelly had run to the fairy detective. Abe liked him, he had always felt a small sense of kindred. Both of them were outcasts in this fairy-world, albeit Abe St. Oker was accepted a little more than 'Filthy' Henry. But there was a risk that Shelly was telling him some crazy things, things that could result in the fairy detective getting a little more curious than would be good for him.

Which meant that Shelly and Henry had just become two more bumps in the road that would need to be sorted. Flattened out on his journey to true immortality.

A dishevelled youth dressed in a hideous tracksuit with bright yellow running shoes approached St. Oker as he continued on his way, turning to walk down Liffey Street. "Spare some change for the bus, bud?" the youth asked.

Abe St. Oker smiled at the perfect example of inner city youth, his fangs extending slightly.

"I have something even better for you," he said, placing a hand on the dirt encrusted shoulder of the youth and gripping it tightly. "Much better."

#

Shelly had taken the seat behind the desk. She sat with her hands out in front of her on the wooden surface, fingers interlaced. Her breathing was slow, controlled. A stare that could have bored a hole through a cinder block in five seconds focused firmly on Filthy Henry. With the fairy-vision turned on it gave her a slightly menacing, demonic look.

The fairy detective was sitting in the chair that Lé Precon had created, loathing the need to use it himself. Magical energies were still crackling throughout the leather, the creation spell still in effect in a small manner. How he had wound up not sitting in his own chair behind the desk was a little unclear. Shelly had just demanded that they have a serious conversation and then taken the best seat in the house.

It was like they were a married couple with a joint bank-account. It was both theirs in theory, but only the wife had use of it really.

"So," Shelly said, " go on then. Just what sort of fairy are you? Unless you expect me to believe that 'half-breed' is now some fairy race."

Filthy Henry groaned and ran a hand across the stubble on his chin.

This was the sort of conversation he had hoped to avoid forever. It was the reason he had stayed alone all this time. Now here was this woman who had had a latent ability to see fairy kind asking the one question he had dodged for years. Giving her fairy-vision was probably the worst decision he had ever made. The fairy world had no need of human tourists, let alone ones that asked questions.

But she had asked a question and he had agreed to answer them. This level of honest rapidly becoming the second worst decision he had ever made.

"I'm a half-fairy," he said, crossing his arms and slouching down in the chair. "A half-breed."

Shelly shrugged, moving her head left and right to indicate that the answer was not satisfactory.

"I am half-human and half-fairy, which makes me somewhat unique in this world."

"How so?" she asked, still not happy with the answer.

"Fairy-folk have strict rules about breeding with humans. They don't! But it has been known to happen over the years and the result is a half-breed like me. A filthy half-breed to use the term of endearment that full fairies have. We are less than Stokers, because at least a Stoker is a turned human not a half-and-half."

The blue glow had faded from Shelly's eyes, seemingly of its own accord. She made a silent 'O' with her mouth.

"So that's why they all call you half-breed," she said. "But if it's possible to have a cross-race baby why are you claiming to be unique."

"Because I am," Filthy Henry said. "Most half-breeds don't live past six months once the fairy-folk find out. They tend to clean up little accidents quickly. You ever hear of a Changeling?"

"Yea they got a mention in that book you made me read. Babies made by fairies that die after a short while?"

"The book is half right," the fairy detective said. "See Changelings are actually a race of fairies that just so happen to look exactly like human infants. For their entire lives. It's hilariously disconcerting when you see a creature that looks like a four month old child sculling beers, smoking and gambling at a poker game. They have no real magical powers, save for one. A Changeling can die whenever it wants to."

Shelly made the appropriate facial expression upon hearing this description. An expression that suggested the person was after vomiting in their mouth and swallowing it back down again, without meaning to do either.

"So they just die?" she asked, horrified.

"Yep. Plus they charge the other fairy-folk for this service. See a half-breed isn't allowed to live as it puts the whole fairy world at risk, it's against The Rules. To ensure little accidents that do happen don't survive the fairy parent, usually the father who has slept with a human without revealing his true nature, hires a Changeling and swaps the real child with a fake. The Changeling then dies and the mother mourns the death of her little bundle of joy. Only thing is once a Changeling is placed into the earth they come back to life. Then a mate comes along and digs them back out and off the go, job done. Of course that was before people started cremating bodies. The Changelings really did not see that one coming."

He laughed. It was a funny story, depending on how you looked at it. A race that had evolved the ability to literally 'play' dead being undone by people who wanted to sprinkle ashes on a river instead of bury the person in the ground.

Shelly looked like she was about to throw up.

"What...," she began, holding a hand up to her mouth. "What happens to the children that the fairy-folk steal?"

Filthy Henry winced.

"It's probably better that you don't know that part," he said. "Anyway, my mother hid me before the swap could be made. Once you survive your first year The Rules say you are to be left alone. So here I am, ninety-eight years later, reviled by every fairy that walks the land. Particularly Changelings. They sort of see me as their very own white whale. Too late to do anything about me but a constant reminder of one who got away. But that's how I got the name 'Filthy Henry', I'm a filthy abomination as far as the fairy world is concerned."

Silence fell between them as Shelly stared at him.

"You're ninety-eight? You look like you're in your early thirties...how...?"

"I age slower because of the fairy-blood in me. It's why I'm the only human that can do real magic. Others that claim to be able to are just channelling the powers of a fairy they somehow captured."

Bombshells of truth always have the same effect on people when they hear them. They are unsure whether to fully believe the truth they have just been told. Shelly was no exception. She just sat still in the chair, silent. He decided to just let her mind take in what had been said, absorbing it like a sponge of bewilderment. Being told the truth about somebody is hard enough without finding out that they are nearly a century old but do not look it. He felt a little naked right then, revealing a lot too much of himself to somebody else. Now all he had to do was wait for the inevitable disgust that would come from yet another person who looked down on a half-breed.

In that respect humans and fairies had a lot more in common than either race realised.

"So which half are you then?" Shelly asked, a hint of a smile on her lips. "Is it like a mermaid sort of thing?"

Then again sometimes people reacted in an entirely new and

profoundly stupid way. Filthy Henry could not help but smile.

"I'm sorry I didn't tell you about Kitty sooner," he said. "Honestly. But I was sort of enjoying having somebody around that I could talk to while working a case. There are not a lot of fairy-folk that look favourably on me. If I had one wish it would be that I was a full blown fairy."

"Really? Why not a human?"

The fairy detective laughed.

"You've seen how cool the fairy world is, right? Why the hell would I want to turn my back on that by becoming human?"

Shelly shifted into a more comfortable position on her chair. His chair!

"I suppose. But I haven't forgiven you for not telling me. I hired you to find my cat, not protect my feelings."

"Well technically you didn't even..."

His sentence was rudely interrupted by the sound of the front door downstairs exploding inwards. Something had smashed into it from outside, sending the door careening up the steps. It broke a few bannister poles as it travelled upwards, before crashing to a stop on the landing outside the office door.

Filthy Henry and Shelly were both on their feet, the fairy detective running to the top of the stairs and looking down. It was a scene of destruction below. The door had been hit so hard that sections of wall were missing where once hinges had been. A cloud of dust and dirt hung in the air, clearing slowly, to reveal a large hole in the wall. Bricks and mortar fell away, enjoying a freedom they had never known.

Shelly had come out of the office and was standing behind the fairy detective, holding tightly onto his arm.

"What the hell was that?" she asked.

He did not answer, instead turning up his fairy vision and staring below.

Any magical spell that powerful would have left a signature behind, a pointer to whoever had cast it. Colours from the real world faded into the background as the magical energies of the fairy-world replaced them. Through the cloud of dust Filthy Henry could see no magical tendrils of power that indicated a spell attack. However, there was a bright red, pulsing, silhouette standing on the street, framed by the destroyed doorway.

"Oh crap," Filthy Henry said in a whisper.

As the dust settled it showed a Stoker, newly turned, standing outside with his fists in front of him. He was dressed in a typical scum-bag style yellow tracksuit, the bite marks still fresh on the side of his neck. Filthy Henry could see the raw magical energies rippling through the Stoker's body. It had only been turned in the last fifteen minutes, its body still full of power. Stokers, vampires in general, were most animalistic when they had just been changed from human into one of the undead. Power coursing through their once fragile body gave them the illusion that anything was possible. But more than that the freshly awakened desire for blood was overpowering, pushing all logical thinking aside like a fat kid running past their skinny siblings in order to get the big slice of cake.

Until that blood-thirst was sated for the first time the new Stoker was a crazed animal with supernatural powers.

Got to get her out of here, Filthy Henry thought.

The fairy detective knew he had enough magic stored up to handle himself against one newborn Stoker, but not enough to magic both himself and Shelly to safety. Teleportation for two full grown adults was a power sucking spell. At least if Shelly was elsewhere it would make dealing with the hungry baby Stoker that little bit easier. Mainly because Filthy Henry would not have to worry about protecting himself and Shelly at the same time.

Without breaking his gaze from the Stoker below, Filthy Henry reached behind and placed a hand on Shelly. There was no time to worry about where she was going, just so long as she was gone.

" *Suíomh bogadh,* " Filthy Henry said, sending the spell towards her.

"What the f...."

A flash of blue from behind, coupled with the lack of finger nails digging into his arm, let Filthy Henry know the spell had worked. Now it was just him and a newborn Stoker.

The perfect way to spend a Thursday evening.

"You know you can't come in here, right?" he shouted down.

"Why not ya bleedin' muppet?" the Stoker asked, pointing at the relocated door at the top of the stairs. "I was able to knock better than the Big Bad Wolf and send your door in, wasn't I?"

"Well anybody can kick a door in, but a vampire has to be invited inside somebody's home before they can enter. Meaning you're stuck out there," Filthy Henry said, keeping a straight face the entire time.

Doubt crept into the Stoker's expression. He looked up and down the street, before frowning and leaning in through the doorway a little.

"Want to invite me in so I can do my job?"

"Not likely," Filthy Henry said.

"God dammit!" the Stoker said, gesticulating wildly. It swung a fist towards the wall, missed, lost balance, and fell crashing to the ground. Lying on the rubble and dirt the Stoker looked up at

Filthy Henry.

"Thought you said I couldn't come in?"

"No, I said you have to be invited inside a person's home to enter. My apartment is the next floor up. Anyway, gotta run."

Running was viewed by many warriors, fighters and manly men as a cowardly act, but that view was subjective. It was only cowardly to the person who wanted to cause harm to somebody. For the person doing the running it was putting into practice Darwin's concept of survival of the fittest. If you were fit and able to run well then you had a much better chance of surviving a fight you ran away from.

Filthy Henry was a huge believer in this school of thought. Right then he just wished that his running partner was not a hungry Stoker out for blood.

Chapter Fourteen

"...uck are you do...," Shelly was saying as the world shifted around her ", ...ing?"

One minute she was cowering behind Filthy Henry, looking down at his exploding door and whatever had caused it. The next she was on the other side of the city, standing outside the closed gates of St. Stephen's Green park very confused and with a sudden urge to vomit.

Nobody had seemed to notice her sudden appearance in the middle of the street, nor the trails of magical blue smoke coming off her. Not even the few fairy-folk that were walking about paid any heed to her. Then again teleporting around the place was probably the fairy version of public transport, although much more efficient. The people at Dublin Bus could make a lot of money if they ever developed a method of instantaneous transport.

Or at least a timetable that resembled reality.

Shelly spun around on the spot and started running through the crowd, crossing the street at the pedestrian crossing with the red man clearly informing her it was not a safe time to cross, and ran down Grafton Street.

Right now Filthy Henry was under attack and the stubborn moron had decided to play the hero by sending her out of harms way.

"Bloody move!" she shouted at the public in general, running as fast as she could.

The sea of shoppers parted in a Biblical fashion, primarily to avoid the wrath of Shelly as she raced along.

As a plan, running was just advancing in reverse. Ground was gained in the exact direction you wanted. Just because said ground was in the opposite direction of your opponent meant nothing, it was all part of the plan.

Filthy Henry was not a big fan of this plan at the minute.

Despite being half fairy his body was mostly human. The ageing thing was a result of the magic in his blood, as was the ability to actually perform spells. But his body was still, when all was said and done, a human body. One that had gone through some serious neglect and was so far from the peak of physical fitness that the mere act of sweating properly felt like a work out in itself. He was already gasping for air by the time he reached the second landing, which did not bode well at all. Being chased by a hungry Stoker was like being a mouse getting chased by a cat on steroids with bionic legs. It was going to end well for one of the players, with very little doubt as to which one.

Right now the fairy detective was buying himself time. Not a lot of time, granted, but time. Time to come up with something that resembled a better plan than just running. There was no point hiding in the apartment. That whole invite-only aspect only applied to a fully turned Stoker. A newborn was still in a state of flux, their body changing over a period of hours. Which meant that they could enter anybody's home without an invitation until their body finally stabilised into its vampiric form.

He ran up to the third floor of the building, the final level, and stopped at the top of the stairs.

This was mainly a floor for junk and the haphazard filing system Filthy Henry had used over the years. Stacks of boxes with old case notes. Discarded phone books that had never been opened. A random assortment of objects that had at one stage been classed as clues in some case but where now just strange souvenirs. Nothing that could be classed as a weapon to take down a rampaging Stoker that was a mere floor below.

"Hennnnnrrryyyy," the Stoker called from below in an almost singing tone. "Why are we playing these games Hennnnnrrryyyy? Mr. Man said I could offer you a choice if you wanted."

The choice to no doubt become a vampire, which was not appealing to Filthy Henry in the least. Becoming a full fledged fairy was definitely high on his wish list, but not one that had to survive on blood. Even though he liked Stokers in general, aside from the one that was currently trying to kill him, changing into one was not something he had ever considered. He would rather be dead. Permanently dead.

Although the manner in which Filthy Henry died was one he would have like to choose himself. Preferably involving a great old age and many nubile young women found in the bed with him.

Panic started to set in. This was one of those no win situations he liked to avoid. If he somehow managed to get out of it the first thing Filthy Henry was going to do was stock this floor with enough Holy Water to drown the Vatican.

Then, at the back of the landing, behind a crooked stack of boxes, the fairy detective saw what looked like salvation in a rectangular form. He reached out to the left, knocked over a couple of boxes so that it blocked the top of the stairs slightly, then ran down to see if Lady Luck had decided to give him one last dance.

Behind the damp pile of boxes was a door, one that Filthy Henry had never used before and had completely forgotten about. But at that moment this door was his most favourite door in all the world. He pushed over the damp stack of boxes, their contents spilling all over the ground, and opened the door. It revealed another flight of stairs leading upwards to the roof top exit.

"Well somebody up there must like me," Filthy Henry said to

himself as he opened the door wide enough to fit through and ran up the stairs.

"Henry have you knocked over you comic books?" the Stoker called out from behind.

Filthy Henry did not look back, racing up the final flight of stairs and pushing open the roof top exit.

Cool night air hit him in the face like a thawing fish as the fairy detective burst out onto the roof of the building. He slammed the door shut behind him and looked around quickly for something to wedge it closed. The improvisation part of his plan had lasted a lot longer than Filthy Henry would have liked it to. Usually he had a rough idea what he was doing, planned with haphazard detail, but right now he was running blind. Running on borrowed time, he knew, as nobody had luck that lasted forever. Nobody was lucky enough to have luck that long.

The rapid search of the roof top for something to wedge the door was proving fruitless. No chairs or broomsticks just happened to be nearby, waiting to be propped beneath the door handle. It was almost like every movie Hollywood had ever produced lied about useful objects being left in random locations during a chase scene.

Before Filthy Henry could contemplate the dilemma further the rooftop door burst open. The Stoker stood in the doorway, smiling.

"Well I've never had to work so hard for a meal before. He said you'd make me work for it, but nothing about it being this hard. I have only ever eaten from the local chip shop. Sure a battered cod isn't going to run very fast. Wonder what you taste like."

The Stoker stepped out onto the rooftop.

"I'm enjoying the game though," he said, running his tongue along the bottom of his newly elongated fangs. "I might play with

181

you for a bit more before drinking. Who knew being a vampire was so...awesome!"

Filthy Henry looked around with a rising sense of panic and saw no way out.

"Ah screw it!" the fairy detective said and broke into a run, heading towards the edge of the rooftop.

The gap between Filthy Henry's building and the one next to it was no wider than a car, easily jump-able. All it would take was the correct amount of speed, a leap of faith at the exact right point and a lot of praying to whoever was listening above for a helping hand.

A foolproof plan if ever there was one and the fairy detective was just enough of a fool to attempt it.

As the edge of the rooftop came closer Filthy Henry held his breath and jumped into the air, pushing away from lip of the roof with his right foot, and hoped for the best. He drifted through the air, limbs akimbo in a useless effort at controlling his airborne movement, and did not look down. Looking down would have been taunting gravity, tempting it to get a little stronger and pull him to the ground.

Time slowed down, creeping forward like an Ice Age with arthritis. The rooftop of the other building inched closer and closer, yet still seemed to be an insane distance away. Then, either by a slight change in the wind or the sadistic personality of Fate, the fairy detective's trajectory started to dip a lot sooner than he had wanted it to. He reached out with both hands and managed to grab the edge of the other rooftop, his entire body crashing into the wall and knocking the wind out of him.

Filthy Henry hung on for dear life. With a considerable amount of effort he started to pull himself up and over the edge. There was a whoosh of air over his head followed by the sound of something cracking as a heavy object landed. A hand gripped Filthy Henry by the wrist and hoisted him upwards. He dangled above the alleyway, a giant worm at the end of a super-strong hook

"Did you really think that would work?" the Stoker said.

In one fluid movement the Stoker spun around on the spot, bringing Filthy Henry along with him. He brought forward his arm and flung the fairy detective across the rooftop like a rag doll. Filthy Henry slammed into a chimney stack on the opposite side of the building. Pain exploded along his spine.

"So," the Stoker said. "We going to finish this? The posh git said that you were some annoying guy who a lot of people wouldn't mind seeing dead."

"Posh git?"

"Yea the guy that turned me into this awesome blood sucking machine. The last thing you'll see before you die."

There was only one Stoker in Ireland that Filthy Henry would have referred to as a posh one.

"Was he wearing a hat by any chance? One of those big one's like Mr. Monopoly?"

The Stoker's eyes narrowed as he prepared to jump.

"Whose Mr. Monopoly? Posh git was wearing some big ass hat. Now stay still so I can eat in silence."

Apparently being turned into a vampire did nothing to increase a person's intelligence levels.

Everything happened in a bit of a blur. The Stoker jumped forward, arms outstretched, mouth wide open, hunger burning in his eyes. He sailed through the air with the grace of a pouncing mountain lion, the street lights below glistening on his fangs.

Generally Filthy Henry preferred to not have to kill a fairy in order to resolve a situation, but that was an idealistic person's way of looking at things. Even a tree-hugging hippie would lend a hand to the mean, cold hearted, lumber corporation if the one hundred year old spruce they had been chained to suddenly started trying to eat them. Which was how Filthy Henry was able to justify his next action without feeling any guilt.

The fairy detective raised up both his hands, pointing the palms at the Stoker, and summoned up every ounce of magic he had left in his body.

"*DÓITEÁIN!!!*" he roared, channelling the magic directly in front of him.

Two jets of white hot flame burst forth from Filthy Henry's hands, hitting the Stoker directly in the face. The vampire was knocked out of the air and fell to the rooftop, clutching his head and rolling around in pain. Filthy Henry kept his hands aimed at the Stoker and carefully stood up. Stepping forward he kept the flames burning so they seared the flesh from the vampire's bones. The rooftop started to bubble as the tar was heated by the magical fire. As the last sparks of magic left the fairy detective's body the fire died out, a final flame coming from his hands and drifting down to land on the charred remains of the Stoker.

Exhausted, Filthy Henry walked over to the remains of the Stoker and brought his right foot down hard on the blackened skull. There was no coming back from having your skull crushed, that was one common weakness all creatures shared.

"Easy," he said to nobody in particular. "Now to go talk with St. Oker about why he broke..."

Then the fairy detective collapsed.

#

Shelly turned down onto Middle Abbey Street, dodging a woman pushing a pram, and ran towards Filthy Henry's office.

She caught sight of an explosion coming from the rooftops and stopped dead in her tracks.

"Henry?" she said in little more than a whisper.

She started running again and crossed the road, narrowly avoiding a car. She stopped at the recently destroyed front door of Filthy Henry's building.

Inside was pitch black, the light from the street just about illuminating the hallway and stairs. From Filthy Henry's open office door some more light lit the first landing. But the entire building was as silent as the grave. No sounds of violence, screams of pain, pleas for mercy. Nothing at all. Either the Stoker and the fairy detective were using some sort of street mime style of fighting or only one of them was left alive. She sniffed the air and smelt nothing. Whatever had caused the fire seemingly had not burnt anything in the building.

"Henry?" Shelly whispered.
There was no reply.
Edging through the doorway, Shelly started to creep up the stairs.

She paused on the second floor. Nothing was broken. The glass pane was still in the office door. There was a distinct lack of overturned desks or burn marks on the wall. Nowhere was there any sign of a struggle at all. Not even a single drop of blood.

Shelly could feel her heart pounding in her chest, trying its best to burst free from her ribcage and escape before something scary jumped out of the shadows. If it got any louder the Stoker would probably be able to hear the thumps.

"Henry?" she hissed into the darkness.

Nobody answered. She had half expected the vampire to reply in a poor imitation of Filthy Henry's voice.

185

Clenching her teeth so their chattering did not give her away, Shelly started to head towards the second flight of stairs. Still there was no sign of a struggle, or even of a marital spat. It was beginning to look like the Stoker had very carefully killed Filthy Henry so as to not leave any sort of trace. From the looks of this floor it was the one that Filthy Henry lived on, but he had decided against hiding in his apartment it seemed.

"Oh I really don't like this," Shelly said to herself as she began to climb up to the next floor.

At the top of the stairs boxes had been pushed over, blocking the way. It was the first indication that anything had happened in the building at all. Climbing over them, taking great care to make no noise, Shelly started looking around. She saw the rooftop staircase and made her way to it.

A staircase had never before seemed so threatening to Shelly in her entire life. Moving with feet that weighed a ton she climbed up towards the rooftop and stepped outside.

Onto an empty and deserted roof.

"This is getting bloody ridiculous," she said, looking to see anything that was on fire.

Even something smouldering would have done at that moment. Anything at all to indicate that she was not loosing her mind and that a vampire had just tried to kill her and Filthy Henry. Which would have sounded a lot crazier if somebody else had heard her thoughts at that moment.

Whatever had caused the flames she saw from street level had clearly not happened here. Flicking on her fairy-sight Shelly started to walk around the rooftop, searching for anything at all that might help her find Filthy Henry.

Trails of magic appeared in the air as her vision changed to see in the fairy spectrum. It drifted on the wind like smoke, all coming from the same direction. She headed over to the edge of the building, towards where the magical smoke was coming from, and saw the charred remains of the Stoker on the opposite rooftop.

But no sign of the fairy detective.

The door to the other rooftop was open, swinging back and forth on its hinges. A feeling of hope blossomed inside her. Maybe Filthy Henry had caused the fire, destroyed his attacker, and then escaped.

"GET YOUR ARSE DOWN HERE. I NEED HELP!"

Shelly leaned over the side of the rooftop and looked down to see Filthy Henry staring back up at her. He was sitting on the ground, back against the wall, arms limply hanging from his side. For all intents and purposes he looked drunk. The magical light that usually shone from him was nowhere to be seen.

"ARE YOU OKAY?" she shouted down to him.

"OH I'M FINE. GRAND IN FACT. TAKE YOUR TIME. NO RUSH. NOT LIKE I AM IN NEED OF SOME REAL HELP OR NOTHING. LET'S JUST SHOOT THE BREEZE FOR A BIT MORE."

Shelly was relieved that Filthy Henry was at least alive. Which was no doubt some sort of miracle, depending on how you looked at it.

With some miracles you just had to look really hard.

Chapter Fifteen

It did not matter what the quality of the food was, just that it was food. It did not even have to be edible, cooked or seasoned to perfection. Nothing. It just had to be food that could be rapidly chewed upon and swallowed with the gusto of an obese child on day release from Fat Camp. Otherwise bad things were likely to happen and Filthy Henry figured he had had enough bad things happen today without voluntarily adding to the mix.

The small mountain of food in front of him meant nothing, he did not even taste it as he ate. All that mattered was the eating and digesting. To avoid owing Shelly a ton of money he had used the last dredge of magic left in him to conjure up some Euro notes. Temporary Euro notes. They would last roughly four hours before disappearing back into the ether, long enough to buy multiple meals and get out away before anybody noticed.

They had stopped at the first place serving food they had passed, Shelly helping the weakened fairy detective amble down the street. A table outside had been empty and Filthy Henry had gratefully dropped into the seat while Shelly went and placed his extreme order of food. She had returned with a packet of crisps for him to munch on while the food had been prepared, a very thoughtful gesture he had found. Once the food had finally arrived Filthy Henry started to devour everything in sight.

Shelly sat across from him, sipping on a cola and trying to not watch him eat. He could not blame her. The only thing preventing him from sucking up everything on the table in one go was the size of his mouth and his poor lung capacity.

"I thought the last time was bad," Shelly said, glancing at him as he munched on a cheeseburger held between two other cheeseburgers.

"Need more," Filthy Henry said between chews. "Absolutely no magic left. Bad. Very bad."

"Why?"

He groaned in mid-chew.

Had she no table manners? Talking while another person's mouth was full. Could she not just sit there in silence and slurp on her soda which had been bought for her with counterfeit money?

Filthy Henry swallowed the massive mouthful of cheeseburger and took a sip of his drink. As he started to dunk some chips into a bowl of ketchup the fairy detective looked at Shelly.

"I need to have magical reserves at all times in my body," Filthy Henry explained, placing his cup back down on the table beside six similar, but empty, ones. "It comes back naturally of its own accord, but food usually gets turned directly into magical energy for me quickly. Since I'm not a full fairy if I ever run out of magic completely my fairy side starts to convert my body fat into magical energy."

Shelly made a silent 'O' with her mouth.

"You mean your magical side starts to eat your human side?"

He nodded, shovelling the chips into his mouth and chewing vigorously.

"More or less. The natural restoration doesn't work fast enough to counter the effect. It would eventually kill me, hence why I gotta eat so much. On the plus side I rarely put on weight. So if you wouldn't mind..."

Once more the gorging continued while Shelly remained silent and stared down the street. She looked at a stray dog that was moving amongst the people, making its way across the street towards their table.

As he munched on the, literally, life saving dinner Filthy Henry started to think about his fight with the Stoker.

A little drop of guilt was clamouring for attention in the sea of his conscience, but it was easily ignored. One could argue that the Stoker had been only doing what any hungry newborn animal would do, that it had no choice in the matter. But nobody would seek justification from a hunter who shot a rampaging bear with a sniper rifle. It was the same principal. The Stoker had been created with the sole purpose of killing himself and Shelly, anything that happened to the creature as a result of that was self defence.

But why would a Stoker create another one without being ready for the Newborn's hunger? Generally Stokers were always prepared for that sort of thing, making a quick withdrawal from a local blood bank before turning somebody. Plus there were strict population controls in place for the fairy-folk who shunned daylight and enjoyed very bloody Bloody Mary's. Even creating a single new one required so much paper work and a sign off from a number of high powered fairies that it would take nearly a century for the Stoker to get permission to turn someone. Anyone turned without the prior paperwork met the very pointy end of a novelty sized toothpick, handled by the only half-breed in the world.

It was a dusty job, but somebody had to do it.

Of course a newborn Stoker would kill just about anything in order to get that first drop of blood. Making them the perfect killer. One without any remorse and simply doing what their instincts told them. You just had to point them in the direction you wanted.

Which made scary sense to Filthy Henry. Hell it would have been the sort of plan that he came up with himself. But why? Unless he was starting to figure out something that somebody would rather not get figured out.

He thought about his current case load but the only one of real importance he was working on was Lé Precon's stolen Mothercrock. It made no sense for the King of the Leprechauns to want him dead, unless he was trying to cover something up. But why would Lé Precon steal his own crock, there was no purpose or benefit to it.

Meaning that whoever had sent the Stoker must, in some way, be involved in the theft of The Mothercrock.

In the fairy detective's mind a clue started to jump up and down, waving a mentally imagined hand in order to get attention.

The Stoker had mentioned a posh vampire wearing a hat, which greatly limited the amount of possible Stokers that had performed the illegal turning. In fact it reduced the list down to a single digit that was greater than zero but less than two. Even calling it a list was insulting to lists. It was more of a name badge at a convention for prime suspects. A badge which read: Abraham St. Oker.

Filthy Henry stopped chewing, swallowed the mouthful of food, and stared at the dog as Shelly scratched the animal on the head.

The wisp had also said it had been turned by a posh speaking Stoker. Two random newborns created by St. Oker, without the proper paperwork being filed. But why did the vampire-author want to have Filthy Henry removed from the picture? They had gotten on so well for years without ever crossing swords. Unless, somehow, the fairy detective had stumbled across something that St. Oker did not want people to know.

But what?

He looked at Shelly. She had come to the office right before the crazed Stoker had attacked. Was it possible that the Stoker had been sent to kill them both or had she merely been in the wrong place at the right time?

Shelly picked up a scrap of meat from one of Filthy Henry's discarded plates and dropped it to the ground in front of the dog. The animal gobbled it down then looked back up at her, licking its snout.

"What was it you wanted to tell me earlier?" Filthy Henry asked her, pushing away some of the empty food packages.

"Hmm?" Shelly said, turning back to look at him.

"Earlier. Tonight. You said you wanted to tell me something but only after I told you about myself. What was it?"

"Oh that," Shelly said, shrugging her shoulders. "That was something stupid is all. Nothing important. A mad idea that I had."

Filthy Henry leaned across the table and stared at her directly in the eye.

"We just got attacked by somebody that can make Stokers and I'm guessing that your mad idea might have something to do with that."

"Well the thing is Bram Stoker seems to be climbing up the best sellers list rather quickly."

"So?"

"So? How is he doing it if he hasn't got millions stashed away somewhere? You said that he doesn't get royalties any more because he should have died naturally years ago, yet in the last two days 'Dracula' has jumped up five places. It will be the number one best seller by the end of the week if it keeps going. Hell by the end of tonight. There you go, boy."

She had taken another morsel of uneaten food and dropped into the dog's mouth.

A rather large penny dropped into the mental piggy bank of Filthy Henry's mind. It clanged around in the empty hypothetical container, growing in size with each bang. Nothing Shelly had said was concrete proof one way or the other, but it was a theory and sometimes a theory was all you needed. Hell Fermat was only famous for coming up with a theorem, not proving that it was valid. Checking his internal magic levels, Filthy Henry picked up four more cheeseburgers and started eating a fifth. He stood up from the table. Shelly picked up a plate that still had a full burger on it and placed it on the ground beside her chair.

"Don't do that," Filthy Henry said between chews. "I was going to eat that."

Quickly he cast a rainbow dome over the plate. It was nowhere near as powerful as a proper leprechaun one and would only last for a few minutes, but it would be enough to stop anything getting at his burger.

"That's so pretty," Shelly said.

She reached down to the moving hemisphere of colour and put her hand against it. It did no get past the shimmering light.

"Won't others see it though?"

"Nope," Filthy Henry said. "Their mind will convince them that it's just lights reflecting off the stores in a puddle or somethi..."

He trailed off as the most amazing thing ever to be witnessed by somebody who considered magic mundane happened. With its head completely covered in coloured light the dog had gone over to the plate and started to eat the burger. It had gotten through a magical shield that stopped anything getting through, without any magically powers at all.

"What's up?" Shelly asked him, then she noticed the dog as well. "Oh, but I thought you said..."

"I did say," the fairy detective said. "Even a weak version of that spell cast by me should stop anything passing through it for a few minutes."

The dog, having eaten the entire burger in three bites, lay down beside the plate and seemingly went to sleep.

"So how did the dog get through if I couldn't?" Shelly said, looking at it with her fairy vision turned on.

"We'll worry about it later," he said, gathering up the last of his food and stepping away from the table.

He turned right and started to walk down O'Connell Street towards the River Liffey. Behind him came the sound of Shelly's chair scrapping on the pavement as she pushed it back and the pad of her feet on the pavement as she followed him.

"You've come up with a nice little theory there," Filthy Henry said, halfway through another cheese-burger. "One that I wouldn't mind testing out. We have until tomorrow morning to get this thing sorted with Lé Precon anyway so what's one long shot really going to cost us?" He finished the burger in one massive mouthful. "But first I need to find me a swan."

#

Running along the River Liffey in Dublin's fair city, hanging above the water, there is a wooden walkway. Meant as a tourist attraction, because people are attracted to the prospect of being able to walk over water without the stigma of being a Messiah, the Liffey Walkway had more or less become just another method for people to get about the city. Dotted along its wooden surface were wooden benches and little coffee kiosks, closed at this time of night. Filthy Henry had entered the walkway via the entrance at the end of O'Connell Bridge and started strolling along, the buns from his last burger held in his left hand. Shelly followed a step behind him.

"Did you say you needed to find a swan?" Shelly asked.

"Yep," Filthy Henry replied, examining the benches that they passed. "Ah, there we are. Just wait here a second will you."

Shelly went to say something, but decided against it. Instead she walked up to the barrier that prevented people from falling off the walkway into the river below and leaned against it.

The fairy detective walked ten feet away from her and sat down beside a stranger on one of the river-side benches. They conversed for a few minutes, then Filthy Henry handed the man the burger buns and stood up. He walked back to Shelly and leaned over the railings. "What was that about?" she asked Filthy Henry as he rejoined her.

"Needed to find a swan," he said.

Shelly looked back at the stranger as he rose from the bench with her fairy-vision. The tell-tale light of a fairy shone from him, similar to the light that Garda Downy had shown. Little feathers floating about his aura.

"He's a Leerling," she said.

"Exactly, like I said. Needed to find a swan. You'll always find a Leerling down here. Needed him to deliver a message to Lé Precon for me."

"And you paid him with...bread?"

"Nah I bribed him with bread. Leerlings are suckers for bread," he said, smiling. "They sit out here all night waiting for somebody to throw bread down to the real birds."

"Why didn't you just ring him?"

Filthy Henry snorted.

"You mean on a mobile? Fairies don't use mobile phones. We've got Leerlings for that, much better. Put the post service to shame so they do."

Shelly sighed, clasped her hands together and stared at the water flowing beneath her feet.

"I'm never going to understand this world," she said. "It's just too weird. How you manage to keep sane is impressive."

Reaching over and placing his hand on top of hers, Filthy Henry smiled.

"I'm not sane," he said, nudging her playful with his shoulder. "I just pretend to be. Besides, you'll get used to this world. Give it a chance and it might show you just how wonderful it really can be."

Shelly looked over at Filthy Henry and saw the city lights sparkling in his eyes. There was something else in them as well. If she had been drinking she would have called it a spark of attraction. Right there, right then, the fairy detective looked like the sort of man that she would gladly...

She closed her eyes, puckered her lips slightly, and leaned in to kiss him.

An eternity passed, the beat of her heart dragging out into infinity. She was in that moment of time when uncertainty reigned on high. When you had thoughts racing through your mind about whether or not this attempted kiss had been a great or stupid move. As her lips met empty air her thoughts aligned themselves behind the 'stupid' side of things. When she opened her eyes Filthy Henry was nowhere to be seen.

"Rat bastard," she said, banging her hand angrily on the railing.

There was no sign of the fairy detective at all.

Chapter Sixteen

Shelly was frozen in place, surrounded by a strange grey fog. In fact it was not just her, the entire city was covered in the grey fog, silent and unmoving. A freeze frame of the world. Filthy Henry looked over the railings at the still waters below. Nothing moved. He stepped back from the barrier and tried to focus on the fog. It was clearly magical in nature, fog did not normally freeze things in time. But what was causing it?

Then the fairy detective detected it, a slight smell of shamrocks in the air.

"Alright Lé Precon, let's stop dicking around," Filthy Henry said.

The King of the Leprechauns popped into sight, sitting on one of the wooden benches with his legs dangling over the edge. Some multi-coloured shamrocks fell from him like magical dandruff. He looked at Filthy Henry and frowned.

"I got your Leerling," Lé Precon said, clicking his jaw. "Lucky for you I just happened to be nearby, otherwise I would have teleported your half-bred ass to me. Not exactly the news I was looking for, by the way."

"What do you want from me?" Filthy Henry asked, walking over to sit down on the bench beside the leprechaun. "I've got a solid lead on The Mothercrock and I was just about to go and see how good a lead that was."

"But you haven't got my crock back," he said. "And time is running out for you half-breed. I've decided that if you don't figure out who, how and where by the deadline...well let's just say that Dublin is going to get a surprise."

Filthy Henry hated veiled threats almost as much as he hated subtle insults. He always figured if you had something to say just spit it out. Nobody enjoyed word games except couples in heated arguments over who was meant to buy a present for the in-laws.

"What would that be exactly?" he asked.

"I'm going to unleash the entire fairy world on the humans. Remove the barrier. Pretty much wipe the country clean to avoid having to worry about some humans stealing from The People again." Lé Precon smiled and gave the fairy detective a cheeky little wink.

"You can't do that! The Rules!"

"Screw The Rules!" Lé Precon said, jumping up so he was standing on the bench and looking Filthy Henry directly in the eyes. "Those maggots have broken The Rules somehow and nobody can figure it out. Ergo they are to be dealt with accordingly. Now tell me what you know or so help me I don't care who your father is I will end you!"

Filthy Henry narrowed his eyes and glared at the leprechaun. The short little runt had somehow figured out who Filthy Henry's father was decades ago and had lorded the information over him ever since. The fairy detective had long since made his peace with not knowing. Things were as they were and there was no changing them. He was a half-breed plain and simple. But every time Lé Precon played the 'Daddy card' it struck a nerve with the fairy detective. He gave some serious contemplation to summoning up some magical fire and burning the beard right off the green garbed git.

But down that road, suicide lay. Lé Precon would be able to counter the spell and retaliate even worse.

"Fine," Filthy Henry said. "Just calm the hell down. No need to go ruining everything for everyone. The humans got inside your little fort because they had fairy in them. They were able to see the world behind the mundane one."

"Impossible," Lé Precon said, dismissing the statement with a wave of his hand. "You're the only freak that has ever survived. There is nothing alive that has a trace of fairy in them."

"No, you're one hundred percent right," Filthy Henry agreed, sarcastically. "Shelly was able to see you the other day outside my office, without any magical help at all. You snobby git, some humans still believe in magic beyond childhood. Hell I was able to give her proper fairy sight and I am only a half-breed. Looks like somebody else figured out how to give humans without a hint of second sight the ability to see things as well. They gave them a potion."

"A potion?"

Filthy Henry could not resist smiling a little. Since fairies rarely had a need to augment their abilities and spells they never dabbled with potions. But Filthy Henry knew that it was possible to create concoctions that could enhance powers or bestow limited gifts. He had learned it from a few druids that managed to get their hands on some fairy ingredients. Ones humans should not know about.

"A potion, mixed with the blood of a Cat Síth. They drank it and it allowed them to see the fairy-world for a while. It would eventually have worn off completely, not like a human that has gone insane and can't control when and what they see of the fairy world."

"Huh," Lé Precon said, looking thoughtfully at the ground. "So my Rainbow Guard might not have been full of crap after all."

"He did say there was a Cat Síth smell coming off them," Filthy Henry said. "It only stands to reason. They drank blood but were not fairies. Somebody out there has been doing their homework. They have figured out a trick that many of us thought impossible."

"Still doesn't explain how they got past the Rainbow," Lé Precon said. "Nothing can get past the Rainbow. Before I pay you in full you better have an answer for that. I don't care if you give me The Mothercrock with the thief sitting inside it. I want to know what the weakness is in an alarm spell that has worked for centuries."

Filthy Henry shrugged.

"No problem," he said. "Just as long as you don't forget about granting my wish. In fact you'll have to do that before I tell you the security hole. Not that I don't trust you, of course."

Lé Precon frowned, clearly unhappy with the counter-negotiations taking place.

"Alright, fine. You can tell me as the wish takes place. That way if I think you are pulling one of your legendary fast ones I will still have enough time to cancel the wish," Lé Precon said. He looked over at the frozen Shelly. "We are going to have to talk about this human female that you've decided to let see our world all the time as well. Can't be having two of you monkeys prying into things that are none of your concern. Now get back to work, you're wasting your time."

The King of the Leprechauns clicked his fingers and Filthy Henry was blinded by a bright white light.

#

Shelly sat down on the nearest bench and sighed. She had been rejected by a few men in her time, but none had ever used magic to disappear just to avoid kissing her. At least not that she knew of. It took a real jerk to use a magical advantage to not kiss a girl. Talk about bruising a person's ego. It was like having an anti-fairy tale romance.

"Jerk!" Shelly shouted at the night.

Some people passing by gave her a wide berth and a strange look.

There was a loud thump as something landed on the walkway in front of her. Shelly jumped up onto the bench.

"Gods dammit," the something said. "My bloody back."

Shelly stopped exercising her neck muscles trying to look for an escape route and looked at the something in front of her.

"Henry?"

"Present," the fairy detective said, groaning.

He rolled over to the railings at the river side and hauled himself up to his feet.

"Little bastard never just shows up for a chat. It's all magic and pain with him. I'm going to have to start dealing with another leprechaun for loans from now on."

Shelly stared at him, mouth open in surprise.

"What the hell happened to you?" she said, climbing down from the bench and walking over to the fairy detective. She punched him in the shoulder, instantly regretting the random act of violence as her hand started hurting.

"Ouch!" Filthy Henry said, clutching his shoulder. "What was that for?"

"You just disappeared," Shelly said, clicking her fingers in front of his nose. "Right when we were about to...you know...and we've got Stokers running around trying to kill us."

"You were fine," the fairy detective said. "The Stokers know The Rules, they would have obeyed them. Worse case scenario a new Stoker would have been created and sent to get you. But sure who'd be stupid enough to try that twice?"

Shelly glared at Filthy Henry.

"Where! Did! You! Go!?"

Rubbing at his shoulder, Filthy Henry glanced up at Shelly and then found something very interesting to look at by his feet. This was the same effect her glare had on most people of a male persuasion. It was one of the tricks she had inherited from her mother. Something that was fondly referred to in the family as 'The Guilty Glare'.

"I didn't go anywhere," Filthy Henry said. "Lé Precon pulled me a second out of sync with the real world to have a little chat. He's getting impatient and wants results soon. Otherwise he is planning on showing the world that fairy folk are real, right before he kills every human he sees. Apparently the little bastard decided to put me back a few minutes ahead, hence why it seemed like I just vanished."

Shelly let the glare ease as the reality of what Filthy Henry had just said sunk in.

"He can't do that. Can he?"

Filthy Henry shrugged, wincing straight afterwards and rubbing his punched shoulder harder.

"My God you have a solid punch. Look we need to get this Mothercrock thing sorted before the end of the night or all hell is going to break loose. An impatient Lé Precon is a stupid leprechaun. I don't have enough magical powers to enforce The Rules against a damn army of Stokers. But I don't want to go taking on Stokers without some form of backup either."

"So what do we do? Go get some help from your fairy friends?"

The fairy detective laughed, then shook his head.

"Nope," he said. "We go shopping. I need to get some big guns."

Druids had been really popular in ancient Ireland during the Celtic times. They had been regarded as wise men that knew a few things about things common people had no clue about. Another topic they knew stuff about, but a lesser documented fact, was magic. Captured magic to be precise, since a human body cannot naturally channel the energies without running the risk of being destroyed. Trying to impress a girl by conjuring fireballs is all well and good, but if the end result is a mild case of death instead of some serious cootie infection then what is the point?

But if a fairy is captured the one thing they will try to do is barter for their freedom. So Druids made a hobby of capturing fairies, using whatever means they could come up with to create the perfect trap. Afterwards the fairy would have to divulge secrets and tricks to the Druid, allowing the human to perform very limited amounts of magic, in a safely controlled fashion, that had been borrowed from the fairy. This gave rise to belief that Druids had magical abilities.

All they really had were some enchanted stones that tapped into the powers of the fairy they had locked in their secret caves.

Filthy Henry had found all this fascinating growing up and actively sought out modern day Druids. These hippie like descendants of the once great and might Druid now used what their ancestors had passed along to sell enchanted objects. A black market for the magical consumer as it were. Filthy Henry had found that using these objects sometimes helped to bolster his magical energy store or allowed him to carry around a powerful spell that cost him nothing to cast.

Plus Druids had a lovely habit of collecting religious objects as well. Some holy water and crucifixes were always handy to have when you went up against Stokers. Even if the Stoker was Jewish they tended to stay away from a cross held in front of them. It was some sort of strange physiological condition every Stoker was afflicted with.

"Why are we standing outside a magic shop on Parliament Street?" Shelly asked. "These places just sell healing stones and tarot cards and all that rubbish."

"I told you," Filthy Henry said. "We needed to go shopping. You know of another place in Dublin that sells magically enhanced objects?"

Shelly looked at the shop front.

True it was not much to look at from outside, but then it did not get much better on the inside either. The outside had been painted in a puke green colour with the name of the shop sprayed in gold over the door. Crystals and charms hung in the window, along side posters advertising tarot card readings and communes with dearly departed family members. There was also an offer currently on, half price junior magician kits now with two plastic wands.

"This is where you go to get the big guns?"

"Just shut up already," Filthy Henry said. "I don't go judging where you buy your magical items do I?"

He headed towards the shop door, pushed it open and stepped inside as a little bell jingled over his head.

"I don't buy magical items," Shelly said, following him inside and closing the door behind her.

"Well then," the fairy detective said. "Whist your noise."

"Coming, coming," a voice called from further back in the store.

Inside the store was gloomy, barely lit by overhead lights. Some displays of books had lights on them, but more to illuminate what was for sale instead of the shop itself. A veritable maze of stands littered the shop floor, each one holding random objects ranging from coloured stones to sticks of wood.

"Those are meant to be wands?" Shelly whispered, pointing at the wooden sticks.

Filthy Henry went to answer, but the store owner appeared from behind a bookcase smiling at the pair of them.

He was dressed in a long flowing grey robe and was as bald as a baby's behind. Hanging around his neck was a large medallion with what looked like Celtic designs inscribed onto it. It was obvious by the extra weight he was carrying that the man was not afraid to ask for second helpings. Or fifth ones for that matter.

#

"Dru," Filthy Henry said in a cheery tone, holding out his arms wide and walking towards the store owner to hug him.

"Get out!" Dru said, his eyes growing wide at the sight of the fairy detective.

"Dru the Druid?" Shelly asked, sniggering.

"Zip it," Filthy Henry hissed back at her. "Dru come on, there's no need to be like that."

Dru the Druid walked over to a counter with a cash register on it and sat down on a stool, crossing his arms and frowning.

"You said you were only going to borrow, borrow, that vial of dragon flame. Next thing I know I have no eyebrows, my car is on fire and there is an angry Puca haunting my flat. Plus, let's not forget, the vial of dragon flame was destroyed in the process."

"Well now your eyebrows match your head," Filthy Henry said with a smile.

That was the problem with borrowing things from people who were good at holding a grudge. If you ever came back to ask for another favour it usually reminded them of what happened last time. Resulting in a rapid response, generally of the negative variety.

"Get out," Dru said once more, emphasising the request by gesturing towards the door.

Filthy Henry turned around and held out his hand in front of Shelly.

"Give me whatever money you have on you."

"Why?"

"Because I need money."

"Just use your spell."

"He's a Druid, not an idiot. I hand him fairy made money and he will see right through it."

"Well I haven't got any money on me," Shelly said. "So you'll have to come up with something else."

A groan was required, so Filthy Henry groaned and rolled his eyes.

"Dru," he said, turning back around. "I need supplies and your the only shop in town. Come on, mate."

"I'm not your mate," Dru the Druid said.

Shelly budged past the fairy detective and marched straight across the shop floor towards the Druid behind the counter. Before the man had a minute to react she reached over, grabbed him by the collar of his robe and hauled him over the counter so that their noses touched.

"Listen here you strange little man. I've had about as much as I can take of this freaky world I've been dragged into. So give him whatever the hell he wants and I will make sure that he is gone from here within five seconds. Otherwise I am going to beat you more bald than you could possibly imagine."

"Fine fine, fine," Dru said, squirming in Shelly's grasp and trying to push her away. "Fine, fine, fine. Whatever he wants. But only because I want you out of the store along with him. You're both barred from now on."

The fairy detective put his hands into his trouser pockets and strolled nonchalantly up to the counter. Shelly released the Druid from her grip, forcing him back on his stool with a shove.

"What do you need?" Dru asked Filthy Henry, keeping an eye on Shelly for any sudden movements.

"I need four bottles of holy water. Two crucifixes blessed by the holy hat wearer himself. Some enchanted garlic and a line of store credit."

Dru narrowed his eyes and glared at Filthy Henry.

"Okay," the fairy detective said with a smile. "We can do without the garlic."

Chapter Seventeen

Filthy Henry and Shelly had found a poorly lit, practically dark, porch on Dawson Street late that night which concealed them perfectly from any nosy neighbours. The porch allowed them to observe the buildings across the street at their leisure. One building was of particular interest to them.

It was a typical building for the area, one that had been built decades ago and kept in minor repair over the years. None of the rooms had lights on in them, but they all seemed to have heavy curtains drawn down over the windows. The building seemed to be empty.

"It's so bloody complicated," Filthy Henry said running the side of his index finger along the stubble on his chin. "I don't like it."

Shelly leaned out a little, looked up and down the street, then slipped back into the shadows.

"What's not to like? Building that probably has a dozen Stokers inside it, each of whom has no doubt been told to drain our blood, and we are contemplating breaking into the place to see if a leprechaun's stolen crock of gold is inside. How is that complicated exactly?"

Filthy Henry laughed. For somebody who had only known about the existence of fairies for little more than a week Shelly was using the term Stokers like a seasoned pro. Even most of the Druids still tended to call them vampires. Sometimes Celtic Vampires, but only at a stretch and even then they were trying to be politically correct and arty at the same time.

"Well for starters they haven't been instructed to drain both of us," he said.

"Really?"

"No. More than likely just you. My blood is tainted with the fairy magic in me. Any Stoker that tried to drink it would end up exploding. That's why the Newborn was sent after us. He wouldn't have known better."

Shelly punched him in the shoulder.
"Well that's bloody reassuring," she said.
"Ouch! Would you stop doing that please!" Filthy Henry said, rubbing his shoulder. "Anyway, we are still only running with the theory that Abe stole the Mothercrock because 'Dracula' has been jumping up the best seller list so fast. The Mothercrock would provide him with enough money to buy the world, so purchasing a few million books wouldn't be all that hard. But right now I am hoping beyond hope that the Stokers haven't changed their eating habits recently and that the building is entirely empty."

"Eating habits?" Shelly asked. "As in that they haven't all turned vegan or something?"

"No, that would be stupid. It's fairly late on a Friday night. Stokers usually have to go to the blood banks and make withdrawals. Tonight is the night of the week that Stokers all go grocery shopping, so to speak."

Reaching into his bag of tricks that Dru the Druid had kindly provided under mild duress, the fairy detective handed over some vials of holy water to Shelly along with a crucifix.

"You see a Stoker, avoid it," Filthy Henry said as Shelly put the objects into her left coat pocket. "If he comes at you, hit him with the cross. If and only if that doesn't stop him, use the holy water. Got it? We can't go breaking The Rules and staking them. Humans have to follow The Rules just as much as fairy-kind do. Even if you didn't know they were there to follow in the first place."

"OK," Shelly said, closing her eyes. When she opened them again they had the blue glow of fairy vision. "Nice and quiet I take it."

"No, no. By all means make as much noise as you possibly can when inside. Just in case the Stokers are in the building and don't know we are sneaking around. In fact if you could yell out your name ever time you take two steps that would be great."

He dodged another punch aimed directly at his shoulder by jumping out of the porch and running across the street. An alley between the buildings allowed the fairy detective to slip around the back, away from the brightly lit main street. Breaking into a place was always easier if there was less chance of a random person driving by and reporting the crime.

A small wall ran around a little garden area at the back of the Stoker building. Some blocks were missing, giving Filthy Henry convenient footholds to climb up and over the wall. Dropping down on the other side he turned on his fairy-vision and scanned the garden. While it was true that Stokers as a race had no magical abilities, beyond living forever and super strength of course, that did not mean they were idiots. You could hire any number of different fairy races to come in and install a magical alarm system for you, one that worked just as well on humans as it would on fairies. But there appeared to be nothing of the sort here. Either The Mothercrock was not here or the Stokers were being very stupid.

"Little help you ignorant bastard," Shelly hissed from above.

Filthy Henry stood up straight and turned around to help Shelly down from the top of the wall. Once she was steady on her own two feet he walked up to the back door of the building and pressed his ear against it. All seemed silent on the other side.

Placing his right hand over the door handle Filthy Henry said

"Oscail!"

A green glow surrounded his hand for a moment, followed by a clicking sound as the lock opened.

"No fancy lock-picks with you," Shelly said.

"You didn't think that was fancy?" Filthy Henry asked as he gently pushed the door open and peered inside.

Aided by his fairy vision Filthy Henry looked in into the dark room beyond. The back door opened up to reveal a kitchen on the other-side, which Filthy Henry found a little ironic since Stokers never cooked anything. They did love playing human though. He stepped inside, looked around to make sure there was nothing waiting to surprise him, then motioned for Shelly to follow.

"How come I can see so well?" Shelly asked in the lowest whisper the fairy detective had ever just about heard.

"Don't worry about it, just make sure that if you see something giving off waves of colour to avoid it. Magical traps can be cast on anything. You see something in a room glowing, don't go into that room. Understood?"

She nodded.

"Great," Filthy Henry whispered. "I think we should split up. Just remember you have the only weapons that really work against a Stoker. If you really need help do what all good horror movie actresses do."

"Which is?" Shelly asked.

"Scream your lungs out."

"You're an asshole," she said.

"True," Filthy Henry replied. "But at least I am consistent."

They left the kitchen and entered a small hallway. Directly ahead was the front door, back to the main street. Stairs on the right led to the upper levels of the building. There were two doors on the left hand side of the hallway, both closed.

"You check upstairs," Filthy Henry whispered into Shelly's ear. "I'll take these two rooms and then follow you up."

She nodded once, then made her way to the foot of the stairs. As she began to climb them cautiously the fairy detective walked up to the furthest door and entered the room.

#

Stealth is a tricky thing to master and an impossible thing to do unless you are part-ninja part-cat. Shelly knew she was neither of these things and even reckoned at that very moment that she had some elephant in her genetic make-up. It was the only way to explain how every, single, softly-softly movement she made somehow created a thunderous noise.

The fear she felt at that very moment was worse than what she had experienced back at Filthy Henry's office after the newborn Stoker had attacked. At least then she had known there was possible danger within the building. Here she could be walking into a nest of Stokers and not realise it. Maybe even a herd of Stokers, she was not entirely sure what the collective name for vampires was.

Up until a week ago Shelly had assumed they were not real creatures at all. Now she was wondering how you counted them. How life changes...

Each step on the stairs creaked a little as she climbed up them. After a minute that lasted an eternity Shelly reached the top of the stairs and found herself on a long landing. There were seven doors, each of them closed, and nothing else. No paintings on the walls or furniture to be seen. Not even a glowing spot on the floor that would have suggested a spell had been placed. From the single window at the far end of the landing some light from the street shone through, casting eerie shadows.

Shelly reached into her pockets and pulled out one of the holy water vials and the crucifix. Bringing the wooden cross up in front of her, she started to creep towards the nearest door. Her heart was racing, yet oddly beating in time with every step she took. It was the most horrific soundtrack she had ever heard. Reaching out with a trembling hand, Shelly slowly turned the doorknob and opened the door. The hinges creaked in a clichéd manner.

Typical, Shelly thought as she tightened her grip on the crucifix.

Peering around the door frame into the darkened room, Shelly used the fairy vision to see what could be seen. It was a relief to see that the room was deserted and entirely spell free as well, yet smelled strangely like a library. She stepped inside and started looking about.

The room was an average sized bedroom, although one without the bed. There were piles of books stacked everywhere. Some of the books had matching copies beside each other. The odd pile had so many mismatched tomes in it that it appeared to be a literary version of Jenga. But every one of them bore the same title and author's name on the spine of the book.

Bram Stoker's Dracula.

There were reprints and new prints, old prints and crazy prints. Some of the publishing houses stamps could be traced through the ages as the style and method used to produce the book changed. Shelly picked a book up at random and flicked it open, just to be sure.

The entire room was just full of copies of the book. Which made sense in a way, since it was St. Oker's decades old hobby. If you bought a copy of a book you wanted to make sure it remained out of circulation. Nobody reached the number one slot on a best sellers list based on second-hand sales.

Checking each of the other rooms with equal measures of care and curiosity revealed more of the same. No furniture, no decorations, but mounds and mounds of copies of 'Dracula'. Some rooms seemed to have been filled with great care from floor to ceiling, a solid wall of books. Others just had the volumes thrown in haphazardly. All of them devoid of any Stokers on guard duty or crocks of gold waiting to be lifted.

Finally Shelly came to the last unopened door on the floor. She opened it and looked around, expecting to see more of the same. Instead it appeared that this room had been left untouched by the growing collection of musty old books. It was laid out like a writer's office. A large wooden desk was pressed up against the window, the chair position so that whoever sat at the desk could stare out at the world beyond the glass. Bookcases lined the walls, mostly filled with copies of 'Dracula' but also books on writing styles, genealogy and fairy mythology. Clearly St. Oker had taken an interest into learning about his new race after becoming a member of the fairy-folk. Two large filing cabinets stood just inside the door. There was even a very comfy looking sofa laid out against the far wall with a blanket thrown on it in a dishevelled manner. Presumably used for impromptu naps during spurts of creative brilliance.

Shelly pulled open the filing cabinet drawers one at a time, searching inside for anything of interest. They mainly seemed to contain old newspaper clippings displaying the best selling books and reviews of St. Oker's work throughout the years. There were even some print outs of online reviews of the book, as well as some movie reviews about the various adaptations that had been made based around the world famous Count Dracula. Nothing of interest regarding the stolen leprechaun crock of gold.

Next Shelly started searching the book cases, but after a few minutes of pulling out books at random to see if there was a hidden section she gave up. There was nothing of interest contained on any of the shelves.

She pulled back the chair from the desk and sat down on it. From here there was nothing to see through the window. It looked out over the backyard and allowed a person to see into the back room of the building opposite. Hardly a place to get amazing inspiration for writing stories. Although it was probably well shielded from direct sunlight, meaning the vampire author could presumably sit there during the day time and not catch fire as a result.

Three drawers were set into the body of the desk, little metal rings hanging from them for handles. Shelly tugged experimentally at one. It slid open without any effort at all. Not that this meant anything, since the top drawer was entirely empty of anything clue like. Pushing it quietly back in, she pulled out the second drawer. "Bingo," she said.

Reaching into the drawer Shelly took out an old, leather bound, book and a paper folder. Putting these down on the table in front of her, she looked over her shoulder to make sure she was still alone in the room. She opened up the old fashioned book, a strong musty smell hitting her nostrils as the covers opened with a creak of leather.

Written on the pages in a flowery, cursive, style of writing with intricately detailed sketches were words that Shelly could not recognise. A language that seemed to rely heavily on doodles to help explain what the words seemingly had trouble doing. Then two words jumped out at Shelly.

"It's Irish," Shelly said, surprised.

Every person born in Ireland had to endure years of learning Irish during their time in school, helping to instil a bit of national pride in a person that they had a native tongue to speak. This despite the fact that English was the more prevalent language spoken in the country. Once people left school at eighteen the practise of speaking poorly formed Irish was dropped by the wayside, becoming little more than a joking habit between friends. But twelve years of learning the same nearly dead language every day managed to ingrain something in the brain, burning it into the very cells of a person.

Right now those cells were getting very excited at the prospect of once more being used. Shelly flicked through some more of the pages in the book, recognising one in every twenty words. It was definitely Irish, possibly a very ancient and old style of the language. Not that she would have been able to translate a modern version of it, but it would have been slightly easier to try and guess what was written in the book.

On one page there was just a large picture of a rainbow on it, with a small paragraph of the ancient Irish scribbled under the arch.

She closed the book and moved it to the side of the table. Filthy Henry might have better luck figuring out what was written in it. Maybe it was some sort of fairy version of Irish that only the fairy-folk could read easily. Opening the folder Shelly found two medical reports with attached Garda reports. One report was about somebody called Frankie Doran, the other dealt with a man called Jim O'Toole. According to the Garda reports they were 'known associates' and 'people of interest' concerning a number of unsolved petty crimes around Dublin. Flicking through everything she found nothing of worth at all, nothing to make it obvious why a vampire would keep the reports in his drawer. The only thing worthy of any note at all, other than the amount of crimes the pair had committed, was a medical entry on the last page of Frankie's report. He had the same ability to see colours as a dog did. It was some extremely rare case which meant he saw the world in black and white. Other than that there was nothing amazingly interesting about either of them. Even their list of crimes was decidedly mundane.

"Stokers are crazy," Shelly said as she started to read the reports again, just to be sure nothing of value was contained in the sheets.

She stopped half way through the second reading and looked up, staring out the window. Henry had created what he himself called a very basic Rainbow, one that Shelly was unable to penetrate. Yet the dog had been able to push its head through without any problems to get the food from the plate.

The dog, who saw the world in shades of black and white just like this Frankie Doran person.

Behind her a floorboard creaked, almost inaudible but in a silent house the smallest of noises is like a thunderclap. Shelly froze. Her stomach clenched into a very tight ball, her heart started to play her ribcage like a human xylophone. Short, shallow, breathing replaced her more natural oxygen in-taking habits.

A hand was placed gently on her shoulder.

"Now my dear," said a voice as smooth as a gravestone. "Why don't you tell me where I can find Filthy Henry and just what exactly you are doing alive in my house?"

Chapter Eighteen

The front room had turned out to be a total loss. It was nothing but a glorified and disorganised library that stocked only one book. The only thing that was mildly interesting in the entire room was a glass case in the centre of the floor.

Walking over to it, keeping his eyes peeled for anything magical in the room, Filthy Henry looked through the glass at a copy of 'Dracula' that was out on display. It appeared to be old, very old. No doubt it was St. Oker's first copy of his book. Something that any writer would keep safe and cherish throughout the years. Even if they did have a house that was home to a million more copies of the same book. You would always cherish the very first copy you ever owned of your own novel. More so because it had been published in serial format before a single bound volume.

"Why not just sell this to get enough money for your little project?" Filthy Henry asked the empty room, intending the question for St. Oker. "It would have meant nobody else got hurt or involved."

Sighing, the fairy detective left the front room and walked down the hallway to the only other closed door. Opening it and looking in he saw a set of stone stairs that led down to a basement.

Filthy Henry had seen enough horror movies in his time to know that walking down into a dark basement in an empty house was the quickest way to catching a terminal case of deadness. He pulled out the crucifix and held onto a vial of holy water. Contemplating conjuring a spell, just to have one at the ready, he thought better of it. The magic required to keep a spell prepared would have cost him greatly. Magic that could come in handy later on if the situation became a little bit hairy.

Tightening his grip on the wooden cross, Filthy Henry slowly walked down the stone steps. He kept his eyes open, denying them the occasional blink. Ears listened for any sound at all, just in case. Nostrils took in as much air as possible on the off chance that a stray fart gave away a would be attacker's position. Filthy Henry was a well tuned, finely wound, ready to burst, hunter stalking his prey. Just prey that was more powerful and better equipped to kill a person, but that was a minor detail that the fairy detective was very much trying to push from his mind.

At the end of the stairs the Filthy Henry found himself in a very well kept and clean basement. It seemed to be organised for holding meetings, with chairs stacked up against the walls. Thick, black, curtains hung beside each of the windows, each glass pane showing a little bit of the street above. The curtains made sense if this was where the Stokers had meetings, since the sun would have shone straight in from above and made every Stoker a little cremated. Two curtains were drawn closed, thick black material hiding the window from sight completely. At the far end of the room a bright golden light caught Filthy Henry's attention. Toning down his fairy-vision made it easier to the source.

Standing on a table was a large metal cauldron.

Lé Precon's Mothercrock in all its financially benefiting glory.

Filthy Henry stared at it for a moment and considered just picking it up and running with it. Riches for as long as his magical enhanced life lasted would be his. The entire fairy-world would fall into financial ruin. Hell even the human world would suffer. More banks were propped up by indirect loans from leprechauns than humans knew about. If all those debts suddenly had to be called in, with magical knee breaking to make sure payments were made, the world would have to resort back to a barter system. All while he enjoyed living in the lap of luxury.

It was a lovely idea, a fantasy. But nothing more than that. Filthy Henry knew that he would forever be on the run from fairy-kind. There would be magical creatures hunting him constantly.

"Beggars can dream," he said to himself.

Besides, as nice as being rich until you died sounded the payment from Lé Precon was worth more. Money could not buy you happiness, but wishes that were granted by a leprechaun could alter reality and make you much more happy.

Filthy Henry did find it a little surprising that The Mothercrock was just sitting out in the open. On a table. In a poorly secured room. Without so much as a spell put in place to make loud noises if somebody went near it. The whole set up smacked of over confidence, an over confidence that Filthy Henry had never attributed to the vampire-author.

But the fairy detective's mother had always told him to never look a gift horse in the mouth because it would just as soon snap your hand off. If St. Oker was willing to leave the most prized artefact in the world sitting on a table in some basement, so be it. It just made the job of retrieving The Mothercrock all the easier.

Which was what was keeping Filthy Henry standing still in the one spot, right at the bottom step of the stairs, staring at The Mothercrock. Something just did not add up. At times like this a person could be envious of somebody who was bitten by a radioactive spider. That sort of genetic mishap at least resulted in a useful ability to predict danger. A half-human, half-fairy had to use sight and sound to detect trouble like some sort of chump. Nothing in the basement seemed out of place. Definitely there was no magic in the room with the exception of The Mothercrock and unless the Stokers were planning on killing him with currency there was nothing to fear from that. Plus there was not another living soul in the room with him. He strained his ears to hear for anything that even hinted at a heart beating.

Nothing.

Maybe I just got really lucky on this one, he thought.

Heading over to the table with The Mothercrock, Filthy Henry dropped the vial of holy water back into his pocket and reached out to pick up the magical money maker.

There was a rustle of cloth, a swish of wind, and a chill that ran down the fairy detective's spine. Two Stokers stood behind The Mothercrock, staring at Filthy Henry like hungry wolves.

"Well now," one of them said. "Who would have thought that would have worked so well."

Filthy Henry risked glancing to the right and saw that the previously curtain-closed windows were now curtain-less. The Stokers had been hiding in the little windows, sitting on the sills and using the curtains to conceal their presence. He mentally kicked himself for trying to listen for a heartbeat. Vampires hearts stopped beating the second they were turned.

Such a rookie mistake to make.

Focusing on the two Stokers before him, the fairy detective brought up his crucifix and held it at eye level.

"You are both hereby implicated in a crime that is in direct violation of The Rules," Filthy Henry said in as authoritative a tone he could manage. "If you stand down now your punishment will be lenient and may be dismissed entirely if you give evidence against the ring-leader of this act."

Neither Stoker responded. They each started to step around from behind the table, circling towards Filthy Henry as he backed towards the stairs. He kept moving the crucifix from in front of one to the other while reaching into his pocket with his free hand, slipping two holy water vials between his fingers, and preparing for the worst.

"You know that won't work on me," the Stoker on the left said, pointing at the wooden cross. "I'm Jewish."

"Plus I don't believe in any of that religious nonsense either," the other Stoker said. "So that means you are just holding up a silly statue."

There is a saying that violence is never an option. The fairy detective had always thought it a stupid saying as most of the time violence was the best and only option a person had.

Filthy Henry had followed this mantra his entire life. Growing up he had found that if you punched the bully in the face, really hard, so that blood flowed freely from their nose, the bullying would stop. If you did this the first time the bully tried anything it nipped things before they even began. He did not consider himself a violent man, more of an opportunistic one.

Without waiting for either of the Stokers to make the first move he pulled his hand free from the pocket. As he pivoted on his right heel to turn around and run back up the stairs Filthy Henry's hand arched through the air releasing the two vials of holy water. Before they knew what was happening the first Stoker was clutching his face as the water burned his flesh. Filthy Henry started running up towards the ground floor. Behind him came the sound of water splashing and more agonised screams. The Stokers were out of action.

He pushed open the door at the top of the stairs, jumped out into the hallway, twirled around and slammed the basement door shut. If there had of been a key in the lock he would have turned it, even though a Stoker could punch through an oak door like kindling.

"Well now Henry," a voice said from the direction of the front door. "If you would be so kind as to turn and face me with your hands in the air we can avoid any bloody unpleasantness."

222

Filthy Henry let out an exasperated sigh and did as he was instructed. He moved slowly to avoid any misunderstandings and was not in the least bit surprised to see Abe St. Oker standing before him with Shelly firmly gripped by her throat.

"My, my, what a pickle we have here," St. Oker said with a fang-filled smile.

#

Shelly was finding it difficult to breath. The vampire-author's hand had a solid hold around her neck and any slight struggle was met with an equal slight increase in his grip. No matter what was about to happen she would not be getting free any time soon.

In front of her stood Filthy Henry, hands raised in the air, trench coat fanned out like a cheap super-hero cloak. Via her enhanced magical sight she could clearly see that he had no spells at the ready. Nothing up his sleeve.

He was apparently giving up.

"Now," St. Oker said, letting his index finger flex a little against Shelly's neck. "We have a bit of a situation here it would seem."

Two Stokers exited the kitchen, standing a few feet behind Filthy Henry. He looked over his shoulder at them, nodding to each in turn, then turned back to meet St. Oker's gaze.

"Don't worry, Shelly," Filthy Henry said. "You'll be alright."

For some reason she believed him, although she was not entirely sure why. He had not winked to indicate that he had some dastardly clever plan waiting to rescue them both.

"I really can't see how that statement will hold true," St. Oker said. "After all, I have found two trespassers in my home. By all rights I could drain the two of you and leave your dried corpses out by the side of the road on garbage night."

"Well you can't drain me," the fairy detective said with a grin.

He was actually grinning. A vampire was talking about draining their blood and Filthy Henry was grinning like an idiot. Shelly would have groaned if her neck was not so firmly held by St. Oker.

"True, my old friend. But we could always drain her while you watch powerless to stop us. Then simply kill you."

"Touché," Filthy Henry said.

All Shelly could manage was to glare at the fairy detective. If he had a plan she wanted him to use it sooner rather than later. Later was a nice concept of time when you had nothing half-strangling you to death. Later meant you had a future. Right now Shelly was worried that her immediate present was all the later she had left.

St. Oker, pushing Shelly before him, took two steps closer to Filthy Henry. He leaned over her shoulder, his fangs extending slightly.

"Shall we just get down to this then?"

"Wait!" Filthy Henry said gesturing for the vampire writer to stop.

The two Stokers behind him took a step back at his sudden outburst.

"Yes?" St. Oker asked, dreamily.

Filthy Henry coughed, clearing his throat. He looked at Shelly for a split second, then back at the vampire holding onto her.

"You are in violations of The Rules and have left me with no alternative but to deport you back to the fairy-realm to await trial by your magical peers and punishment in accordance with your crime."

He sounded like he meant every word. If there had been a badge in his hands it would have looked all the more official. Yet the fact that one vampire was slowly chocking her to death and two more were standing behind the fairy detective sort of made the whole thing a bit farcical. It was like walking into the middle of a Mexican stand-off where everyone but you had an automatic weapon in their hands, the barrels of which were suddenly pointed at you.

St. Oker started laughing. The pair of Stokers joined in. All three laughed, loudly and deeply.

After twenty seconds all three vampires stopped laughing. St. Oker used his free hand to wipe away tears from his eyes.

"Henry I do like you," he said, still shaking a little with laughter. "I'm going to miss you."

The vampire-author nodded his head and the pair of Stokers behind Filthy Henry stepped forward, each grabbing one of the fairy detective's arms.

"No!" Shelly managed to say.

"Don't worry my dear," St. Oker said. "I won't make you watch. Plus he won't be long in joining you in the afterlife."

For a sentence that was meant to reassure it had the exact, no doubt desired, opposite effect. Shelly felt a cold sensation fill her stomach.

"Just hold on," Filthy Henry said, struggling against the grip of the two Stokers who had twisted his arms down so they were behind his back. "How about we make a deal?"

"There's nothing you can offer the boss," one of the Stokers said to Filthy Henry. "You're dead half-breed." He leaned in close to the fairy detective's ear and hissed. "Finally."

St. Oker raised his free hand and gestured for calm.

"Let's hear what he has to say," the vampire-author said. "After all, every creature is entitled to his last words. Henry's should be heard."

The fairy detective let out a long sigh and visibly sagged in the grip of the vampires. To Shelly it was as plain as the nose on her face. He had given up the fight, without starting the bloody thing to begin with. Some brilliant magically powered detective he had turned out to be. The slightest bit of trouble and that was it, game over.

"I remain here, you do whatever the hell you want with me. Kill me, pull me apart, distil my blood to get some magical juice. Whatever. Just let her go. Come on, she's a nobody. A nothing. She can only see fairy-kind out of the corner of her eye because she is an artist. Even then the spell that let's her see everything all the time is linked to me. Once I die, she looses the ability. She can't even do anything to threaten you. Who is she going to talk to? A fairy? She doesn't know how to find them. A Garda? They'd lock her up for being nuts. You simply move out of here and you are done, she'd never been any bother to you again."

Scratching thoughtfully at his chin St. Oker looked at Shelly, lifting her up by her neck a little, then back to Filthy Henry.

"That is true," he said. "She is only human after all. But she knows too much. I don't need Lé Precon, the ignorant little half pint with his over stringent rules for loaning money, finding out that I have his crock of gold."

"But he won't," Filthy Henry said shaking his head. "If she can't see a fairy how can she spill the beans to one?"

"Sounds reasonable boss," the Stoker on the left said.

"It does," St. Oker said. "It really does. Once we make you a dearly departed, this lovely young lady goes back to being fully normal. Another crazy person that talks about seeing leprechauns and talking to thin air. Assuming of course that Lé Precon doesn't bend the rules himself and appear to her without her magical vision in place."

"He can't risk it," Filthy Henry said. "He would no longer be the king if it got out!"

St. Oker's grip lessened around her neck.

"Just, before you let her go free. Which, by the way, I assume means you will never hassle her again and that she will be walking out the door safe and unharmed. Can we share one, last, kiss."

St. Oker let Shelly go and guided her over to the fairy detective.

"Well Henry, you old romantic. Forfeiting your life to save that of your woman. I never would have guessed. She may leave and I will trouble her no more. Let one arm go."

This last part was directed to the Stoker on Filthy Henry's left. He let go of the fairy detective's arm.

"Make it quick though," St. Oker said, " we have books to buy."

Shelly could feel herself welling up with sadness. This was not how things should have gone. A single tear built up on the bottom of her right eye, sliding down her cheek.

Filthy Henry looked up at her and smiled.

"Don't worry," he said. "It was all part of the plan."

Without any warning at all he reached up with his free hand, pressed the palm of it against the side of her face, pulled her down and kissed her passionately on the lips. It was the most amazing kiss she had ever had in her life. All memories of previous kisses cowered away from this one, knowing that they could not compare in the least. There was warmth and passion and emotion pouring from his lips into her. The pressure was just right, not too much nor too light. The perfect Goldilocks' bowl of porridge made with oats that were kisses. It even had a strange sensation, like the magical spark of a first kiss. Her whole mouth tingled with it, then her cheeks and finally her eyes.

She was lost in the moment and wanted it to never end.

"As an old romantic I am loath to do this, but you really must be going."

St. Oker firmly pulled her away and escorted her to the front door. He opened it, walked her down the steps to street level, and let go. It took Shelly a moment to realise the kiss was no longer happening and she was outside.

"I do hope you won't judge me too harshly based on your experiences thus far," St. Oker said. "Now run along and enjoy the rest of your life. Forget about the past week, it is no longer relevant."

He turned, walked back up the steps, entered the house and closed the door behind him. Leaving Shelly on the street, alone, and heart broken.

"I've got to find help," she said to nobody.

Making sure that her fairy sight was turned on, Shelly ran away from the building of vampires and started looking for any fairy that might be willing to help Filthy Henry. After a kiss like that the least she figured she could do was save his life.

Chapter Nineteen

Nothing had ever sounded more ominous to Filthy Henry than the lock of the front door clicking as St. Oker closed it behind him. The vampire-author slid into place two bolts, one at the top of the door and the other at the bottom, then turned a key and locked the door completely. Seemingly just to make sure that the door was well and truly closed, St. Oker tugged on the handle twice and nodded with satisfaction when it failed to open.

He turned around, picked up some gloves from a table beside the front door, and pulled them on.

"Now, if you would just remain as you are," St. Oker said, walking up to the fairy detective.

Filthy Henry was starting to panic. Plans that rescued a person generally kicked in sooner rather than later. He was putting a lot of trust into Shelly right now and it did not seem to be paying off as quickly as he would have liked. He felt like he was playing a solo game of Russian roulette with a loaded double-barrelled shotgun.

St. Oker reached into the fairy detective's pockets. He pulled out the crucifix. Behind Filthy Henry the two Stokers took a step back, putting some distance between themselves and the holy item.

"It is okay, gentlemen," St. Oker said. "It is out of his hands now."

He snapped the wooden cross in two and tossed the pieces over his shoulder.

"Well I guess that's Plan B ruined," Filthy Henry said, smiling at St. Oker.

"If that comprised Plan B I think you can safely give up on Plan A," St. Oker said, reaching past Filthy Henry and opening the door down to the basement. "Whatever that may have been. Now, I do so hate the sight of blood on my freshly painted walls. So we shall move this little conversation down to the basement. Just remember our deal, Henry."

With a little shove from the Stokers behind him, Filthy Henry started walking down the stairs into the dark basement below. He tried to remain calm, wishing he had something to eat so that he could fill up the magic tank. Kissing Shelly had cost a bit more than he had intended it to. Right now he had enough in him to take out one of the three bloodsuckers. Possibly. To be sure he would have had to knock several shades of brown stuff out of the Stoker to weaken it a little first, which would have taken hours if he was lucky to last that long. Even then, without magic to aid him during the fight, there was still only a ten percent chance of it working.

At the foot of the stairs were the smouldering remains of the guard Stokers that had been watching The Mothercrock. The fairy detective gingerly stepped over them, showing some respect to the dead-undead because that was how his mammy had raised him, and was led into the middle of the floor. One of the Stokers holding onto his arm growled at the sight of his fallen comrades.

"Oh that is a shame," St. Oker said as he sat down on the middle steps of the stairs and looked at the bodies. "One of those was a sibling of the man holding onto your left arm, Henry. I can only imagine that he may want to make this last a little bit longer. I had hoped for a clean execution."

"Brilliant," Filthy Henry said, sarcastically.

That was always the problem with the mastermind behind any crime. They generally loved to hear themselves talk. The sound of their own voice was like some sort of soothing music that they figured should be shared with everyone in the world with ears.

But it was a trait that Filthy Henry was happy St. Oker had right now, because it meant he could buy some time.

"So," he said, hanging limply between the two Stokers. "Was this all really about you getting onto the best sellers list?"

St. Oker sat bolt upright, pride surging through his body.

"Why yes, Henry. Yes it was, because…"

Filthy Henry only half listened to what was being said. His eyes were scanning for anything that could be incorporated into Plan C, since Plan A was really taking its sweet bloody time.

#

Shelly ran down Duke Street, heading towards Grafton Street, in search of help. It was late at night, or early in the morning depending on which way you looked at your watch, but Grafton Street was usually busy at all times of day.

Except tonight. As she stepped out onto the cobble-locked street Shelly was met with a sight she had never seen in her entire life.

The street was deserted. Empty. Devoid of another living thing. Neither human nor fairy nor animal was wandering around for as far as the eye could see. There was not one single soul available to come to her aid. For the first time in recorded history the street was completely empty.

This hit her like a slap to the face. Filthy Henry had literally sacrificed himself to let her live and in a few minutes he would be dead and she could do nothing to help him. She had never felt so useless in her entire life.

Shelly dropped to the ground, defeated. There was no point in running any further for help, they would never make it back to Dawson Street before St. Oker had killed Filthy Henry. She looked around with the fairy-vision, a great sadness welling up in her heart. Once the world stopped looking so magical that would be it. The Stokers would have killed Filthy Henry and her connection to the fairy world would be no more. It would be like watching him die; she would know the exact moment.

Tears brimmed up in both her eyes. One rolled down her cheek, hung dangerously from her chin for a moment before dropping to the ground like a suicidal lemming. As it splashed on the stones Shelly noticed a strange golden light in the tear drop. A strange golden light that her tears normally lacked.

Shelly stared at the drop and watched the light intensify as a few more glowing tears were shed.

"Well now that is new," she said, amazed.

#

St. Oker had been rabbiting on for the past three minutes about his little master plan. Buying time had never been such a costly experience. Filthy Henry had always enjoyed conversing with the vampire writer, but now he was starting to wonder how he had not staked him years ago. There was so much hot air spewing from the fanged mouth that it could have inflated a fleet of balloons. Even the Stokers holding the fairy detective in place were showing signs of getting agitated. Both of them were flexing their hold on Filthy Henry's arms, wanting to get down to the violence they had been promised.

Plan C had failed to materialize, much to Filthy Henry's dismay. There was nothing in the basement that could be used to escape. No conveniently placed garden posts that could be made into impromptu stakes. Not one full canister of petrol, just waiting for a well placed fireball to be flung towards it. It was almost as if the Fates had decided to sit this one out and let the fairy detective figure things out himself. Then he felt it. A tingle that ran through his entire body, like pins and needles starting in his feet and working upwards to his head.

Finally, Filthy Henry thought.

"Well Abe," he said, interrupting St. Oker's monologue. "This has been great. Nice catching up with you and all that. But tell me this, before you kill me, how did you get around the Rainbow?"

St. Oker stopped talking and stared at the fairy detective.

"Well that was very rude, but I'll tell you and then kill you. The Rainbow was simple really, I'm actually surprised it had never been tried before. A Rainbow only works so long as the thing observing it knows what colours are. A being that can only see in black and white would just see spinning lights of varying shades of grey. They would have to be one hundred percent colour-blind you understand, but so long as they were then the Rainbow had no effect on them."

The tingle was growing stronger throughout his body but Filthy Henry knew he needed a few more seconds before the spell would kick in fully.

"So...," he said, taking his time to speak. "Since there is no such thing as a colour-blind fairy, because the magical powers are full of colour, you figured a human would be perfect. Why not use a dog?"

"A common misconception about dogs is that they see the world in black and white," St. Oker said. "Dogs actually see the world in blues and yellows with some grey thrown in for good measure. No I needed a human that could function normally and see the world of the fairy folk as well. Not some lunatic from the crazy house, they would be no good. Gibbering mess the lot of them."

"Which explains the Cat Síth blood," Filthy Henry said. "You gave two humans a way to see the fairy world knowing that one of them was completely colour blind. But he wasn't a crazy person and you had no intentions of leaving them around as witnesses anyway. I assume that there would have been no bodies or Newborn Stoker dust in the warehouse if the Leerling had not interrupted you."

"Got it in one," St. Oker said. "The potion was something I found in a book twenty or thirty years ago. With the right ingredients and some fairy blood a normal human could be given limited abilities to see the fairy world. Something the Ancient Druids used a lot, along with copious amounts of magic mushrooms. I recalled seeing an elderly Cat Síth out on one of my walks around the city one night and figured why not. Spill a little blood for the greater good and all that. It was pure coincidence that the Cat Síth was friends with Shelly, I just thought she was homeless."

"Well thanks for that. You've cleared a lot of things up for me," the fairy detective said with a smile as he felt the tingle throughout his entire body. "But I really have to be going now."

"What are you talking about Hen...ry?"

Filthy Henry knew why his name had been dragged out a little. It was because of the golden glow that was coming from his body at that very moment. The tingling sensation had intensified as the spell kicked in, growing in strength so that his whole body was enclosed in a shell of light. He felt both Stokers let go of his arms.

St. Oker stared open-mouth at the fairy detective.

The basement seemed to get bigger from Filthy Henry's perspective, but he knew it was not really the room increasing in size. Rather the spell was adjusting his body so that the teleportation took effect easier. Which was why Filthy Henry hated using the spell to get from A to B unless he was sure that the exit point at B was bigger than he was. When you had to be condensed in order to get flung out magically at your destination it became a little bit uncomfortable. Judging by how much he was shrinking Filthy Henry reckoned that Shelly had shed one or two

234

tears nowhere near another body of water.

Which was impressive given how wet and rainy Ireland's weather tended to be.

The spell sped up, making him get smaller quicker, until the three Stokers looked like giants staring down at a helpless villager.

"STAND ON HIM WITH YOUR FOOT YOU MORONS!" St. Oker shouted.

Both Stokers brought up their right feet, aimed, and stomped down at the tiny fairy detective a fraction of a second too late. He had reached the required size and felt his entire body being ripped apart as the spell transported him out of the basement.

The last thing Filthy Henry heard was St. Oker screaming his name at the top of his voice.

You could always rely on Plan A!

#

Shelly watched her glowing teardrops with great interest. They had joined together, seemingly of their own accord, to form one larger drop. Just to make sure that it was not some strange effect of looking at a tear through fairy-vision, she turned off the magically enhanced sight.

The glowing drop of moisture remained, intensifying with each passing second. It had even started to ripple, wobbling from side to side. Slowly two little trails spread out from the sides of the drop, with two more pushing out from the bottom of it. At the top of the drop, or at least the part that had no lines coming from it, the water started to bulge slightly. Almost as if something in the teardrop was trying to force its way out. Presumably whatever was causing the light had decided to make an appearance.

"GARRHRH!"

235

Shelly fell backwards, away from the glowing drop on the ground in front of her, and scuttled away. The shout had come from within the teardrop, the glowing light brightening with the noise.

"GGRRHRGHAAAHH!" the tear drop shouted once more, the entire water body bulging upwards. Even the little trails of water had started glowing now, moving independently to the rest of the drop.

It was incredibly worrying to watch. Her first thought was that this could be some sort of creature sent by St. Oker to renege on his deal with Filthy Henry. But then vampires were apparently very limited to the magical abilities they had. The fairy detective had told her that.

Right then the glowing drop exploded, growing in size on the cobble-locked street. Water rushed out in five directions and a liquid man shape formed on the ground. Inside the watery form golden light raced around, seemingly pushing the water onwards. There was a brief moment when all movement ceased and then the water splashed, as if it had been dropped from a great height onto the ground.

Shelly covered her eyes from the droplets that rained on her. When she took down her hand she saw Filthy Henry, lying on his back, completely drenched from head to toe with rivulets of water running off his body.

"Couldn't have cried near a river or puddle or something, no?" he said, sitting up. "Or at least found some drunk's wee or something in a store doorway."

She blinked twice.

The wet fairy detective remained. Sitting there. On the street. Soaking wet. In front of her. Alive.

"Who are you?" she asked, searching in her pockets for anything that could be used as a weapon and only finding the crucifix.

"I'm Filthy Henry," he said, wiping water off his face. "Now put down that cross will you. It's me. Not some Stoker."

"How? What?"

"Transferred my essence to you when we kissed. Once you cried the spell used water as a conduit to teleport me to the source of water my essence was in. But because you didn't cry near water I had to be made tiny and then very painfully regrown to my original size. Thanks by the way."

She just stared at him.

"For saving me," Filthy Henry continued, taking her silence as a question. "Sorry that may have sounded a tad sarcastic, but you try being shrunk and enlarged rapidly. Anyway thanks, seriously. If you hadn't cried right then I would be dead by now. Although you could have shed a few tears a little sooner, just an FYI. You'd swear I meant nothing at all to you."

He got to his feet, walked over to her, and offered her his hand.

"Now come on," Filthy Henry said as he helped her stand up. "We have to run!"

"No half-breed you should have already been long gone!"

They both looked down the street and saw St. Oker standing there, hands bunched into fists, looking annoyed.

"I really wish I had a Plan D right about now," Filthy Henry said and started running away from St. Oker, pulling Shelly along with him.

Chapter Twenty

Running was not something Filthy Henry had ever enjoyed doing; yet lately it seemed to be taking up large portions of his life. True, the running did give him improved chances of survival and medically a little exercise never hurt anybody, but he was starting to pine for the days when he never ran. His main problem with running was that it made you tired, meaning it was little more than a stalling tactic when up against a Stoker.

A whoosh of air from behind indicated that St. Oker had moved at vampiric speed. The sound travelled overhead and was punctuated by stones cracking as something heavy slammed into them from above. In the blink of an eye the empty street ahead was crowded with one vampire writer, grinning like a wolf.

Filthy Henry looked about quickly, searching for a side street that they could use as a means of escape. Shop fronts ruined the horizon of possibilities. St. Oker had landed in the perfect position, blocking them completely. They had no hope of running around him. His vampire speed would have made the attempt as futile as a hare racing against a steroid enhanced tortoise.

The fairy detective wheeled around, making sure his grip on Shelly's hand was tight, and ran back the way they had come.

"Can't. We. Just. Use. Magic?" Shelly asked, panting as they ran.

"Not enough to take him down. Need to weaken him somehow," Filthy Henry said. "Why, you have some magic I can borrow? I sorta used up all of mine escaping him the first time."

Another whoosh, another destroyed section of pavement and St. Oker was once more in front of them. He had jumped sooner this time, preventing them from even reaching the spot where they had started running in the first place.

"Tick tock, half-breed."

That was starting to annoy Filthy Henry. Of all the races a Stoker had no right to call him a half-breed. Not to mention that Abe and he had been associates. Just because a man had his plans of becoming the all-time best seller ruined was no reason to resort to derogative name calling.

Once more Filthy Henry spun around to run the other way. However, as he reached the exact halfway mark of the move he slowed down slightly and listened. There was the rush of air as St. Oker jumped again. The fairy detective continued wheeling around, essentially turning on the spot, and ran up the street. A perfectly simple ruse, one he had not expected the vampire-author to fall for.

"Niii....," Shelly said.

Filthy Henry was yanked backwards and slammed into the ground, the wind knocked out of him. Shelly's hand was ripped out of his grasp. He rolled over onto his stomach and looked up.

St. Oker had grabbed Shelly as he jumped over them and was holding her by her neck a foot above the ground. She was kicking at the air, clawing at his fingers to try and break free.

"One less loose end to tie up," the vampire writer said. "We were going to kill you then one of the lads was going to track down Shelly and finish her off. I know, I know. We had a deal, but I never said I wouldn't get one of my workers to clean up loose ends. Little word-play trick I learned from you. Besides you would have been dead, hardly the best position to notice such changes to agreements. Alas you shall just have to bear witness..."

With a flick of his wrist, St. Oker snapped Shelly's neck. Her lifeless form dangled from his fingers for a moment before he discarded her body like a morbid banana skin, throwing it to the ground.

"Such a pity, I bet her blood tasted fantastic."

It happened so fast that Filthy Henry had no time to react. He could not scream. Could not shout out a plea for mercy. One second Shelly was alive, struggling to breath, the next her lifeless corpse was just more litter on Grafton Street.

He could not believe it.

Deep inside, in a place that Filthy Henry had never been aware of, a powerful ball of emotion sought to be heard. It whispered promises of vengeance and justice and the iron cold resolve required to make sure everyone got what they deserved. All it asked in return was to be let out, let loose, let drive the body it inhabited for only a few minutes.

Only a few minutes, sure what could happen in a few minutes? Filthy Henry closed his eyes and agreed to the internal request. He did not care where it came from or what it was. If it could give him revenge it was welcome. Without a second thought he allowed the inner voice to take control.

Suddenly magic coursed through every fibre of his being with such strength as he had never felt before. It was almost as if his body had been lying to him all these years, showing him only the barest amount of potential to make sure he never got any bright ideas. But now as Filthy Henry's rage sought an outlet his body had decided to bend the rules, just this once. Every muscle was infused with energy, every limb powered up beyond all reckoning.

The fairy detective opened his eyes and saw the world through a magical haze of pure, rare, power fuelled by the darkest emotions buried deep within a man's soul. His hands started burning with a bright blue light, dark trails of magical energy sparking off them in the air. He felt powerful, ready to do anything and destroy everything. Right then the world was his plaything and he had just been given a new set of fully charged batteries.

Pounding both his fists into the ground, Filthy Henry fired himself up into a standing position. The street now sported two new potholes that crackled for a few seconds with magical energy.

He looked at St. Oker as the vampire slowly walked towards him without a care in the world. The sight of Shelly behind the vampire writer caused another surge of power to run through Filthy Henry's body.

"RRRRRRRAAAAARRRRR!!!!" Filthy Henry screamed, rushing towards St. Oker with his right hand in the air ready to throw a punch.

For a moment St. Oker seemed to not register what was happening. Normally humans ran away from vampires, it was instinct. Then his eyes widened as he clearly realised that Filthy Henry was moving at a greatly enhanced speed.

The punch caught St. Oker completely off guard. Filthy Henry poured every ounce of strength and magic he could into the right hook, aimed it at St. Oker's jaw, and let rip. The magically encased hand slammed into the vampire's face and kept on going, lifting St. Oker off his feet and sending him careening down the street. He crashed into the ground and slid along the stone surface, leaving a trail of broken bricks and cobblestones in his wake.

The fairy detective did not wait. He leapt into the air like a super hero leapfrogging over a tall building, brought both his arms up at the peak of his jump, and pounded them on top of St. Oker as he landed.

"HOW!" Filthy Henry shouted, grabbing St. Oker by his collar and smashing him in the face. "HOW!" Punch. "COULD!" PUNCH. "YOU!" PUNCH!!!

"HENRY!"

Filthy Henry barely heard his name being called. It was an annoyance to be dealt with later; his vengeance told him to ignore it.

"SHE!" PUNCH!!! "WAS!"

His hand stopped pounding the vampire in the face. It met resistance from some unseen force that wrapped around his blue glowing arm. Filthy Henry looked at his fist, his fairy vision turned up to a level he never knew it could be, and saw the magical blue flames on his hand were being pushed backwards by tiny little rainbows and multi-coloured shamrocks. A spell had been cast and aimed directly at him, the trajectory of the spell leading back up the street.

The fairy detective followed the trail of energy and saw Lé Precon surrounded by his Rainbow Guards standing in the middle of Grafton Street, beside Shelly's body. Each of the brightly dressed leprechauns had both hands pointed at the fairy detective, magically restraining him. Sweat was pouring down their faces.

Filthy Henry registered surprise for a moment. Leprechauns were full-blood fairies, teeming with magical power. One of them would have been able to hold a human half-breed back with ease, yet an entire Rainbow Guard were seemingly having trouble keeping Filthy Henry immobile.

Just how much raw power is in me? The fairy detective thought as he struggled to land another punch.

The Rainbow Guard visibly moved an inch forward as they were tugged along by their collective spell.

"Stand down Henry!" Lé Precon ordered.

The King Leprechaun was not adding his own magic to that of his guards but looked like he was considering it. For the first time in his life Filthy Henry saw concern on Lé Precon's face. If it was taking seven powerful fairies to keep one half-breed at bay something had obviously gone terribly awry.

The momentary pause in delivering righteous justice had caused the flow of power in Filthy Henry's body to subside slightly. Calm returned to his thinking, the magical blood-rage fading a little.

Beneath him St. Oker let out a groan of pain, blood streaming from everywhere on the vampire's face. What was left of his face. The parts that were not swollen and bruised were battered and bleeding. Filthy Henry pitied the creature a little. Vampires were used to dealing out pain, rarely had one received so much of it from a less powerful being. The spell coming from the Rainbow Guard pushed Filthy Henry back a few inches, the strain on their faces lessening.

As suddenly as it had come over the fairy detective, the magically fuelled strength vanished. His hands stopped burning with blue flames and the world returned to normal. He let go of St. Oker's collar, dropping the unconscious vampire writer to the ground, and stood up. The holding spell was released and the Rainbow Guard stood down. The yellow one fell over, clearly exhausted from the effort of controlled magic.

Lé Precon walked down the street towards Filthy Henry, glancing at Shelly's corpse.

"Looks like you got your daddy's temper as well," Lé Precon said, indicating the bloody mess that was St. Oker. "I never knew you had it in you. The magic or the maniac." He stared at the blood-covered body on the ground, clearly disturbed. "That was quite the display of violence."

Checking his internal magic reserves Filthy Henry was surprised to learn that he was still an eighth full. A show of power like that should have emptied him and put him into a magical induced coma. It scared him a little to think that such a dark

243

emotion as anger was able to unleash so much raw power in him. It made him wonder if the rumour about who his father was had some truth to it. But none of that mattered now. Shelly was dead. There would be time later to find out about his father. Right now was for mourning her.

Filthy Henry looked back at the Rainbow Guard. They had taken a defensive stance, forming a semi-circle at one end of the street. Lé Precon had stopped walking and was standing two feet away from the fairy detective.

None of the leprechauns had any magic or spells at the ready. Filthy Henry noted this and let it sink in as an idea formed in his head. He started to slowly conjure a fireball in his hand, keeping it behind his back so that nobody else could see. The levels of power kept to a minimum as it built up, delaying any chance of detecting the spell.

"So," Lé Precon said, " where is my crock of gold? I'm guessing the Stoker of all Stokers was involved somehow."

Filthy Henry gave the King of the Leprechauns a condensed summary of what had happened. How the Stokers had been involved, why humans had been used, even what St. Oker had planned to use The Mothercrock for. Unsurprisingly Lé Precon was not impressed that his crock of gold had been stolen for such a pointless reason. As a race, leprechauns preferred their stories to come from bards instead of books.

"It's in a basement on Dawson Street," the fairy detective finished.

A Rainbow Guard, the red one, vanished in a puff of smoke and reappeared a second later holding The Mothercrock in his arms. At a nod from Lé Precon the entire Rainbow Guard vanished, taking The Mothercrock with them.

"It will be in a safer location now," Lé Precon told Filthy Henry. "One with an improved Rainbow protecting it. Funny how something completely colour-blind could penetrate a spell that has been around since the Old Times."

"What about him?" Filthy Henry asked, nudging the unconscious St. Oker with the toe of his shoe. His spell was just about ready to be cast, the heat from the fireball warming his hand.

"I suppose we have a situation there alright," Lé Precon said, scratching his chin through his beard. "He has broken a lot of The Rules."

Filthy Henry acted before Lé Precon could stop him.

"*Sruthán!*" he said, pouring as much hatred and power into the spell as he could while aiming his left hand at St. Oker.

The vampire's body burst into flames, disintegrating quickly into a mound of blackened ash as Filthy Henry kept the spell in place until a light breeze carried the black specks away. When it was gone all that was left on the cobbles of Grafton Street was a dark smudge that outlined a man shape on the ground.

Filthy Henry felt no remorse or guilt at all. He closed his hand, stopping the spell, and looked down at Lé Precon.

"Any questions?" he asked.

Lé Precon took a minute to stop staring at the spot where St. Oker had been. He slowly turned his head to look up at Filthy Henry and shook once in the negative.

Filthy Henry said nothing and walked away from the leprechaun, down the street to where Shelly's body lay. The sight of the lifeless woman brought tears to his eye. It had been a long time since somebody had managed to work their way into his life so deeply. He avoided making friends or even associates that were mortal, human, because they had no real reason to get mixed up in the fairy world. They were either in danger all the time from a fairy with a grudge against humanity or died from old age and left him alone again. But Shelly had been different and for the life of him the fairy detective was not sure why that was.

"So...um...payment," Lé Precon said, staying in the same spot and looking at Filthy Henry fearfully. He had tucked his cane underneath his left arm and both his hands had the glow of a prepared spell in them. Precautions were clearly being taken. "You're debt has been cleared as agreed. Plus you have one wish, which I am guessing you will use to have granted what you always desired."

The fairy detective kept staring at Shelly's face.

He had almost forgotten about the payment for completing the case. Debt free and with one reality altering wish in the bag. A wish to fulfil that which he had desired since the age of twenty. Being a half-breed, let alone the only half-breed, was tough. You never really fitted into either world. Humans would never understand your troubles and fairies saw you as nothing but trouble. Neither world wanted you and yet you had to find a way to fit into both. Every half-breed would have had the same wish: to not be a half-breed. To become a full-blood fairy. To finally fit into a world at last.

Filthy Henry looked up from Shelly's corpse and wiped away the tears from his eyes.

Then he made his wish.

Chapter Twenty-One

The funeral service had been...well...a service. Some lovely words were said, a bit of dirt was thrown onto the lid of a coffin and a nice bunch of flowers had been placed beside a big hole in the ground. After it had all been said and done Filthy Henry remained by the graveside and let out a yawn that he had been suppressing for the past fifteen minutes.

He had a dislike of funerals as a rule. Funerals made things seem very final, but this one in particular had been a tough one to get through.

"Well that was bloody pointless," he said, pulling out a chocolate bar from his coat pocket and opening it.

He broke off a piece and popped it into his mouth. The priest gave him a dirty look before closing his Bible and walking away from the grave, heading in the direction of the car park.

"Well it meant something to me," Shelly said, dabbing at her eyes with a handkerchief. "I wanted to say goodbye to my friend properly. It was nice of the priest to give her The Last Rites. Supposedly they only do that sort of thing for people. He said it was the first time he had had to ask that a cat be let into proper Heaven and not that made up one that you tell kids pets go to."

Filthy Henry looked down at the tiny grave and chewed thoughtfully on the piece of chocolate in his mouth.

It had been a nice ceremony for Kitty Purry, there was no denying that. Plus he did get a nasty little chuckle from the fact that a priest had just given The Last Rites to a fairy. Those were two sets of people that just never mixed because of such wildly contrasting beliefs.

He glanced over at Shelly as she stared down at the tiny coffin.

Filthy Henry had figured it was wiser not to let her know she had died. People tended to get all caught up in emotions when they found out they had been brought back to life. Sometimes they ran around the place preaching to anybody that would listen. Messiah Madness would set in and they would try to convince the world that every religious belief was spot on that money. It was a nightmare to keep quiet. That was why it took the reality altering power of a leprechaun wish to pull a resurrection off correctly. Any other race generally just wound up creating a zombie, only good for drooling all over the furniture and washing the dishes. If you could get them to stop gnawing on people's brains, of course.

But to see Shelly up and about again, even if she had no memory of actually dying, was a wish well spent as far as Filthy Henry was concerned. Besides, there would always be other opportunities to trick Lé Precon into giving him another wish. One that could be used to make the fairy detective a full fairy. Of that he had no doubt.

"You want to go get some coffee?" Shelly asked him, looping her arm in around his. "After all. Big magical battle last night, bound to need to recharge the magic batteries. Maybe talk about why you killed Bram Stoker?"

Filthy Henry looked over at her and smiled.

"Yes to the food but not a hope about the other bit. Let's just say that he deserved it. When he ... knocked you out. Well I thought he had done something much worse. Sort of lost control, anger issues. Yada, yada."

A Leerling flew down, stopped on the opposite side of Kitty Purry's grave, and transformed into human form.

"Filthy Henry," he said, nodding politely to Shelly.

"What about it?" Filthy Henry asked.

"Well I've been sent to hire you. A case."

"A case?"

Shelly let go of the fairy detective's arm and pulled out a notepad from her coat pocket.

"What are the details?"

"What are you doing?" Filthy Henry asked her.

"Taking notes," she replied. "Like a good partner does."

"Go on," Filthy Henry said to the Leerling, frowning at Shelly.

"Well there is a haunted bus," the Leering said, "and somebody figured you'd be the best person to sort it out. Sort of falls into your area of expertise."

Filthy Henry broke off another chunk of chocolate, popped it into his mouth and started chewing. He smiled at Shelly.
"First you get me lunch," Filthy Henry said. "Then we go have a look at this case. Sound like a plan?"
Shelly stopped writing in her notepad and looked up at him.

"Sure thing," she said with a half-smile. "Partner?"

The fairy detective grinned, reaching over and taking the notepad and pen out of her hands. He tossed them into the grave.

"Hell no!" Filthy Henry said, turning around and heading towards the graveyard entrance.

249

CPSIA information can be obtained at www.ICGtesting.com
Printed in the USA
LVOW05s2356281114

416147LV00016B/480/P